FAE'S PRISONER

QUEENS OF THE FAE: BOOK FOUR

MELISSA A. CRAVEN

M. LYNN

Edited by Cindy Ray Hale
Proofread by Caitlin Haines
Cover by Covers by Combs

For those who tell us a realistic story has to have cursing.
Gosh. DARN it. We never listen.
:)

PRISON REALM

NORTHERN VATLAN

LOCH VILLANDI

FARGELSI KINGDOM

SOUTHERN VATLA

DRAGUR FOREST

VINDUR CITY

ISKALT KINGDOM
EASTERN VATLANDS
ELDFAL
SANDUR
SOL LOCH
UR KINGDOM
TEOTANN OASIS
ELDUR DESERT
CH LANGT
RADUR CITY

Ten years of cruel darkness and starvation.

Ten years of scraping by in a prison realm, of bowing before a king who liked nothing more than seeing his people on their knees.

But Griffin O'Shea had no delusions. He deserved his fate, deserved the punishment that sent him across the powerful barrier surrounding the fae prison realm, to have everyone outside that barrier forget he ever existed.

He tried to forget too, tried to put his brother from his mind, to forget the woman he'd married—not that she'd wanted to marry him. He'd felt it all those years ago, the moment their marriage bond shattered the day he left his old life behind.

There were only two ways to get out of a fae marriage.

Death.

Or a fate worse than death. The prison realm.

Griffin's anger had long since subsided over the fate his brother and his wife allowed him to choose, the one they'd accepted without a fight. There was no time for hatred anymore, no time to do anything but survive.

Which was what Griffin tried to do.

The cheers from the gathering crowd reached him where he leaned against the cold stone wall of the tunnel beneath the castle. For ten years, he'd managed to avoid the notice of King Egan Byrne, but that wasn't possible anymore, not when the people he'd grown to care about were in danger.

But he'd failed them.

Failed to infiltrate the castle, failed to save the little girl who looked to him with so much trust.

He pushed off the wall and paced the length of the tunnel.

He didn't deserve Nessa's trust. When Nessa's sister, Shauna, found him on his first day here, he hadn't deserved her kindness or her friendship. She'd saved his life that day.

But he deserved this day, now.

The crowd, come to watch the newest battle, would assume Griffin had betrayed King Egan. He supposed he had, but that wasn't why Griffin wanted this, why a fight for his life was long overdue.

If they knew the true reason he was here in the prison realm, he'd lose their trust.

He'd been an ally of Queen Regan O'Rourke, the now dead sorceress of Fargelsi. If word got out, not even Nessa would look to him with trust.

Because the queen he'd spent most of his life in service to sent a good many of them here—to a realm the rest of the fae world forgot existed. The fourth kingdom of Myrkur. The realm of the Dark Fae, where it was always night and Griffin O'Shea held no magic.

If he died today, he would die still feeling like a traitor.

Light footsteps echoed through the tunnel behind him, and he lifted his head to find Gulliver, an orphaned kid Griffin found about a year after joining Shauna's village. They'd been together ever since.

But he shouldn't be here. "Gullie, what in the name of all the realms do you think you're doing here?"

Gulliver narrowed his cat-like eyes. His tail curled around his middle. He wasn't the first Dark Fae Griffin had met with such features. Before crossing the prison barrier, he hadn't thought fae like him existed.

But they did. Here in Myrkur some fae had tails or tusks, others had horns or wings. They were the Dark Fae, exiled to this realm generations ago.

"I came to see you." Gulliver crossed his arms, trying to project strength like he always did when he thought he was in trouble.

Griffin sighed. He didn't want his last words to his twelve-year-old charge to be a chastisement. "If the king or his men catch you here—"

"I know. I know. They'll take me as an indentured servant to work in the mines." He flashed Griffin a grin. "Good thing they never catch me."

"Yet," Griffin grumbled. "They haven't caught you *yet.*" Gulliver was a thief. A good one. He had the ability to move around unseen, unheard. And his tail was lightning quick, shoving his stolen bounty away faster than a blink. It came in handy. "Were you trying to sneak up on me?"

"No. That would be useless. You always seem to know I'm there." Gulliver kicked at a rock on the ground before lifting his vulnerable eyes to Griffin "The crowd says you're going to fight the king's greatest warrior."

"Gullie, I'm going to be okay."

"Do you promise?"

Griffin sighed but didn't respond. They both knew it was a promise he wasn't sure he could keep. "You've never seen me fight." He'd had many chances to wield a sword over the years but mostly to protect their secret village from other Dark Fae. There was a difference between that kind of fight and single combat with a trained swordsman. "Have you seen my competitor yet?"

Gulliver shook his head. "Do you think it'll be a Dark Fae?" His eyes narrowed to slits. "Or Tuatha De Dannon?"

"Probably Dark Fae." The king only took Dark Fae into his employ. Light Fae, those like Griffin, were more likely to be indentured servants, and the Tuatha De Dannon were land fae, like Gulliver. An ancient race of fae born here in Myrkur but enslaved all the same.

"What if it's a mountain ogre? Or a Slyph with great bat wings?"

Griffin planted a hand on each of Gulliver's shoulders and dipped his head to look him in the eye. "I don't want you watching this fight."

"But—"

"When you leave here, find Shauna and get as far away from the castle as you can."

Gulliver's bottom lip quivered. "What about Nessa? The king still has her."

"Practice patience. I will do my best for Nessa but I don't want my fate to be yours. You're a good man, Gulliver, but I need to know you'll be safe."

He puffed up his chest even as he fought back tears. Griffin yanked him into a hug, not wanting to let go.

Since entering the prison realm, Griffin had found what he'd sought his whole life, what he'd once deluded himself into thinking he'd found with Regan—the queen who raised him.

A family.

He had to fight for them now, to honor them until his last breath.

Which could very well be today.

Releasing Gulliver, Griffin pushed him back the way he'd come. "Go before someone sees you."

Gulliver took a strengthening breath, giving Griffin one last look, before running down the tunnel, leaving Griffin alone once more.

He'd never been strong in his convictions. At least, not until coming here. He'd had a tendency to let people down, never being who they wanted or needed him to be. The day he'd found the three-year-old Gulliver sleeping on the street, he'd made a vow to himself. He would always be there for him, and he'd try to be better, to do better. For the kid.

But now, it was time to break that vow.

It was time to say goodbye to the best friend he'd ever had, Shauna. Time to leave Gulliver as he promised he never would.

Time to give up on saving the young Nessa, who'd only had eight years of freedom and would spend the rest of her life in captivity.

He'd failed them all. Because he wasn't going to win this fight.

The crowd outside grew louder, their stomps over the

tunnel making dirt rain down on him. They came to see a battle, to see blood.

Footsteps echoed through the tunnel from the arena ahead, and Griffin turned to see the king himself approaching, the short tusks protruding through his beard made his smile seem even darker.

Griffin didn't bow, instead he straightened his shoulders and narrowed his eyes.

A loud clang echoed as King Egan threw a sword at Griffin's feet. He bent to pick it up, examining the rusted blade and cracked hilt.

"The great Griffin O'Shea." The king crossed his arms.

Griffin didn't make a habit of sharing his last name, but something told him he didn't want to find out how the king knew it. Yet... "You don't get to speak my full name."

"Your little Nessa has been a great wealth of information."

Griffin lunged for him, slamming the king against the stone wall. "What did you do to her?" Even as a kid, Nessa wouldn't have given information freely to this man, information only Shauna was supposed to know.

The king smiled. "The child is strong in her convictions. I quite like that. She wouldn't give me information to save herself. But to save you..."

Griffin cursed. Nessa must have thought telling the king Griffin was of royal blood would earn him a place of power. She was wrong about one thing. Griffin didn't want that power.

The king pushed Griffin away and righted himself. "It doesn't have to come to this. Join me now and this all goes away. I could use a soldier with the royal blood of Iskalt running through his veins."

Royal blood. The blood of Iskalt, one of the other three fae realms where his brother now held the throne. But Griffin had never honored his blood. He hadn't chosen Iskalt in the war that brought him here. He'd served the Fargelsi Queen all his life, fighting against both Iskalt and Eldur.

"I will never join you." Griffin spat.

King Egan's lips ticked up into a pleased smile behind his unkempt beard. "Let's make this interesting, shall we? I don't believe you will win, but if you do, the girl's contract is yours, and you're free to take her home."

"The girl... you'd give Nessa to me?"

His smile widened. "Of course. Though, she could have value as an indentured. She's beautiful. A bit young and weak, but perhaps she'll prove useful in many ways."

Griffin gripped the hilt of his sword tighter, wishing he could drive the rusted blade straight through Egan's belly. But it was no secret the paranoid king surrounded himself with loyal servants who wouldn't let Griffin take his next breath if he slayed the king where he stood.

Griffin stepped closer to Egan, dropping his voice. "One day, I'm going to kill you."

A booming laugh echoed against the stone. "Well, my boy, you must win this day first. I'll see you in the arena."

When he was gone, Griffin leaned his head back against the wall, finding a new strength in himself. If he won today, maybe he wouldn't fail Nessa after all.

This was for her and every other fae who'd made Griffin one of their own.

He ran a hand through his long auburn hair, adjusting

the ribbon that held it away from his face.

Ogres were big and dangerous but also slow. He could use that to his advantage. A Slyph however, with their powerful wings, they were fast and difficult to catch.

A key rattled in the lock at the end of the tunnel that led into the arena. A bald man dressed in the king's colors stepped in. Black ragged wings protruded from his back. "It is time." The Slyph spoke with a gravelly voice that matched his countenance.

Griffin was ready. He would save Nessa or die trying.

He stepped away from the wall and followed the man through the opening. Rough stone turned to fine sand beneath his feet.

He couldn't make out the faces of the crowd in the inky darkness, but that wasn't unusual. The sun never rose in Myrkur. It was one of the harshest things about this broken and cruel realm. Griffin had almost forgotten what it felt like to have sunlight warm his skin.

Or magic sparking at his fingertips.

Upon entry into the prison realm, all magic vanished from those who could wield it. Griffin hadn't been able to call forth his own magic in more than a decade.

Torches lined the arena and the platform on which the king sat, creating a circle of light. Griffin wiped a sweaty palm on his linen pants before tearing his white shirt off over his head and tossing it to the ground.

The crowd chanted and cheered along with the rhythm of a heavy drumbeat coming from somewhere behind the king.

The king stood, and the crowd quieted, straining to hear his every word. "My fae friends, thank you for coming today." Egan turned to the crowd, raising his hands at their applause.

Griffin wondered if the crowd was full of only Dark Fae, the ones who were loyal to their king. Or had they forced others to attend these macabre fights?

The king continued. "This morning, the young man before you was given a choice. Serve me or face his own mortality."

The crowd booed and hissed at Griffin.

But he wouldn't let himself become an indentured servant to a corrupt king. He'd faithfully served Regan despite knowing it was wrong.

Never again.

"And he has chosen death!"

The crowd roared with anger at Griffin's audacity to deny their king.

Griffin refused to look at the fae calling for his demise.

The king held up a hand to quiet the cheers. "Now, I am not a heartless fool. On the chance Griffin manages to defeat my best warrior, he will win the contract of my newest servant, Nessa." His eyes drifted to Griffin. "The rules are simple. Fight to the death by any means necessary."

If Griffin managed to kill an ogre, he'd have no regrets. He'd take Nessa home, and they'd tell stories of tonight for years to come.

The thick metal grate blocking the entrance to another tunnel lifted. Griffin braced himself, ready for whatever fae beast came for him.

Out of the shadows came a warrior.

Not an ogre.

And not someone Griffin wanted to kill.

Griffin had never laid eyes on Riona Nieland, but that didn't mean he couldn't recognize her.

Unlike the crowd chanting her name, Riona had no smile on her face, no indication she took pleasure in this fight.

She stood with her back to him, her face lifted in respect to regard the king on his dais far above the arena floor.

Griffin had none to give either of them.

"My king." Riona lowered herself to her knees as if this was a practiced performance. The crowd quieted, leaning forward to hear her words.

Riona was the king's most loyal soldier, despite her youthful appearance. She'd made a name for herself overseeing village raids when those villages refused to pay the king's high taxes that demanded too much of their meager yields.

Bright tattoos in an array of colors and ancient symbols wound up her arms, disappearing under the capped sleeves of the thin shirt she wore under her chain mail. The tattoos seemed to breathe, like they had a life of their own.

As the king's warrior, she had the advantage of proper armor and weapons.

Griffin only had himself and a rusted sword with a crack running the length of the hilt.

The balding winged man who'd led Griffin from the tunnel clamped a hand on the back of his neck. "Kneel to your king." He tried to force Griffin to his knees, but Griffin stood his ground.

"That man is not my king."

"Did you say something, prisoner?" King Egan perched on the edge of his half rotted throne, looking down his long nose into the arena, waiting in anticipation for Griffin's words.

Griffin strengthened his voice. "You are not my king. I have no king."

It was the truth. Griffin was a man without a home. With Queen Regan dead and her niece, Neeve O'Rourke, on the Fargelsian throne, that kingdom was no longer his. In Eldur, Queen Alona most likely cursed his name for everything he'd done to harm her people.

And his brother... Lochlan held the throne of Iskalt, but he'd be the last person to welcome Griffin.

So, it came down to the king of the prison realm, the man starving his people and forcing them to fight to the death when it amused him. Griffin would never call such a man his king.

Egan stroked his long wiry beard. "Well, it's no matter now. Even kingless men can die at the order of a king."

Riona shot Griffin a venomous look over her shoulder before focusing on Egan once more. "I will do you proud, Majesty. Please allow your humble servant your blessing this day." She pressed her forehead to the ground before Egan.

The king stood and lifted a hand. "Riona Nieland, you are blessed. This fight will end when one of you dies. Should Griffin prevail, he wins the contract for the indentured child, Nessa." He stared down at Riona with a lecherous gaze. "Should my favored warrior, Riona succeed, she will earn herself a promotion in rank."

"Thank you, sire." She lifted her face to him, gazing at him through the veil of her lashes, as if she welcomed his attention. "You honor me."

Griffin snorted, but he doubted anyone heard him. Even when he was loyal to Regan, he wouldn't have groveled like this woman. But Egan demanded such fawning from his loyal subjects.

She pushed to her feet, and Griffin faced her, the rusted sword firm in his grip.

Riona gave him a fearful look as she slid her sword free. Was she scared?

Griffin dropped his sword to the sand. "I won't fight you."

Riona cocked her head to the side. "That's a shame because I will fight you."

She lifted her sword in a wide, uncontrollable arc, missing Griffin entirely.

"Have you ever gone to battle?"

Riona narrowed her eyes. "There is no need for battle in Myrkur."

"Maybe not in the castle." Had she lived a comfortable life being told her sword skill could beat anyone's?

"Fight her, Griffin!" Gulliver's scream rose above the crowd.

Griffin couldn't find his charge in the dark, but he sighed, wishing the kid would heed his command to leave. For once.

"I won't fight you," he repeated.

She advanced on him, tossing her sword from hand to hand, her eyes narrowing. That was when he saw them.

The wings unfurling from her back.

Riona Nieland was a Dark Fae. A Slyph, and a rare one at that. He couldn't take his eyes from the fine white lace-like wings that spread in a wide arc around her. Delicate and beautiful, they looked out of place in the dirt arena. With a sweep of his rusted sword, he could sheer her wings right off her back and leave her lying helpless in the sand.

How was this woman Egan's prized warrior?

The crowd cried out for blood, for violence.

And all Griffin wanted to give them was surrender, peace.

This time, when Riona lifted the sword, Griffin had to duck her attack from above.

"You cannot win if you do not fight," she growled, landing behind him.

Nessa's face had been a permanent fixture in his mind since she was taken. Normally, thinking of her made him feel vulnerable. A reminder that he couldn't save her.

But now, those thoughts gave him strength. He still had a chance to walk away from this.

Griffin lunged back from Riona's air attack, sprinting to where he'd left his sword. Riona wasn't far behind. As soon as he gripped the hilt and whirled around, he blocked her sword, the blow far heavier than he'd expected from such a small fae.

In the orange glow of the torches, they danced together, her wings fluttering like a dragonfly's.

"I thought you weren't going to fight me?" she grit out as their swords clanged once more.

When Griffin didn't answer, she went on. "What changed your mind? Fear?"

"I'm not scared of you." He drove her back with another attack.

"You should be."

He met Riona's cold blue eyes. Ebony hair fell loose from her single braid.

He didn't want to fight her, even though she was loyal to Egan. He'd been in her shoes once before.

But still, this was for Nessa, for his makeshift family.

"Why aren't you scared of me?" She jumped back to avoid his blade.

"Because." He kicked her, sending her sprawling to the sand. "I have something to fight for."

They were the truest words he'd ever spoken. For the first time in his life, he wasn't torn between what was right and what was his duty.

And it was freeing.

"The girl?" She jumped to her feet, sword in hand. "She means something to you?"

He didn't answer as his chest heaved with his labored

breath. Riona didn't look as tired as he felt. She circled him, her breath even and her brow free of sweat.

The crowd jeered above them, but even that noise faded away, and it was just Griffin and Riona.

Sweat ran down Griffin's face as they circled each other, neither making a move.

"Fight!" the king yelled.

They both ignored him.

He might rule the prison realm, but down in this pit, there were only two people who got to decide what happened next.

With a growl, Riona sprinted toward him, her sword raised. He blocked her attack, the momentum pushing her back. She came again, this time sweeping her sword at his legs.

He jumped over the blade and ducked her sudden move into the air above him.

Something clattered to the sand, and they both looked up to see a jewel encrusted dagger the king threw for his champion.

Riona looked from the dagger to Griffin.

"Go." He clenched his jaw. "I never expected this to be a fair fight."

She shook her head. "There will be honor in your death. I will not cheat to bring it about." She wasted no time advancing on him once more.

Pain seared up his side as her blade glanced off his ribs. Crimson blood trickled along his bare skin.

Pushing the pain aside, he blocked her next attack, twisting to the right before jumping toward her with his sword raised. She slipped out of the way just in time.

Griffin's wound opened wider, letting blood pour down his side. But there was nothing he could do about it. Not now.

Now, all he could focus on was staying alive long enough to end this fight.

Commotion on the king's platform stole his attention for a moment. Nessa appeared carrying a tea tray for the king.

If Griffin failed, that would be her life if she were lucky. More likely she'd end up in the opal mines or worse.

Nessa's eyes drifted to him for a brief moment, and Griffin wished he could see her more clearly, that he could know if she was okay.

With renewed energy, he rushed for Riona, meeting her move for move. His body began to recall his former training, like muscle memory.

She had nimble feet and lightning fast wings, yet he suspected she had an even quicker mind. But everyone was beatable.

"I won't let her become you," he bit out. Riona groveled before the king, flattering him and taking whatever scraps he gave her. Today it was a jeweled dagger, but tomorrow it could be rags.

The words surprised Riona, and she paused long enough for her sword to drop just the slightest bit.

He knocked the sword from her hand, kicking it across the arena. She'd duped him in the beginning. "You weren't scared before. Do you feel it now?" He rested his sword against her throat and a hand at her back, gripping her wing joint. One twist, and she'd never fly again.

She swallowed, the truth evident in her eyes. She knew she'd lost.

She closed her eyes for a brief moment before settling them on Griffin. "At least grant me a warrior's death."

Griffin nodded and pushed her down to kneel before him, his sword still at her throat. He stared down at his rusted blade as the sounds of the crowd swept over him.

They wanted someone to die, and to them, it did not matter who.

The king rose from his seat, anger flashing across his face.

Griffin ignored him as he wiped sweat from his face. His entire body was hot, exhausted. Not only from the fight but the days leading up to it. Finding Nessa, trying to set her free, knowing he'd lost when the king's men found him.

It all brought him to this moment. He glanced from Riona to the crowd chanting for her death. Only moments ago, they'd cheered for her to prevail.

He circled her, lifting his sword. He rested the tip on her back, her tattoos disappearing and reappearing along her arms. This was what she wanted, what the people wanted.

He lifted his voice to the crowd. "You want her death? You call for her blood?" He sucked in a breath. "This isn't right. The people of Myrkur should not be fighting each other. We're all stuck here, we're all forgotten. And yet ... you wish for barbaric practices." He looked to the king. "I reject your demands."

He lowered his sword and threw it across the arena to join Riona's. "I reject death. I reject blood." He circled Riona again, and she lifted her eyes. They weren't icy as before, only confused. Anger coursed through Griffin as he watched her odd markings snake along her arms. This was what his life had become, a constant struggle for survival. And he had no one to blame but himself.

If he wanted to end the cycle of struggle, he first needed to change himself.

Dropping to his knees, he winced at the pain in his side. Blood oozed out with nothing to stop it. He focused on the girl in front of him. "I will not kill you today." His voice was meant to be soft, reassuring.

Riona's eyes narrowed, and a scowl formed on her face. "You are a fool, Griffin." Her voice was so low only he could hear. "There will be consequences."

"There always are." He lifted his voice once more so the crowd could hear him. "I will not kill Riona Nieland." Cheers and boos provided a mixed reaction, but they weren't Griffin's concern. The little girl standing next to the king was. "I won this fight and the prize."

He stood near the platform, his eyes never leaving Nessa's fearful brown ones.

"Griff!" Gulliver's yell of warning was enough to make Griffin turn as Riona ran for him, sword in hand.

Griffin scrambled for his own sword and managed to block a series of rapid attacks. His strength out dueled her waning speed.

Ice raced through his veins as he readied for another attack. But it didn't come. Riona stopped, her hand drifting up to cover her mouth. "Your eyes."

"My eyes?" It took him a moment to realize what she'd meant. He'd felt the surge of magic in his veins. The ice. But it wasn't possible. The prison barrier meant anyone who crossed it did so without their magic. It had been a cruel part of his imprisonment, and one he hadn't expected.

Only one thing could have stopped Riona's attack. Magic. The Dark Fae feared magic because they'd never had it.

His eyes flashed violet, a reaction to the Iskaltian magic he wasn't supposed to have. It was fleeting, only enough to surprise Riona into stopping her attack. Then, it was gone.

The king lifted a hand. "I declare this fight over. My greatest warrior lives. Though Griffin has bested her. For that he has earned his freedom."

Griffin stiffened. "No, not my freedom. I did this for the girl. I won her contract."

The king stroked his tangled beard. "And yet, Riona still lives. I don't think you're in a position to negotiate."

Riona stepped in front of Griffin, a thoughtful look on her face. Griffin braced himself for her to reveal what she'd seen. Instead, she met the king's gaze head on.

"Sire." She spoke loud enough for the king to hear but not the surrounding crowd. "It will benefit you to be seen as merciful and honest. It's just one girl."

Griffin looked from Riona to the king and back again. Moments ago, they'd tried to kill each other, and now ... now, she was his only hope of saving a girl he loved like his own kin.

The king's gaze softened as he considered Riona's words, studying her face with a fondness that surprised Griffin.

Egan's expression brightened, and he snapped his fingers. "Excellent idea, dear. Nessa, come here."

She took a tentative step forward but didn't say a word.

"Do you want to be released?"

She nodded.

"No one can say I'm not a merciful king." Griffin saw it

happening in slow motion. King Egan shoved Nessa forward. She teetered on the edge of the platform before he pushed her again. Only air greeted her on the drop.

Griffin ran past Riona as Nessa's cry rang in his ears. He lifted his arms, but the momentum of catching her drove him onto his back with Nessa thudding into his injured side. Pain seared through him, but it didn't matter. He had her. He hadn't failed this time.

Nessa's little hands clung to him.

Griffin sat up, keeping a hold on her. He brushed a hand over her hair, down her shoulder, looking for any sign of injury. "Are you okay, Ness?"

She nodded as tears slipped down her cheek.

The world grew hazy, the sounds fading away into the dark. He tried to look around, assuming Riona had already left to join the king. A pool of dark red blood seeped into the sand at his side.

Blackness crept into his vision.

"I've got you," he whispered to Nessa.

But it may have been a lie because his arms slipped from her and weakness tingled throughout his body.

He put a hand to his wound, trying to stem the bleeding. Blood oozed between his fingers moments before he fell into a different kind of darkness.

It was an immense thing: Dying. A life could be summed up in one's final acts. At least, he hoped so. No one remembered the Griffin who'd chosen the wrong queen and done truly evil things. The prison magic wiped those memories from the realm.

The Griffin O'Shea the prison realm would remember,

the one it would mourn, was a man who'd protect the people he loved no matter the cost.

And he figured that was a pretty darn good way to leave this life.

Nessa's sniffling receded into the distance as Griffin fell onto his back, letting his last sight be of the stars overhead.

Chapter Three

A stabbing pain shot through Griffin's side, and he came up swinging, fearing he was still in the king's fighting pits.

"Calm down, you big baby, it was just the first stitch." Shauna pushed him back down on the table in her kitchen—a kitchen where he'd eaten most of his meals since his arrival in Myrkur. The day he'd stepped through the border magic that separated the three fae realms from the prison world, Shauna basically saved his life. She'd brought him to her home before the king's guards could take him to the castle. As a new arrival, he would have had a rough initiation into Myrkur society as an indentured servant.

She'd guided him through the mountain pass where it grew darker and darker until they arrived in a land where the sun never shone.

"Are you trying to flay me alive, Shauna?" Griffin grit his teeth as she bent over his injured side.

"No, the king's favorite did that for you. Hold still, you've got a gaping hole in your side." A frown marred her face as she went about her work. Even after ten years without magic, his first instinct was to call on his power to ease his pain.

"This is how the humans do it." He reached for the bottle of spirits she'd used to clean his wounds, taking a long drink before she wrestled it away from him.

"That's my last bottle." She set it back down and passed him a wineskin instead. "Tell me one of your humantales. It will distract you." Shauna had lived her whole life in Myrkur and stories of humans were as bizarre to her as fairytales were to humans.

"It's more likely to entertain you than distract me." Griffin glanced down at the long gash from arm pit to waist, hoping it would grow numb soon.

"Humor me." Shauna leaned closer to see in the candlelight. He hated to waste her candles. They were such a precious commodity in their small community.

"They have this place," Griffin began. "A sort of tavern called McDonald's."

"And this Mr. McDonald serves good ale?" Shauna asked, stabbing her needle through his skin again.

"No ale." He winced, taking another drink from the wineskin. "He serves a sort of sweet, bubbly drink called Coke. Ice cold and refreshing on the hottest days."

"Your humantales always revolve around food and drink." Shauna's stomach gurgled.

"But that's not the best thing Mr. McDonald serves." Griff sneaked one last sip of her spirits. "The food. Oh, Shauna, the food is divine at McDonald's. Cheeseburgers and fried potatoes with ketchup and salt."

"I know what cheese and salt is, but that's about it," Shauna murmured.

"Imagine thick slabs of meat between slices of soft bread and melted cheese with onions and pickles. And ketchup is this tangy tomato sauce that makes everything taste better. And for the kids." He turned and smiled at her, the spirits warming his face. "They have Happy Meals that come with a toy."

"Now you're just making things up." Shauna shook her head with a smile.

"I'm completely serious."

"This Mr. McDonald can just afford to give away toys with a meal?"

"The human world has so many wonderful things. I used to think I could never give up magic to live there, but I've since changed my mind." He winced as she pulled her thread tight. "Tell me she's okay, Shauna."

"Nessa? Of course she's as right as rain, tucked into her bed, dreaming of her hero, the great Griffin O'Shea." She smoothed his hair back from his face. "Thank you for bringing my sister home safely. Even..." She sucked in a breath. "Even though she eavesdropped on our conversations and relayed parts to the king."

"She's just a kid. I can't hold that against her. You know I'd do anything for you two, but I sure thought I was going to fail this time. How did I get out of there alive?"

"Gulliver, who else?" She went back to her stitching.

"Of course." Griffin sighed. The boy was going to find himself at the end of a hangman's noose one of these days.

"After you passed out, the guards dumped you and Nessa in the slums outside the castle gates. Gullie found you just as some scumbag was trying to take off with Nessa. He stole a cart, and they managed to get you in it and pushed you all the way back here before you could bleed to death. It took them most of the night."

"Guess I should probably go easy on the boy."

"Seeing as he saved your life, probably so."

"Where is he now?"

"I fed him some scraps for dinner and sent him to bed an hour ago."

Griffin scoffed. "I've never known that boy to do anything he's told. He's probably out skulking around for his breakfast, the little thief."

"You take good care of him, Griff. You take good care of all of us in Fela."

"That's not how it works, and you know it. In Fela, we take care of each other." Their village was unlike any other in all of Myrkur. Those in the castle lived well on the king's wealth. The indentured who served him ... did not. And the ones who refused to work for the king, or were cast out as useless, lived in slums and poor villages throughout the kingdom, each doing the best they could to survive.

Not everyone in the prison realm was a criminal. There were good fae here. Some were born in Myrkur—the descendants of those criminals sent here from generations past. And some were sent here for small crimes, while others were the Dark Fae of Myrkur, imprisoned here in their home realm long ago simply because they were different from other fae, the Light Fae Griffin had always known.

When he first arrived in Fela, it barely qualified as a town. But it always had one thing all the other places lacked. People who still cared about each other's well-being and weren't simply out for themselves. In the years since, Fela had grown into a community where everyone worked together for the good of all their citizens—right under the king's nose. Hidden among the rockiest mountains of Myrkur, the valley they called home was known only to those who lived there.

"You nearly done?" Griffin's words slurred a bit from the drink. He wasn't much of a drinker anymore. Once upon a time, when he lived among royalty, he drank nothing but the sweetest wine. It was much harder to come by here, and he'd lost his taste for it.

"Not yet, keep drinking. We're going to be here for a while longer," Shauna murmured, focused on her task.

"Where's Hector?"

"At his mother's. Hush now, I need to focus." She prodded his arm, pulling the mangled flesh back together as best she could.

"When's he going to make an honest woman of you?" Griffin took a long pull from the wineskin, grateful his side had grown numb.

"He has a family to take care of already, and I have Nessa. The little ones need him now that his father is gone."

"So, you're both going to sacrifice your youth to care for your families and not seek a little happiness for yourselves?"

"We are happy in our own way, Griff. And we don't need any more mouths to feed."

"I'm just saying you love him, Shauna. You deserve to be together. He's a good man, and I only say that because I am drunk. On any other day, I'd say no man is good enough for you."

Shauna snorted, pulling her thread tight again.

"Are you done yet, or do you intend to knit a sweater out of my hide? I'd like to sleep in my own bed at some point tonight," Griffin said with a grimace.

"You'll sleep on the floor in front of the fire when I'm done with you. You can go home after I'm sure there's no infection. But you will hold still if you ever want to move properly again. There is muscle damage here."

"That damnable Slyph woman and her sharp sword." He growled as Shauna tied off the last of her stitches and splashed mineral spirits across the inflamed wound before she wrapped it with clean linens.

"You'll heal, you stubborn lout." She stood to stretch her tired limbs. "And just where do you think you're going?" She eyed him as he tried to stand.

"I need to check on Gullie."

"Gulliver is fine. You can check on him after you've had your tea." She moved to her small counter where she crushed herbs and made potions for everyday ailments for her family and their neighbors. She was both midwife and healer for their small community, and she'd worked hard to learn her craft from her mother before she passed.

"Fine." Griffin shoved off the rough-hewn table and staggered to the rocking chair across the room by the fireplace. The room started to spin as he collapsed into the chair.

"Drink this." Shauna shoved a warm cup of herbal tea into his hands.

"Mmm." He took a long sip and sighed, leaning his head back. "You shouldn't waste your honey on me."

"It tastes awful without the honey." She propped his feet up on a stool and checked his bandages.

"Stop fussing over me, I'm fine." He sipped the fragrant tea, letting its warmth ease his tensed body.

"Thank you for saving Nessa, Griff." She leaned down to kiss his forehead. "But don't you dare get yourself killed, you hear me?"

"Yes, ma'am." He slurred and frowned. "What'd you put in the tea, Shauna?"

"Just a little concentrated lavender and elderflower syrup to help you sleep, so you don't run off when I'm not looking and re-injure yourself."

"Shauna." He groaned, his eyes drooping.

"Hush and finish your tea so you can sleep and let your body heal."

Griffin leaned his head back against the headrest and did as she said.

"Night, Shauna," he murmured as she went to find her own bed.

Griffin gazed around the small room that was as familiar to him as his own home a stone's throw from Shauna's door. It was funny how it had taken a prison sentence to give him a life he could be proud of. They didn't have riches or power, or even magic, but they had what mattered. Friendship. Community and family. And that gave him a reason to get up in the mornings. Still, Myrkur wasn't the kind of land dreams were made of. Far from it. It was always night in the realm of the Dark Fae. And that meant precious little grew here, so they relied on the few crops they could cultivate, hunting and gathering. Whatever they didn't have, they either went without or improvised.

It wasn't always that way for the people of Myrkur. Only a few generations ago it was a land like all the other fae realms. A kingdom of its own, ruled by the Dark Fae kings who were good to their people. But the Dark Fae didn't always get along well with the Light Fae. Particularly those from Fargelsi, where Griffin grew up. For the Dark Fae, their magic came from their defining characteristics that allowed them the power to fly or the ability to see in the dark or a host of other physical traits that made them different.

Over the years, Griffin had pieced together the history of how Myrkur had become a prison realm. Queen Sorcha O'Rourke of Fargelsi—Queen Regan's grandmother—was often at war with the Dark Fae kingdom who shared a border with her far to the north. She persecuted those Dark Fae within her borders.

Her persecution grew so heinous that the other fae realms, Iskalt and Eldur fought against her in a great war that no one outside Myrkur could remember. To protect the Dark Fae from annihilation, a treaty was signed among the four kingdoms, agreeing to isolate Myrkur behind a barrier spell to protect the Dark Fae from Queen Sorcha and those like her. To save the last of his people, the Dark Fae king agreed, and the boundary spell was erected around Myrkur, utilizing the magic of Fargelsi, Eldur, and Iskalt—only Queen Sorcha changed her part of the spell, causing everyone outside the boundary to forget those on the other side. In the generations since, Myrkur came to be known simply as the prison realm —a place fae criminals were sent as punishment for their crimes, knowing the world and all those who loved them would forget they ever existed.

In the years after the boundary went up, the Dark Fae began to thrive again in their own kingdom. But there were many who hated the king for agreeing to the boundary, and a rebellion ensued. Anarchy and chaos reigned for years until a new king seized the throne. King Egan's grandfather. Under the Byrne Kings, Myrkur had become exactly what Queen Sorcha wanted it to be, a prison.

Griffin's eyes drooped as he set his empty mug aside. His belly was warm, if not full, and his mind fuzzy from Shauna's herbs. He fell into a dreamless, peaceful slumber in front of the fire.

He hadn't slept long when the back door crashed open. Griffin was on his feet before he was fully awake.

"Get inside you little thief, before Chieftain Kvek's men come to drag you to the gallows." Hector marched Gulliver into the kitchen by the scruff of his neck.

"What's he done now?" Griffin yawned, ignoring the ache in his side.

"Stole a hoard of food from the Chieftain of Drykur." Hector crossed his arms over his chest, letting out a snort of disapproval. With his great bullhorns and the ring in his nose, Hector was an intimidating presence.

"Just a couple of eggs and a ham." Gulliver squirmed in Hector's grip, the flat of his tail thumping against his captor's chest. "That greedy old Kvek had at least forty hams in his smoke house, he ain't going to miss one, is he?" Gulliver broke free of Hector's hold.

"Just a ham and eggs?" Griffin stared down his long nose at his charge. "Empty your pockets."

"Come on, Griff, the old toad doesn't need all that food." Gulliver pulled a dozen eggs from his hat and a smoked ham he'd tucked inside his worn coat.

"It doesn't matter how much Chieftain Kvek has. The

point is that food isn't yours, and it's not worth your life to risk taking what doesn't belong to you."

"But look at it, Griff. It smells so good." Gulliver stared at the ham, practically drooling. The flat, leaf-shaped end of his tail tapped against Griffin's face. "You can't tell me we're not going to eat it. Besides, you brought Nessa back home. I thought a nice breakfast feast would be a good way to thank you."

"Gullie." Griffin bent to Gulliver's level. "Next time you want to thank me, just do your chores."

"What's he done now?" Shauna shuffled into the kitchen, her hands on her hips.

"Stealing food, as usual." Griffin folded his arms across his chest, trying to keep a stern frown on his face.

"You listen to me, young man." Shauna cuffed him on the back of the head. "When you stay at my house and I send you to bed, you stay in that bed until you're called for. You don't sneak out. Griffin almost died trying to save Nessa, and that's the thanks you give him?" She tapped her foot on the stone floor as Gulliver hung his head in shame. His long wiry tail thrashed in agitation behind him.

"And don't flick that tail around my kitchen either." Shauna went to brew a pot of tea.

Gulliver grabbed his tail, and the end of it snaked around his arm, twitching with his pent up frustration. Gullie could never hide his feelings. His tail gave him away every time.

"Empty your pockets," Griffin repeated.

"I did." Gulliver's voice went up a few octaves.

"Your other pockets are bulging, Gullie." Griffin pressed his lips together.

Heaving a sigh, Gulliver pulled a loaf of bread from his

coat pocket, followed by a wedge of cheese and a string of sausages from under his shirt.

"Bring your mother and sisters over, Hector." Shauna settled a skillet on the stovetop. "They can help us eat the evidence."

CHAPTER FOUR

Griff stretched his arm over his head as he ran a hand along the wound in his side. It ached when his skin stretched and pulled, but he'd had worse pain since coming to the prison realm.

Nearly a week ago, he'd almost died. Almost faced the fact he'd leave this world with few people to remember he'd ever been there at all. His brother, Lochlan, wouldn't mourn a brother he couldn't recall.

The woman he once called wife wouldn't cry for him.

He stood in the center of their rudimentary village, watching his people going about their daily tasks. He wasn't sure when it happened, but the people of Fela were his family now.

A group of men and women walked along the dirt path through the village carrying buckets of water in each hand, water that would be boiled and made safe for drinking. The nearest water source was a small mountain spring near the cliffs that bordered their land.

Life here in the night realm wasn't easy. He glanced down at his hands, a prince's hands, that had been made rough with work. He cleaned, cooked, harvested meager food supplies, and ventured out to nearby villages for trade. Here, nothing was beneath him. There was something freeing in that thought. No one expected him to change anything or make the hard decisions.

For the first time in his life, there was no pedestal under his feet. He was truly one of the people.

"You should still be resting." Shauna stepped up beside him.

"It's been almost a week. I've had enough rest. There's work to be done."

"There's always work," she scoffed. "But we also need to take care of ourselves. These people count on us."

That was their first mistake. Even a decade later, Griffin didn't think of himself as someone to be trusted or relied upon.

A sigh rattled through his chest. He'd done his penance, ten years of it, so why did he feel like it would take the rest of his life to earn the forgiveness he wanted?

His eyes found Nessa trying to help unload one of the trader's carts. Leaving Shauna behind, Griffin snuck up behind the kid. "Ness."

She screamed, and he laughed.

"Relax, Nessa. It's just me."

She turned around, a frown turning her lips down. "Don't sneak up on me."

He sent her a wink. There weren't many people who could drag smiles out of him. Nessa was one of them. Once upon a time, he'd been a happier sort.

But he was a young fool back then.

"Come on." Griffin lifted a crate of eggs into a small wagon. "You can carry the torch and help me make some deliveries."

Nessa's eyes lit up. For some reason, the kid idolized Griffin. He wanted to tell her he wasn't the kind of man who deserved adoration, but he held his tongue, not wanting to break her heart.

To her, he was the man who'd risked his life to protect her.

He didn't need to look to know she followed him. The first house they came to looked like a strong gust of wind might topple it. Griffin gestured for Nessa to knock, and she did, placing their torch in the old cracked urn in the yard.

An older woman with tiny horns on top of her head answered, a bright smile on her face.

"Lady Walsh." Griffin bowed.

The woman laughed. "I ain't no lady, Griff, but I could get used to your bowing."

He rose. "Not a chance, my dear. But who needs a bow when they have eggs?"

Mrs. Walsh opened the door wider. "You should have led with that. Come in, come in."

Griffin nudged Nessa forward into the house.

Mrs. Walsh pursed her lips. "And just how many of these eggs do I get?"

"As many as your heart desires." Griffin winked. The old women of the village saw right through his charm. "Seems our foragers were lucky on the morning hunt."

They hadn't had eggs in weeks other than the occasional

ones Gulliver pulled from his pockets. One day, Griffin would have to deal with his thievery.

"I'll only take a few quail eggs." Mrs. Walsh reached into the bin Griffin brought in from the wagon. "Others need them much more than an old woman like me."

Griffin had never before lived in a place where each and every person thought of the other residents before themselves.

"Now scoot, children. I have some meditations to do." Once Griffin stopped at the door, she called to him. "Oh, Griff, you might want to check in on Sinead. She hasn't been feeling well, and those children of hers are quite useless."

Griffin nodded. "I will. Thanks."

Once outside, his eyes found the glow of the cook fires in one of the communal shelters at the center of town. Large pots hovered over the fires, filled with water for boiling.

"Ness, you think you can make some deliveries while I go check on Sinead?"

Nessa pushed a dark lock of hair behind her ear and nodded. Taking the torch in one hand, she pulled the wagon behind her with the other.

Griffin put a hand on her head. "You know what to do."

Even the children in the village pitched in, just trying to survive. There was no such thing as a childhood spent playing games and running amok. Not here. This place forced them to grow up fast.

He watched Nessa make her way over to Mrs. Walsh's neighbor and turned to cross the street. Lifting a hand, he knocked on Sinead's door.

No one answered.

He knocked again before pushing it open. Griffin's eyes

found Sinead. She lay in a small bed with a flattened straw mattress, and the remnants of a thin blanket covered her. Bright red hair clung to the sweat on her face.

"Sinead?" Griff rushed forward. She was even worse than Mrs. Walsh implied. Sinead Ryan wasn't much older than Griffin. He scanned the one-room home, looking for her three boys.

Sinead shook as a coughing fit overcame her.

"Where are your boys?" Griffin knelt beside the bed and put a hand to her forehead. She was burning up.

She coughed again. "They were assigned to the harvest today."

Their village had small fields near the cliffs. They didn't yield much, but what they did was vital for their winter stores.

Griffin closed his eyes. It wasn't the first time in the last ten years he wished they had access to healers from the other three realms. Sinead wasn't the first villager to fall ill over the last year. It had happened more and more frequently. A few recovered. Most did not. Yet, they hadn't found the cause.

In Myrkur, lives were brutal and short. It was everything to survive one day at a time. He'd buried too many friends, too many good fae.

And he knew just by seeing her, Sinead wouldn't cling to life much longer.

"I'm going to get Shauna." He pushed to his feet. "She can help you."

He practically ran from the room until he reached the fresh air. It was happening again, the loss. But he couldn't tell anyone how sick she was.

He sprinted across the village, finding Shauna surveying

the pots of boiling water as they were poured into wineskins to be rationed out for the day.

Stepping up to Shauna, he dropped his voice. "I need you to come with me without causing a commotion."

She looked to him in question. "Has your wound reopened?"

"No. It's Sinead."

Shauna's eyes widened. "Show me."

Together, they made their way back to the sick woman. Shauna lowered herself next to the bed. "Hello, darling." She pushed hair out of Sinead's face, a tiny smile on her lips.

But there was something about the action... Shauna looked at Sinead the way Griffin had once looked at his wife.

A wife who'd never truly loved him, but that hadn't seemed to matter at the time.

It made so much sense now, why Shauna and Hector were only friends. She was in love with someone else. Someone she might lose. Tears streamed down her cheeks.

The door opened again, and Nessa slipped in.

Griffin blocked her path. "Ness, you shouldn't be in here." The fewer fae exposed to whatever ailed Sinead, the better.

Shauna looked over her shoulder at Nessa. "Run home and get my kit."

Nessa nodded and disappeared.

"You should go, Griffin." Shauna lifted a tear-stained face to him. "Did you touch her?"

Griffin shook his head.

"Okay, good. Now, go."

Griffin didn't make a habit of disobeying Shauna. The

people looked to her as a leader. Shauna was their healer, and she protected them.

Griffin no longer wanted that kind of responsibility. He'd seen what true power did to him before. He couldn't handle it. In his experience, power corrupted those who wielded it.

He walked back through the village, completing the deliveries Nessa didn't get to. He greeted everyone by name, taking pleasure in the familiarity of the act. Small tasks suited him, they made him feel useful even as his thoughts turned to Sinead.

He returned to the cart loaded with the available goods and moved all the meat into the main cellar beside the cook shelter.

This haul would feed the village for at least a week. More if they were careful.

A young boy streaked through the village, colliding with Nessa who was racing back to Sinead's house with more supplies for Shauna. The boy picked himself up off the ground.

Griffin reached Nessa and helped her up so she could run along to help Shauna.

"Sir." The boy met Griffin's gaze.

"I'm not a sir." Not anymore. He searched for the name in his mind. "Patrick?"

The boy nodded. "That's my name, si—Mr. Griff. I was with Gulliver just now," he gasped. "We was just playing on the road through the mountain pass, and they came."

"They who?" He stepped closer to Patrick. "You were playing outside the gates?" Fear sliced through him.

"Yes, sir. Sorry, sir—Mr. Griff. The king's soldiers. They

was with Chieftain Kvek." His voice dropped. "I hid among the trees, but Gullie..." His voice shook.

Griffin took a fortifying breath. "Are you saying the king's men have Gulliver?"

Patrick nodded. "They was saying he'd hang for his thievery."

Griffin's gaze hardened. The king had taken so much from them, he wouldn't have Gulliver. "Patrick, fetch me a horse."

"You can't be meaning to go up against the soldiers, Mr. Griff?" The boy trailed along behind him.

"That's exactly what I mean to do." For Gulliver. He'd save him and then never let the boy out of his sight again. They'd always known his thievery would catch up to him one day. Today was that day.

Patrick ran for the village stables which only consisted of three stalls and a small exercise pen. Cart-pulling mules took up two of the stalls. And the third... an aged horse that was better suited for the pasture.

Well, staying here suited Griffin too.

Hector jogged toward him before matching his stride. "I just heard. Griffin, I don't care how good you think you are in a fight, it's only been a few days since your injury. You are not at full strength."

"You sound like Shauna." He pushed into his own small home, one he shared with Gulliver.

Hector followed him in. "I'm coming with you."

Griffin raised one brow before bending to pull his sword free from its hidden place beneath his bed. "Going to walk now, are you? Kvek's stronghold is only a few hours away by horse, but longer on foot."

"I still won't let you go alone. I'll take one of the mules."

Griffin straightened to regard his friend. Over the years, he'd developed a relationship with Hector, similar to the kind he wished he'd had with his own brother. "Okay."

Griffin used to think magic made a fae who they were, but then he'd come to the prison world. He'd met fae like Hector who'd never had magic. Nor had he ever seen the sun. He was a Dark Fae who'd lived in this realm his entire life. And he was Griffin's friend, a brother. Magic didn't matter so much when no one had it.

Once outside, Hector ran for the stables.

Patrick led the ragged horse to Griffin. The village took good care of the horse they'd named King, but still, this was a kingdom that beat down even the noblest of its creatures.

A kingdom that let fae like Kvek carry out the king's justice anyway he liked. If he got his way, Gulliver would hang. And soon.

Griffin only hoped he wasn't too late.

Pain seared through his side as he pulled himself onto the horse. Hector joined him a few moments later, pulling his large frame atop the mule.

By the time they left, word of Gulliver's fate had made it around the village, and fae stepped from their homes to wish them well.

The journey to Kvek's stronghold and the village surrounding it seemed to take forever, though it was only a few hours. Griff didn't know what time it was, but his eyes had become adept at seeing in the dark over the years.

They reached the far pass where stone walls rose high. Kvek was a loyalist, never forsaking his king, and he was well compensated for it. Hours from here, fae struggled just to survive.

And Kvek lived like a king. Beyond the stronghold, a village stretched into the distance, many times as large as Fela.

Hector whistled low and long. "And just how do we get into the stronghold?"

Griffin scanned their surroundings. He blew onto his hands to warm them as he thought back to the first time Gulliver came back with stolen goods from Kvek. Griffin told him it was too dangerous, that thievery never ended well.

He'd been right.

"We need to get around the stronghold to the village." There was a way in, he was sure of it. He pictured the dripping wet clothes Gulliver had come home in, despite the hours-long ride on the horse he'd stolen the year before.

The horse Griffin currently rode. Gulliver had been sneaking into the stronghold for years. "Did you know Gullie was the one who brought us King here?" He patted the side of King's neck. Gulliver named him, saying he looked like King Egan himself.

A fact Griffin did *not* share with Egan when he was his prisoner.

He shook his head with a laugh that didn't belong here. Shauna might have saved his life all those years ago when he first arrived in the prison realm, but Gulliver had saved his spirit. Before Gullie, Griffin hadn't wanted to survive. He hadn't known if he had the strength to make it in such a place. Everything he was had been stripped down to the core, leaving behind a version of himself he hadn't recognized.

Until he found the tiny, malnourished Gulliver. The kid gave him a purpose, he gave him strength.

"We need to take the high mountain road to get in." Griffin pointed to the hills in the distance.

Hector didn't argue. His mule would do much better than Griffin's horse on the high road with its narrow path and sheer drop.

Griffin clicked his tongue, and the horse climbed. And climbed. When it got too narrow, he slid from the saddle in favor of leading the horse.

Rocks shifted beneath his feet, falling down into the pass.

Griffin could hardly breathe as the path started its descent. The closer they got, the more he could make out smoke coming from chimneys, turning the dark sky into a hazy gray. He spared a glance for the stronghold with only two sentries manning the tower.

An ogre paced down below, looking for any wrongdoers. Griffin had only faced an ogre once before on a trading trip to a village near the shores of Loch Villandi. He'd led his party too close to the ogre encampment. That ogre was the first Dark Fae blood he'd ever spilled.

But it wasn't the last.

The path widened, and Griffin looked back at Hector to make sure he was still with him.

They both mounted up, preparing to ride into the village. The small cottages were in much better shape than any Griffin had seen in other villages, proving riches poured into this part of the realm.

Griffin spent ten years refusing to pledge an oath to the king. Maybe if he had, life wouldn't be so hard for his people.

But he was done compromising his morals.

He was done seeking riches and power.

Now, he only wanted to be left alone with his family and friends.

The ogre had his eyes trained on the horizon ahead, leaving his back turned to the mountains, allowing Griffin and Hector to slip into the village unseen. A river ran straight through the center of town and under the stronghold. That was their in.

He tried to remember everything Gulliver once told him.

There was a thick metal grate blocking the entrance from the river, but the spikes didn't reach the river bottom.

"Hector, I hope you know how to swim." He waited for Hector to catch up on his thinking before the two shared a smile.

They backed up into the trees obscuring the end of the path from view. They slid down and tied up their mounts. If everything went well, they'd be back in no time.

But one thing Griffin learned in the war of the fae queens... nothing went according to plan.

The two men walked through the village as if they belonged. Stone roads cut through town instead of the dirt paths he was used to. Long bridges spanned the river at intervals.

And looming over everything was the seemingly impenetrable fortress.

They reached the bridge closest to the stronghold. The current rushed beneath them but not in the direction Griffin needed to go.

He studied the water for a long moment before making his way down to the riverbank under the bridge, heaving a sigh before slipping into the cool dark water. Hector followed without a sound.

It took every bit of strength Griffin possessed to swim against the current. And that strength? It was much less than he'd once had outside this dark world.

"Griffin!" Hector yelled. "I can't..."

Griffin spared a glance behind him where Hector was losing his battle with the current. "It's okay," he yelled back. "I won't fail this time!"

Whether Hector was with him or not, Griffin had to do this.

For his own heart as well as Gulliver's. As he neared the grate, his eyes caught on the gallows, built right up against the walls. No one would ever forget who hanged the enemies of Myrkur.

And Gulliver could be next.

With renewed energy, his arms sliced through the water, the chill of the river numbed his wound until he reached the grate blocking the tunnel under the keep. Gripping the metal bars, he let himself rest a minute.

This was for Gulliver, he reminded himself before plunging below the dark water, using the metal bars as a guide. Water pushed at him, trying to make him loosen his hold.

He pulled himself deeper and deeper until he felt the spikes on the bottom of the grate.

Gulliver was right. They didn't reach all the way down. His lungs screamed for air, but he didn't turn back.

Instead, Griffin kicked against the current, pushing himself deeper, using the metal spikes to swing his legs under before pulling the rest of his body free.

He kicked as hard as he could, his head going fuzzy.

When he broke the surface, he gasped for breath, letting his lungs fill again and again, gripping the grate as the current rushed against him.

He wiped the water from his eyes, and that was when he noticed it. The torchlight.

He wasn't alone.

He searched the open landing beside the rushing river until his eyes fell on someone he never expected to see again.

Riona crouched near the edge of the river, swirling a hand in the water. She didn't look at Griffin as she spoke. "When one of my men alerted me to the man in the river, I didn't expect to see you." Her voice held no emotion, no indication of what she'd do.

"Did you call the guards?" he asked. "Or Chieftain Kvek?" Griffin hesitated to move closer to the landing.

Her nose scrunched in distaste. "Kvek is sleeping. If I wake him, I won't get to be the one who decides what to do with you."

Griffin knew almost nothing about Riona other than she was the king's favorite and a heck of a swordswoman. "I've come to make a deal." A deal he hadn't told anyone about. "Kvek holds one of my men, a boy really. Gulliver is young. He doesn't deserve to hang. Me, however... Kvek would do just about anything to get his hands on me."

He didn't know if that was true, but Griffin was willing to divulge his connection to Regan if it meant he could switch places with Gulliver.

Riona stood, torch still in hand. "Climb up here. You can wait."

She turned and left without an explanation, locking a heavy wooden door behind her.

Griffin pulled himself from the water, wringing out the bottom of his shirt. He wasn't afraid of his own death, not when he knew he was already living on borrowed time. Shauna once told him the past couldn't haunt him forever.

He'd proven her wrong.

Griffin watched the door, waiting for guards to arrive and arrest him. He wished he'd said goodbye to Shauna, to Nessa. They'd hate him for his decision to sacrifice himself. But there was no other option for Griffin.

His eyes drifted to the river, and thoughts of Hector worried him. He hoped the man had made it back to the horse by now.

The lock rattled before the door opened, and Gulliver stumbled in.

Griffin lurched to his feet, his healing wound twinging in pain as he wrapped the boy in a hug.

"Ew, you're wet." Gulliver laughed, but he didn't push Griffin away.

"We have to get you out of here. Take the river." He pulled away.

Gulliver smiled. "You have been listening to me, haven't you? I told you it was a good way in."

Griffin scanned Gulliver's face, taking in the bruises stretching over his boyish face. He didn't deserve to live in a world like this.

Riona entered the room, and they froze. Her tattoos shone in the orange glow of her torch.

Griffin gave Gulliver a sad smile. "You go home and tell everyone I love them, okay?"

Gulliver looked from Griffin to Riona, his eyes lighting with understanding. "No. Griff." Tears gathered in his eyes. "This is my fate. You can't take it upon yourself."

Griffin put a hand on each of his shoulders. "I can, and I will. This is what we do for the people we love. Take care of our fae, Gullie. Be what they need. Always."

Gulliver's lips quivered as tears spilled down his bruised cheeks. "No... I..."

Griffin pulled him into one last quick hug before pushing him toward the water. Gulliver didn't take his eyes from Griffin as he submerged himself. It wasn't until he ducked under the water that their eye contact broke, shattering something in Griffin. He always knew he'd die at a king's order. Winning in the pits was only a delay.

He turned to face Riona and held out his wrists. "I won't fight you if you need to chain me."

Her brow furrowed. "You... care for that boy? You'd sacrifice yourself for him?"

Griffin looked to the water once more. "I'd do anything for him."

She stepped forward, her eyes studying him. "Go." She jerked her head to the water.

"What?"

"I said go, Griffin O'Shea. You spared my life in the fight, now I repay my debt to you. Next time I see you, I *will* kill you."

Griffin raised a brow. "You'll try. What about Kvek?"

"He'll wake to find his prisoner gone, and he will search for him. Hide that boy well."

Griffin didn't know what to make of this soldier, one who was loyal to King Egan, yet let Griffin live. Twice.

He slipped into the water. "Thank you."

She didn't respond as he pulled himself under the grate and let the current take him to the boy he'd give up everything for. The boy he'd raised as his own.

The boy who'd be in danger until Kvek grew tired of the search.

Hide him well.

He intended to.

CHAPTER FIVE

Griffin ran up the trail through the mountains to catch up with Hector and Gulliver, his clothes dripping and sodden, making him shiver in the darkness. He didn't trust Riona at her word, that somehow by releasing him the score was settled between them. It was too easy. And nothing was ever easy in Myrkur.

"Griff loves you like you're his own son." Hector's voice reached him across the rocky terrain. He could just make out their forms ahead. Gulliver's tail dragged sadly behind him, and his shoulders drooped.

"Griff would never let them hang you, Gullie. He'd die first before he'd let anything happen to you." Hector draped a strong arm across Gulliver's slim shoulders as they led the horse and mule along the narrow path.

"But it's all my fault, Hector. He's going to die because I was careless."

"And you best remember that next time." Griffin jogged to catch up with them. "I'll not make the same sacrifice twice." Though Griffin knew he'd do it a hundred times over to save the boy he'd grown to love as his own.

Gulliver turned at the sound of his voice. "Griff!" His tail swished, slapping Hector's face side to side.

"Gulliver." Hector yanked on the boy's wayward tail.

"Sorry." He snatched his tail out of Hector's grasp and ran for Griffin. "You escaped!"

"Something like that." Griffin swept the boy up in his arms. "Don't ever scare me like that again, kid." He hugged him tight.

"I won't if you won't." Gulliver squeezed him back, his tail wrapping around Griffin's neck to thump against his head.

"Mind your tail, Gullie. You're choking me." Griffin made a strangled noise in his throat.

"Oh, sorry." Gulliver forced his tail to behave.

"I can't believe we both got away with it." Gulliver lunged ahead with a spring in his step. All worry gone from his mind.

"That's the lesson you take away from this?" Griffin dragged him back by his shirt collar. "We didn't get away with anything, kid. We've got to hide you. Chieftain Kvek will not be happy if he doesn't have someone to hang come morning. He'll send his men out to look for you."

"Aw, don't make me do it, Griff." Even Gulliver's pointed ears seemed to wilt along with his tail at the mention of hiding.

"Oh, you did it to yourself this time. You know where to go once we're home. There'll be plenty of supplies in the cellar. You stay put until I come get you, or so help me, I will hang you myself."

Gulliver heaved a dramatic sigh. "Can Nessa come visit me at least?"

Griffin paused on the trail just on the outskirts of the valley where Fela lay hidden from most of Myrkur. He bent down to Gulliver's level and placed a hand on each of his shoulders. "This is serious. You will stay in the cellar and not make a sound, you hear me?"

"Yes, sir." Gulliver's head fell forward.

"Your life depends on it this time. We got lucky tonight. We won't get a second chance to save your neck again, so for the sake of us all, try to sit still for once in your short life."

Gulliver made a face at that and ran ahead to open the gates that no one outside of Fela would even notice were there.

"You know it will be a miracle if that boy makes it to adulthood alive." Hector slapped Griffin on the back, shaking his head. "It's good to see you alive, Griff." He shuffled along behind Gulliver, leading the mule through the open gate.

"If he does make it, I'll surely have a head full of white hair, or none at all," Griffin murmured as he tugged on the horse's reins, pausing to close and lock the heavy gate behind them. The gates were an engineering marvel and brilliant camouflage that protected the existence of Fela from outsiders. Made of rocks and vines on the surface, it blended with the landscape, making it look just like the cliffs and crags surrounding the narrow entrance to the valley where they lived. Passersby would never know a valley lay behind the false cliff.

Underneath the camouflage, a strong metal structure

held it in place with a lock only those of Fela knew how to open, and they guarded that secret with their lives.

"I'll see to King." Hector took the reins from Griffin. "You see Gullie settled in the cellar with something to keep him busy."

"And quiet," Griffin added. Villagers were already up and moving about their homes in the stillness of the morning. When Griff first arrived in the night realm, he struggled to adjust to the constant darkness. It had always felt like endless night to him, but over the years, he'd learned to see the subtle nuances of a Myrkur morning, and this was shaping up to be a beautiful one. In the absence of sunlight, mornings here were cool and calm. There was a serene stillness about the dawn in Myrkur just before the birds began to sing, and the morning dew covered their world in a clean blanket of sweet smelling freshness. It was Griff's favorite time of the day.

It was late morning before Griffin made his way to the small orchard where Gulliver was to hide until the danger had passed. Naturally, he was out climbing trees and not hiding below ground in the natural cellar they used to store their seasonal provisions. It occasionally served as a hideout as well.

"Gulliver, what will it take to get through to you this is no game?" Griffin stood beneath the oiche fruit trees. The dark tangy fruit was one of the few things that grew hearty and healthy in the land without sunlight. Griffin and several of the men from the village had worked hard to plant the seedlings and cultivate them into a viable orchard over the years. They'd only just reaped the benefits in the last few years as the trees grew strong enough to yield a harvest. This year's harvest would be the best yet. If the village boys didn't pick them clean before harvest time.

Gulliver dropped down from the branches, dark juice running down his chin. "I was hiding, Griff. I swear. Just up in the air instead of underground."

"I saw you from the road, and my night vision isn't like the Dark Fae's. If Kvek's men come for you, they'll find you with little effort."

"No one knows about Fela though. So, why can't I just hide at home?" Gulliver crossed his arms over his thin chest, his tail swishing behind him, swirling up a cloud of dust.

"It's called being extra cautious. Now, get below. I brought you something to keep you busy while you're here."

"Is it work?" Gulliver reluctantly followed him into the woods surrounding the orchard.

"Of a sort."

"You know how I feel about work." A clear spring trickled through the woods, disappearing into a crevice in the rocky ground at the base of a sheer cliff. It was the farthest corner of the valley, their most protected spot. Griffin stepped through the thick creeping vines that covered the cave opening.

At first glance the space seemed nothing more than a mountain crag worn away from erosion as the spring ebbed and flowed with the rains. And anyone looking for a hiding spot would seek somewhere with less mud and muck.

Just as the gates that guarded the pass into the valley shielded Fela from the eyes of the king, the rear wall of the crevice protected their winter stores. Together, Griffin and Gulliver shifted the false wall to create an opening they could slip through.

Beyond the wall, a huge cavern opened up before them. Crates of provisions the villagers had managed to put up for the coming winter season stood along the far wall. The underground spring surged and gurgled at the back of the cave where a small mossy field of mushrooms, root vegetables, and onions grew in the dim light of the glow worms that illuminated the ceiling.

"When I was a kid, I would have jumped at the chance to play here." Griffin gave his ward a little shove into the room. "You can hunt for the biggest mushrooms, pick shadow berries by the stream. Collect a couple of glow worms, and you can catch some fish for your dinner. You can even go swimming and wash up in the spring. You could use a good wash."

"It's boring here." Gulliver kicked at a barrel of cider.

Griffin smiled at the sullen boy. He didn't do well without playmates to get in trouble with. "Let's sit, and I'll get a fire going for you in the oven."

The camp at the back of the cellar had everything Gulliver would need while in hiding, but he had to be very careful with the fire. Hector had engineered an underground oven that would keep the camp warm. It would funnel the smoke through a mud brick chimney that dispersed it through the mountain tunnels and crevices, but it could only handle a very small cook fire.

"Look in my bag," Griffin said as he fanned the small flame in the deep fire pit. "It was going to be your name day present in a couple of months, but I thought you could make good use of it now."

Gulliver rooted through the bag to find a rock carving kit Griff had traded for with the cooper in Drykur. He'd also collected an assortment of ivory and jade stones.

"This is mine?" He ran a hand over the smooth wood of the box. "Thanks, Griff!" Gulliver settled down on a log stump by the fire to examine the tools. "What should I make?" He held up a large jade stone from the box, his eyes round with delight. Gulliver was a talented craftsman. Give him a stick and a knife and he'd whittle the most beautiful figures faster than one could blink. If the boy ever lived to become an adult, he could make an honest living as a tradesman.

"I thought you could make us a chess set." Griff stoked the fire and slid a large flat rock over the pit to hide the flames and heat the stone for warmth later in the night.

"What's chess?"

"A human game. I've sketched the figures we'll need. They're in the box."

"Will you come teach me to play when I get it done?"

"Of course." Griffin sat on the log opposite him. "I'll stay the night with you tonight and come back soon to check on you, and we'll have a lesson then."

Gulliver was already busy shaping the largest rock with a flat-edged chisel.

"I'm sorry to have to ask you to stay here, Gullie."

"It's okay, Griff. I know I messed up." Gulliver swiped the flat end of his tail over the stone that was already taking shape under his skilled fingers.

"It's not just that, kid. You know who I am," Griffin said gently. "Who I really am."

"You know I'd never betray your secrets, not like Nessa—but she's young so you have to forgive her. So, you once loved and respected Queen Regan. She was your sort-of mother, and you didn't know she sent innocent people here. Of course you loved her. It's like how I love you. We don't have anyone else, you and I. But together we're a family."

"That's right." Griffin smiled. "And I know you'd never betray me. But I followed Regan even when I knew she was wrong."

"She took you in after your real parents died." Gulliver shrugged as if it were that simple. To him, it was.

"The point I'm trying to make is that I don't want to ever see you in a position where you'd have to tell my secrets."

"Well, you don't need to worry about that because I wouldn't tell."

"What have I told you a thousand times?" Griffin leaned forward.

Gulliver snorted, narrowing his cat-like eyes at him. "If I'm caught and anyone asks about you, I'm supposed to spill my guts."

"That's right. You tell them what they want to know about me, and I will handle it. You're not to put yourself at risk for me."

"Why is that? Didn't you put yourself at risk today to save me? What's the difference?"

Griffin smiled at that. "I'm the adult, that's why. It's my job as your—whatever I am—to look out for you. Not the other way around."

"You can say it, you know." The tip of Gulliver's tongue

poked out between his lips as he concentrated. "You're my father."

***

Griffin headed back to his small cabin early the next morning, feeling confident Gulliver would stay hidden this time. For a moment, the light along the horizon reminded him of long-forgotten sunrises. And then he smelled the smoke. Thick, dark clouds billowed into the star-lit sky, tinged with the light of flames.

Soldiers were in Fela. Griffin ran, ignoring the pain in his side from his still-healing wound, the wound that hadn't fared well in his river rescue. "Shauna!" he shouted as he ran to where her house had gone up in flames right next to his.

"Griffin." She stumbled to reach him. "They're here for Gulliver." She clutched his shirt in her fists, her eyes wild with fright. "They must have followed you here."

"Gullie is safe." Griffin grabbed her hand, trying to make sense of what he saw. The village was gone. Everything they'd worked so hard to build had gone up in flames. The king's men swarmed the center of Fela, rounding up its inhabitants. His gaze zeroed in on the woman in the midst of the chaos.

"Riona." He stalked toward her, rage consumed him just as the fire consumed everything he and his neighbors had. "We had a deal!" He slammed into her, knocking her to the ground.

She lifted a hand to halt her men as she picked herself up, flicking her delicate white wings behind her. "That was yesterday." She narrowed her dark eyes at him. "Before you led the king's men to a secret village that shouldn't exist. You're all guilty of theft."

"Theft?" Griffin crossed his arms over his chest. "Taxes you mean?"

Riona nodded. "Half of everything you own belongs to King Egan."

"We are just surviving here. There's nothing left for the king." Griffin refused to live in a world where one man took half of everything. That was why he and the others built Fela into the communal village it was. They couldn't survive without each other.

"The wealth you've accumulated here says otherwise. How have you managed it with such small numbers?"

"Wealth? We barely get by." Griffin's hands balled into helpless fists at his sides. This was why they went to such lengths to hide their community. There were countless villages all across Myrkur who slaved away to pay the king's taxes, leaving little for themselves and their families.

Riona glanced around at the villager's sooty faces. "Where are the rest of them?"

"The rest?" Griffin shook his head in confusion.

"Surely there are more of you. These few families can't account for the large crops and livestock—the mill and the smithy. Where is your chieftain?"

"We have no chieftain." Hector stepped forward. "We are a communal village."

"Communal?" She scoffed at the very idea that they would all work together for the good of the community.

"Everything you've burned belonged to Fela." Griffin moved to stand with his neighbors. "Nothing we have here belongs to any one fae, and certainly not to a chieftain—

therefore, no taxes are owed, and no crime has been committed." They were careful to adhere to the letter of the king's law in that regard. It was a loophole they'd found that gave them the idea for the communal crops and farmland to begin with. If no one owned it outright, then no one was responsible for the taxes. "You're welcome to take half of what each family owns, but seeing as you've burned it all, there is nothing left."

"What about your grain stores?" Riona demanded.

"You burned the grain house," Hector said.

"Surely each family has their own stores for bread making."

"No, ma'am." Hector's mother, Kiaran stepped forward. "The grain is stored at the grain house. The women gather there once a week to bake bread for the village, and the children deliver the loaves to each of the families."

"You just give the food away?" one of the king's men asked, scratching his head in confusion.

"Yes," Kiaran said. "It is our way."

"It is your way no longer." Riona wiped a hand across her sweaty brow, her ebony hair falling over her shoulder. "You may rebuild, but you will pay the king's taxes, or we will return, and you will all wish you'd never been born. Now, where is the boy?"

"What boy?" Shauna lifted her chin, shoving a sobbing Nessa behind her.

"The thief with the twitchy tail. He escaped his punishment and led my men here. He will pay for his crimes in service to the king."

Griffin was grateful he'd left Gulliver where they would never find him and only hoped the boy would stay put.

"I've got the wee pest right here, lady." One of the soldiers entered the village center with a wriggling Gulliver hanging from his meaty palm by the scruff of his collar. "Caught him trying to shoot your men with a slingshot."

Griffin's heart stopped in his chest. This was what it was like when a parent knew their child was in danger and could do nothing to intervene. He turned pleading eyes to Riona. She'd let him go once.

She shook her head. "I tried. It's beyond my control now. I'll see to it he doesn't hang from Kvek's noose. The king will have use for his skills. That is the best I can do for him now.

"Move out." Riona shouted to her men, leaving Griffin and the inhabitants of Fela to the ashy remnants of the village they'd called home.

CHAPTER SIX

Griffin couldn't take his eyes from the road. The dust kicked up by the horses settled back down to the ground, and still, he watched.

He could hear Gulliver's pleading until one of Riona's soldiers knocked him over the head to shut him up.

Riona, the soldier who'd let him escape Kvek but came back to do what? Get revenge? He refused to believe she was powerless to stop what happened. The soldiers listened to her as a favorite of the king's.

The same king who now had Gulliver.

"Griff." Shauna gripped his arm. "I know what you're thinking."

If anyone knew his mind, it was her. He hadn't hesitated to infiltrate the castle when Nessa had been taken. And he'd ended up in the fighting pits facing Riona. Now, it was Gulliver in the king's grasp. He'd do no less for the boy he'd raised as his own. But this time, he had no illusions that the king would allow him to win his freedom.

Shauna kept talking. "You can't go after him."

"I have to." He turned his gaze on Shauna.

"Look around, Griff. You're needed here."

He turned, taking in the still-burning structures that once served as homes for their people. Many gawked at the flames, frozen in shock at their meager possessions now turned to ash.

The village never had much, but now they had nothing.

"Sinead." Shauna ran toward the two men carrying the dark-skinned woman away from the burning flames of her home.

Griffin followed his friend and looked down into Sinead's golden eyes. "How is she?"

Shauna crouched down at Sinead's side. "Not good. Before the king's men came, I tried all my herbal remedies on her, but they didn't seem to make a difference. I don't know what's wrong with her."

Nessa sprinted across the broken village, barreling into Griffin's legs and wrapping her arms around him. "We didn't know if you'd come back."

Griffin bent to look into the angelic face. "I'll always come back to you. I'll always save you, protect you, and teach you to protect yourself."

Griffin had known many strong women who didn't need him at all. If he had any say in it, Nessa would grow to be just like them.

But she wasn't the only one he'd made promises to.

He straightened and turned to address the gathering crowd. Heat from the flames licked along his skin, and he knew they'd burn long into the night until there was nothing left. "Have we lost anyone?"

Hector came to stand at his side. "We'll get a count."

Griffin nodded. Since coming to this village, he'd always said he didn't want to be a leader, that he couldn't trust himself with an ounce of power. But his people needed someone to lead, especially with Shauna worried over Sinead.

Hector sucked in a fortifying breath. "Gather what you can. We'll move to the caverns at the orchards until we can rebuild."

"Rebuild?" Kiaran's voice was so quiet only Griffin could hear. "Now that they know we're here, there's no point in rebuilding. They'll come again."

"You know that, and so do I, Mother, but right now our people need hope." Hector squared his shoulders and gathered his family close to him.

"What do you need, brother?" Hector asked.

Gulliver. Griffin needed Gulliver. But he didn't say it, didn't reveal his secrets. Because the truth was, Griffin changed because of Gulliver, became a better person for a child who needed him. If something happened to him... it scared Griffin... what he might do. The lengths he would go to save Gulliver.

There was a darkness inside him, a darkness that lost him everything he could have had and sent him to this horrible place where not even an innocent child was safe.

"I have to go to him." Griffin looked from Hector to Shauna and the rest of their people. He'd break into the castle a thousand times to save his people. "Hector, I need you to hide our people, protect them. You're their leader." He always had been. The people looked to both Griffin and Hector, but most of the fae here were Dark

Fae. Hector was one of them in a way Griffin never could be.

"I don't like the sound of that. Don't speak as if you aren't coming back."

Griffin sighed. "Would you rather I lied to you?"

First, he'd save Gulliver. If he survived that, he'd find Riona. This was her fault, and he'd make sure she faced consequences for betraying his people in favor of a king who cared nothing for them.

Goodbyes were never easy, especially when one didn't know if they'd ever see the people again. He left the caverns days ago on a morning marked by dewy grass and a cleansing breeze. He'd long stopped measuring his days by the rising and setting of the sun.

He'd spent the previous night trying to call on his magic. He'd felt it in the fighting pit, he was sure of it. And Riona had seen his flashing eyes.

How had it returned? And why was it so weak he couldn't use it?

Had the king seen it?

But now, the magic wouldn't come. It was as dormant as it was the moment he stepped through the barrier into the prison realm.

What would Brea think of him now? Would she be proud of her husband—if she knew he existed?

It had been a long time since he'd done something purely because he hoped to erase some of the deeds of his past. He'd learned it wasn't possible, that good did not outweigh bad.

Yet, that wasn't the reason he headed to the palace now.

This was for his family.

Hector stayed behind to take care of their people, and Shauna wouldn't leave Sinead's side as long as she was ill.

So, it was just Griffin. Alone.

How it was meant to be.

He reached the king's forest near the castle early in the evening, but he spent another day scouting the area. Tomorrow morning, he would make his move. Beyond getting inside and finding Gulliver, he had no plan. Before, when trying to save Nessa, he'd stolen the clothes of a king's guard. It got him in, but hadn't offered him any protection.

That wouldn't work this time. It barely had last time.

The closest village to the castle stood at the edge of the king's forest and showed all the signs of prosperity that came with loyalty to the king. But the slums that rose up just outside the castle gates were proof of what happened to those who fell out of favor.

Griffin set up his camp right outside the slums, blending in with the teeming crowds. He tied King beside his camp and lifted his saddle off. He didn't dare leave it out in plain sight for the thieves. Weary to his bones, Griffin didn't bother to start a fire or eat the meager food stores he'd brought before he bedded down for the night. Failure weighed on his mind, more prominent than he'd ever felt before.

When would it stop? When would the king let his people live in peace?

Griffin wanted to be done with fighting. If he never picked up his sword again, it would be too soon.

He rolled over on his hard bedroll, resting his head

against King's saddle, thinking of all the people he'd let down in his life. It was hard to think of his former life as belonging to him because it was a different world. He closed his eyes and pictured the cottage in the idyllic Fargelsi countryside he'd once called his own. It was surrounded by rolling hills and green grass, like an image from a painting.

So different from the dark and mountainous Myrkur.

He'd started drifting off when footsteps had him jerking upright. He couldn't make out a face in the dark until the man grew closer. The first thing Griffin noticed was his uniform. One of the king's men.

"What do you want?" Griffin reached for his sword, pulling it free of the scabbard.

"I have a message from Riona Nieland. Are you Griffin O'Shea?"

"That's me."

"Riona will meet with you in the woods near the northern gates." The man turned away, and his footsteps grew quiet as he faded into the darkness.

"Wait," Griffin called. "When will she be there?"

The man didn't respond.

Griffin cursed as he rolled to his feet and made quick work of saddling King. He didn't bother packing his belongings. Things could be replaced, but he wouldn't miss his one chance to rescue Gulliver.

He pulled himself into the saddle and clicked his tongue, nudging King forward. Together, they raced across the night.

It was most likely a trap. He knew that just as much as he knew Riona couldn't be trusted. Her loyalty to Egan was bone deep.

He reached the trees, slipping under the canopy cover to

avoid being seen by the guards in the northern tower. He slipped off King, letting him take a rest in the relative safety of the forest.

Riona wasn't there.

For what seemed like hours, Griffin paced back and forth, one hand on the hilt of his sword. It was hard to keep track of time in the prison realm, and he didn't know how long he'd waited before snapping twigs alerted him to another presence.

Griffin pulled his sword free, brandishing it in the direction of the noises.

Someone groaned and fell to the ground. Griffin would recognize that groan anywhere.

"Gullie?" He sprinted toward him, finding the kid sprawled on the forest floor, his eyes closed. Fear gripped Griffin as he dropped to his knees and patted the side of Gulliver's face. "Hey, buddy, wake up. You can do it. Open your eyes."

Another groan was the best thing Griffin had ever heard.

Gulliver's eyes slid open, and Griff couldn't take his gaze from the puffy bruises circling each eye.

"Stay with me," Griffin whispered, bowing his head.

"G-Griff." Gulliver's chest heaved like breathing was the most difficult thing he'd ever done.

A tear slipped down Griffin's cheek, and he wiped it away. The prison realm hardened people, and Griffin was no different. This boy was the only person who could bring tears to his eyes.

"What did they do to you?" Griffin checked Gulliver for further injuries, finding raised red stripes along his arms and back. "They whipped you?" He couldn't keep the horror from his voice. King Egan's punishments were legendary, but Griffin doubted he'd have gone to such lengths to punish a small crime against a chieftain.

No, this had another purpose.

Information.

A cry left Gulliver, and tears built in his eyes. "I betrayed you, Griff." He closed his eyes. "They wanted to know all about you."

"The king already knew I was an O'Shea."

"He didn't care about that. I told them everything, Griff. I tried not to, but it hurt so bad, I just wanted it to stop. They... they..." He moved slowly as if everything caused him pain as he rolled onto his side.

Griffin didn't understand at first. He looked for further injuries before his eyes landed on what was missing.

His eyes widened. "Gullie."

The king's men had cut off half of Gulliver's tail, the thing that made him who he was. The flat leaf shaped tip was gone.

Having never known Dark Fae existed most of his life, it took a while to get used to seeing wings and horns and tails.

But he knew what those features meant to the people who had them. It was their version of magic.

The remaining part of his tail didn't flick with Gulliver's emotions, it didn't wrap around him. Instead, it sat lifeless, dormant.

"I'm going to kill them for this." Griffin grit his teeth. "One day, Gulliver, we will rid our home of the noose the king places around us."

"Don't say that," Gulliver whispered. "I didn't come alone."

Griffin's eyes shot to the trees as soldiers materialized.

"Back away from the boy." One of the soldiers aimed an arrow his way.

"He's hurt. I can't."

The soldier stepped closer. "You will do as we say."

Griffin leaned down to speak to Gulliver, ignoring the soldiers. "I guess this is where I sacrifice myself."

"No, Griff. You can't. They'll kill you now that they know you were one of Queen Regan's loyalists."

The only thing Dark Fae, prisoners, and the king agreed on was their hatred of the Fargelsian royal line who developed the magic that trapped them here. That he'd served one of their queens made Griffin an enemy of all who resided in Myrkur. "I'll be okay. Do you think you can ride?"

Tears flowed down Gulliver's cheeks. "I..." He paused as a sob shook him. "I can ride."

"That's good." Griffin brushed hair back from Gulliver's forehead. "Our people are in the caverns. You'll be safe there."

"But you? How will you be safe?"

Griffin didn't answer. He didn't deserve safety, didn't deserve mercy. It took ten years for his deeds to catch up with him in the prison realm. And now that they had, he welcomed the end of his torment. If this was how he could atone for his mistakes, then he'd gladly go with the soldiers.

As he stood, he broke all the promises he'd made to the people he cared about. That he'd be okay. That he'd return to them.

They were impossible words.

Two soldiers gripped his arms, pulling him away from Gulliver. "You're going to be okay, Gullie."

Gulliver struggled to sit up, his eyes never leaving Griffin. "I'm sorry, Griff. I failed you. This is because of me."

Griffin shook his head. "Don't ever blame yourself. The king wants me because of the actions in *my* past, not yours."

Gulliver got to his feet. "No, Griff. Nothing you did matters. Not here."

"I wish that was true. Don't wait until you're too far down a dark path to become the person you want to be." Griffin didn't fight the men holding him. He deserved this fate. "Be good, Gulliver. Whatever your life becomes, be a good man. Because there are no regrets in goodness. And regrets can shatter the soul."

Gulliver leaned against a tree for support as the soldiers chained Griffin's wrists together.

Griffin spent the last ten years trying to make up for the person he'd been before coming to the prison world.

But in the end, redemption didn't matter.

"I'll admit." King Egan poured Griffin another glass of bitter red wine. "I was a bit surprised when my guards told me they'd captured the man who'd fought for his freedom in the fighting pits." The king's toothy smile and thunderous laughter made Griffin cringe with disgust. The man was vile, but this reception was not quite what he'd had in mind when the king's soldiers dragged him into the castle. "For a moment, I regretted not letting you keep your freedom. But just for a moment."

Griffin grew up in the finest palace across the three realms, but the Myrkur castle was little more than a crumbling ruin. What was once a mighty fortress was now a hovel the king and his loyal servants called the Great Castle of Myrkur, the seat of the lord of the prison realm. The drafty halls and fortified battlements seemed as if one good storm would level the whole structure, but the king concealed those flaws under a layer of fancy furnishings crafted with gold and silver-plated designs.

Even now, the ancient oak table was covered in the finest linens, stained with wine and what looked like blood but fine, nonetheless. What infuriated Griffin was the veritable feast laid before the king. A prime cut of beef, roasted vegetables, fried fish, stuffed peppers, fresh crusty bread with melted butter, and three kinds of pie for dessert. It was enough to feed all the people of Fela for several days, and most of it would likely go to the pigs when the king was finished.

"Another steak, O'Shea?" Egan carved a thick slab of meat from the rare and bloody roast at the center of the table. "That one not to your liking?" Egan gestured with his dagger at Griffin's full plate. He refused to eat from the king's table.

"No, thank you." Griffin took a sip of dark red wine from the gaudy silver goblet at his elbow. He recognized the flavor of oiche berries. He watched as the king cut his meat, stabbing it with his ruby dagger before stuffing it into his mouth. The rich juices dripped down the short tusks protruding from his jaw and flowed into his beard.

When one thought of a fae king—even a Dark Fae king—Egan was not the image that came to mind. Rough around the edges, dirty and without the benefit of a single table manner, he disgusted Griffin.

Egan leaned back in his throne-like chair, propping his feet up on the table and resting his plate against his broad barrel chest where he continued to shovel food into his mouth. "The O'Sheas of Iskalt were a mighty clan long ago. You are the last of them. You and your king brother."

"We are." Griffin didn't feel the need to mention his uncle, Callum O'Shea, who was currently a prisoner in the deepest darkest cells of Iskalt.

"I could have use for a man like you." Egan nodded, managing to chew his food with his mouth closed for once. Taking a deep gulp of his wine, the king spilled more into his dark gray-streaked beard than he managed to get into his mouth. His hair wasn't much better than his beard. Long and stringy and threaded with braids and bits of leather and beads, he looked more like a battle-worn warrior than a king. Griffin supposed that was what it took to control a prison realm once ruled by true kings. "I could offer you and your lady friend a comfortable position at my court."

Griffin snorted at that, taking up his wine goblet to cover his sneer. This was no royal court, and Egan was no true king. And Shauna would have a few choice words to the king about being any man's *lady friend*.

"I apologize, your Majesty." Griffin pasted on a smile. "What lady friend?"

"They call her Shauna, I believe. Her and her little girl. The one you fought for. Bring them to the castle, and they'll have everything they could ever want."

"And what role would you have me play among your... court?" Griffin leaned forward as if he was highly interested in what the king had to say.

"The O'Sheas have a singular magic, I am told." The king abandoned his meal in favor of more wine. "I can offer you much wealth for the use of your magic."

"I have no magic, your Majesty." Not anymore. Griffin folded his hands in front of him. He'd grown weary of this dance.

"Magic can be restored," the king said with a wave of his hand. "Did you like your taste in the fighting pits?"

That was him? Griffin met his dark gaze. "You..."

"Yes, though I am but a lowly Dark Fae, I managed to return a sliver of your power, just enough for you to feel it, for you to trust me. I can return it all."

"How?" Griffin would never trust this fae, but he needed answers. Griffin ran through everything he'd learned about the Dark Fae in his mind. If one of them had magic, it changed everything. Was that how the king kept his throne?

The king shrugged. "I have my ways. There is a spell that even a Dark Fae can perform, if you know the words that will direct the magic back to its owner."

Egan leaned forward, droplets of wine hanging in his beard. "You will serve me."

"At what price?"

"Serve me." The king leaned forward. "Give me your loyalty, and I will restore a portion of your magic to you. To use in my service, of course." His rough voice shifted like gravel in his throat. "You are a nobleman, O'Shea. I can give you your life back. Wealth. Status. I can restore you to power... of a sort. You and your woman will rise head and shoulders above the rest of my court. I can give you riches beyond your wildest dreams." He sat back as if he'd just offered Griffin the world on a silver platter.

"And what do you believe my magic can do for you, your Majesty?"

"You can create portals, yes?"

Griffin's brow furrowed. "What do you want with the human realm?" That was the only reason he'd want Griffin's portal magic.

"You will learn in time."

There was no way Griffin would bring this man into the human realm. None.

"And if I can't open a portal?" He didn't completely believe the king could return that much magic to him.

"Then, you are useless to me. It is well known what happens to those who prove useless to the king. Particularly those with a past loyalty to Queen Regan O'Rourke." Egan refilled his goblet, sloshing wine onto the tablecloth.

The king's outcasts either ended up dead or living in a slum unable to get work. Those rejected by the king were the untouchables of Myrkur society. To help an outcast was to become one. They didn't live long.

"And what of my ward?" Griffin drummed his fingertips on the table.

"Ward?" The king frowned.

"The boy your people tortured for this information you've discovered about my past. The one you nearly killed to get to me."

"The slum rat?" The king paused with his goblet halfway to his mouth.

"Your men cut off his tail." Griffin slammed his fist against the table, itching to get his hands on the king's dagger. To the Dark Fae, their unusual features were a matter of pride. What they'd done to Gulliver was blasphemous and cowardly.

"Aye, I can see how that might anger you. Didn't realize he was your ward." Egan ran a finger over the smooth ivory tusks that were his defining feature, in addition to his pointed fae ears and smooth flawless skin—under a layer of dirt. "We shall do what we can for him. He will live here at the castle with you and your woman."

"And if I refuse your kind offer?" Griffin folded his arms across his chest.

"Then, you are free to go." Egan shrugged. "You are welcome to try to outrun your secrets, but things have a way of catching up to a man in Myrkur when he has nowhere left to hide."

"I see." Griffin drained the wine from his goblet. He was screwed either way.

"Walk with me, Griff." The king rose from his chair and led him from the dining hall.

Griffin followed him down a long corridor, the floor strewn with crumbling rock and litter gathered in corners from years of neglect and a general disregard for cleanliness and good housekeeping. The air was stale and hot. Too little fresh air came in through the arrow loop openings in the walls.

"You're an honorable man, I can see that now," Egan said. "You aren't motivated by the riches and comfort you see here. I can respect that." The king clapped him on the back as they stepped through an open gate into the castle bailey—an inner courtyard behind the safety of the castle walls—what remained of them. The dark green grass spanned the width of the courtyard. The night air was thick with sweat and the musky scent of too many unwashed bodies.

"Stay the night and think on my offer. We can talk again over breakfast. Donal here will see you to your rooms." The king left him with a stooped young man with no remarkable features. An indentured servant.

"This way, my lord." The man bowed.

His formal address took Griffin by surprise. He hadn't been addressed as such in more than a decade. He'd once responded to such epitaphs as "your Highness," or "my lord" as was his right by birth. To hear it now though, it sounded foreign to his ears. That wasn't his life anymore.

Griffin followed the steward across the bailey to the soldiers' barracks. The move was strategic. Rather than wow him with the *elegant* comforts of a guest suite, the king chose to put Griffin in with the soldiers. Egan wanted him to see his army. And see it he did. Hundreds of men and women trained in the inner courtyard. Dark Fae creatures he'd never seen before stood in organized ranks. Great lumbering ogres with their long arms, saber teeth, and mottled moss-like skin. Tall men and women with ram's horns or tusks like the king's. A sea of winged Slyph trained in the skies above the castle. And beyond the castle walls, stretching toward the Black Sea, were thousands upon thousands of soldiers, Dark Fae and indentured, criminals and non.

Beyond the land, to the sea, were the Asrai. What Brea had once called mermaids. He'd scoffed at his wife's human notions of the fae back then. The Asrai were natural habitants of Loch Villandi, the pristine lake that separated Fargelsi and the Northern Vatlands. But when Queen Sorcha banished the Asrai to Myrkur, they made their home in the Black Sea. Griffin didn't know much about them or the Slyph of the sky, but something told him he should find out.

Not only did Egan have a vast army, but he had a navy and air-force too. The king had big plans, and those plans now included Griffin and his ability to portal to the human realm.

Chapter Eight

When Griffin walked into the dining hall the following morning, the atmosphere had changed dramatically. Scores of tables stood where none had the evening before. Egan's court raised a ruckus as they broke their fast on glazed ham, eggs, bacon, and fresh baked bread—more food than Fela had seen in a month. As Griffin made his way to the king's table, his "court" cheered and raised their flagons of ale, calling out Griffin's name like he was already one of them.

"Lads, bring our guest to the table," the king roared above the din. "He's just in time for the morning's entertainment." Egan's jeering smile sent warning bells off in Griffin's mind.

Meaty hands grabbed him by the shoulders and dragged him to sit in the chair beside the king. They bound his hands with shackles and strapped him to the chair.

"I take it you've had a change of heart, your Highness?" Griffin arched a brow at the king.

"You had your chance to accept my offer last night, and you didn't take it." Egan shrugged, spearing a slab of ham on the end of his dagger. "I thought you could do with some proper motivation." He gestured toward the end of the hall with his greasy knife.

Griffin struggled against his restraints, gripping the arms of his chair until his knuckles turned white. At the apex of the hall, Shauna and Nessa were tied to blood-stained posts, their backs bared to the waist. Angry red welts stood out on Nessa's smooth dark skin, but Shauna had taken the brunt of the punishment. Blood streamed down her back, and her head hung limp between her shoulders. Gulliver was nowhere in sight. "Let them go." Griffin turned angry eyes on the king.

"Aye, she's your woman." Egan's thunderous laughter joined that of his court. "Is the wee one your get?"

"What are your terms?" Griffin growled. As he'd suspected the night before, he was screwed either way. He had no choice but to follow the king's lead.

"Your women will work for me as indentured. As long as you serve me loyally, they will clean and see to my chambers. They will eat well and rest easily under my protection. Should you defy me, I will send them to the brothel tents, where they will serve my soldiers, to breed along with the other women of little use."

"And what shall you have me do, my king?" Griffin's voice dripped acid. He would die before he let that happen to Shauna and Nessa, and Egan knew it.

"Walk with me, young Griffin." The king swilled the last of his ale and gestured for his soldiers to release Griffin from his shackles.

"My... women." Griffin glanced to the end of the hall.

He couldn't meet Nessa's terrified gaze. Thankfully, Shauna had passed out.

"The healers will see to them immediately." Egan gave a careless wave in their direction, and Griffin let out a strangled breath when soldiers moved to release them from their restraints.

Griffin followed the king from the hall, surprised when he guided him into his private chambers. He'd expected a pig's sty but was surprised again to see the king's lounge was neat and orderly with simple furniture and not a speck of dust in sight.

"Sit." Egan lowered himself on a chair covered in supple leather, gesturing for Griffin to take the one opposite him. He reached for a sleek ebony box, retrieving an elegant pipe from its velvet-lined interior. He packed the bowl with pungent tobacco and bent to light a long splinter from the low burning fire in the brick fireplace.

He offered the pipe to Griffin, but he declined.

"Your queen's grandmother was responsible for turning Myrkur into a prison." He leaned back in his chair, puffing on his pipe. "Have they truly forgotten us?"

Griffin nodded. "To the outside world, Myrkur never existed, and Dark Fae are the stuff of human imagination. They believe Myrkur is a prison world, created as a punishment for those who break the laws of the fae. The torment of knowing you will be forgotten by all those who once loved you is widely considered the worst possible punishment."

"Sorcha was responsible for that. But her granddaughter is as bad as she was from what I hear."

"Was," Griffin said. "She is dead."

"I suspected." Egan nodded. "We noticed a substantial

drop in new citizens a few years ago, and it has be a very long time since I've welcomed someone of your stature into my fold. It is good news to hear she is dead." He leaned forward. "Tell me, who rules each of the realms now? Your brother is King of Iskalt, but is Faolan still Queen of Eldur? I heard some nonsense from an indentured who came here only a few years ago that a human woman rules Eldur now."

"It is a long story, but Queen Alona is Faolan's human daughter. She's inherited the throne."

"And Gelsi?"

"King Brandon's daughter, Neeve O'Rourke is Queen of Fargelsi now." Griffin gave the facts as they were and offered nothing more.

"Aye, another O'Rourke woman." Egan spat into the fireplace. "We have been captive behind the walls of the border spell for far too long. I mean to bring it down."

"And how am I to help with such an endeavor?" Griffin asked. The thought of bringing down the barrier spell sent both fear and excitement through him. Then, he thought back to the army Egan was building. What happened if they got loose in the three realms?

"We cannot pass through the barrier, but I believe you can portal from Myrkur to the human realm."

"What do you hope to find in the human realm? There is no magic there."

"A backdoor," Egan said. "Open a portal to the human realm and from there—"

"You want me to open a portal into any of the fae realms," Griffin finished for him.

"It can be done?"

"There's only one way to find out," Griffin said. "But

magic has rules. When I travel to the human realm, I can go anywhere I've been before. But when I portal back to the fae realm, I can only return to my original location, which means if I leave from Myrkur to enter the human realm, I have to return here. But with the magical barrier in place, my O'Shea magic might not allow me to pass through the barrier spell."

"That sounds awfully convenient," Egan replied.

"Rather inconvenient for Shauna and Nessa, if you ask me," Griffin said. "I need some assurances, your Majesty. If I am unable to do what you ask, what will become of them?"

"Best you succeed so we don't have to find out. It would be a shame for such a fine young girl to end up in the tents at such a tender age."

"And if I manage to create this backdoor, where would you have me go?"

"Fargelsi. There, you will search for anyone who knows what went into creating the barrier spell. Then, you can find a way to bring it down."

"You want me to search all of Gelsi for a person who might remember what happened three generations ago?" The task was impossible.

"I suggest you start with Brandon O'Rourke."

"And if I may ask, what do you plan to do once the barrier falls?"

"Take my revenge on the Light Fae." King Egan took a deep pull of his pipe, the tendrils of smoke drifting up to the ceiling. "These young kings and queens will have no chance against my army."

Griffin nodded as if in agreement. But he knew one thing Egan didn't. The new generation of Fae rulers might be young, but they were united in a way the realms had never been before. Egan wouldn't see that coming.

The king stood, dashing out the contents of his pipe into the fireplace. Standing behind Griffin, he placed his huge hands around the base of Griffin's skull and recited words Griffin couldn't understand. Long-forgotten but familiar magic surged within him, filling a hole that had stood empty inside him for more than a decade. The icy tendrils of O'Shea magic stretched inside him, lighting the violet fire in his eyes.

Iskalt magic was night magic, and in the night realm, Griffin O'Shea should have been more powerful than he had ever been, but something was missing. He stared down at his hands, trying to create a ball of light or anything so simple. Nothing happened.

"I have returned your portal magic. Nothing more."

Griffin looked to him, wanting to destroy him for everything he'd done, but he couldn't think past the O'Shea magic surging through him.

"You will leave in two days' time for the human realm," Egan said, stepping away from Griffin. He was weakened after returning Griffin's magic to him. "One of my trusted soldiers will accompany you on your journey. You will carry out my wishes, or I will hear about any disloyalty, and your woman and her child will suffer."

"I will serve you well, your Majesty. I will find a way to do as you ask, but I have a few requests. Something to give me some assurance while I am away."

"You may ask, but you try my patience, young Griffin."

"I just need to know that while I am away, Shauna and Nessa will come to no harm."

"I give you my word as king that they shall remain untouched while serving in my household as long as they behave."

His word meant next to nothing, but Griffin pushed on. "And my people? Your men destroyed our village."

"Ah, yes, Fela, I heard about that. Sorry business, taxes. If they pay, I see no reason to deprive them of the crown's assistance in rebuilding. Is that all?"

"One more thing, your Majesty." Griffin paused. Making another request was tricky, but it wasn't about him this time. "I would like to take one of my men with me on this journey. Between the human realm, Fargelsi, Eldur, and Iskalt, we have much ground to cover. I would be grateful to you if I may take a man I trust to help me along the way." Was that enough groveling?

Egan nodded. "Very well. My steward will see to your provisions for the journey."

"We will need money while in the human realm."

Egan snorted his annoyance. "You will be there but a moment."

"Your Majesty is aware that Iskalt magic only works at night?"

Egan nodded. "So, leave at night."

"Time is skewed between the fae and human realms. It will be daylight when we arrive in the human world. We will have to wait for nightfall. There are things we will need for this journey that we can only get there."

"Fine. I'm sending one of my people with you. They will have the means to purchase whatever you may need while in the human realm." Egan urged him toward the door.

With that, Donal appeared from the king's inner chambers and whisked Griffin back to his rooms in the castle. Once alone, Griffin paced the confined space, running his hands through his hair in frustration.

"How did I get into this mess?" He tried the door but wasn't surprised to find it locked. He had little more than a day to figure out how he was going to accomplish an impossible task. He didn't want to think about the possibility of failure. At least not while the king had Shauna and Nessa in his clutches.

But even more, he didn't want to think of returning to a land where his own brother wouldn't know him.

Griff couldn't stop moving. He sat. He stood. He paced in the moonlight streaming in through his window.

The prison realm was supposed to be a one-way ticket. The magical barrier kept it that way. As soon as a prisoner set foot across it, their magic disappeared as did the world's memory of them. No one could explain the ancient magic that had doomed them all.

But now… Griffin stared down at his hands, willing himself to do something, anything. The magic sparked along his fingertips, a familiar and unsettling feeling.

He'd resigned himself to his fate, to living out his days among prisoners and the Dark Fae, all united in one thing.

No one else knew they existed.

Griffin tried the door again. He tried to summon his magic to force his way out. But the power didn't come. The king returned his O'Shea magic, the kind that opened portals to the human world, but it wasn't enough. Griffin had the tiniest taste of the magic that left him many years ago. And he wanted more.

Uncurling his fingers, he flattened his palm against the scratchy fabric of his pants.

Images flashed through his mind. Shauna and Nessa and their terrified eyes. The wounds they'd suffered because of him. It was his fault, their captivity.

And he'd do anything to set them free.

The images changed to people he'd done his best not to think about for years. Regan. The woman who'd been like a mother, the evil queen he'd abandoned too late and wouldn't be waiting for him in Fargelsi.

He'd known Queen Neeve as a servant girl, the one offering kindness in a palace devoid of such things. They hadn't known then she was the daughter of King Brandon, or that Brandon was even alive. Not even Griffin imagined Regan locking her brother away in a cell for almost twenty years.

That would be the smart place to go in search of a way to bring down the magic surrounding the prison world. The histories of Fargelsi were no doubt lost when the palace crumbled in the final battle of the Queen's War.

But there was one person there who might be able to help.

The question was would he? What lie would Griffin have to tell? The prison realm had been created for a reason. None of the three kingdoms would want to mess with that magic.

The image changed yet again, and this time, he saw the people of Fela. A mixture of Dark Fae and those unfortunate enough to be sent to Myrkur. Didn't they deserve for the

Light Fae to know they existed? To know that the three kingdoms didn't only belong to those with traditional magic.

For them, he'd do this. For them, he'd seek a way to bring the barrier down just enough to create an escape route for the good people of Myrkur. And if it didn't work? If Griffin helped to set all those in Myrkur free to ravage the kingdoms he'd once called home? What would he do then?

The kingdoms would have to prepare for war.

Most inhabitants of the prison realm wouldn't want a fight, but tell that to the king's horde of an army eager for war.

The horrors he might unleash on the three kingdoms would be unimaginable.

And yet... he covered his face with his hands. His O'Shea portal magic turned his blood to ice, chilling his skin in a way he hadn't felt in too long.

Still, the portal magic reminded Griffin of his past and where such powerful feelings led. He jumped to his feet and paced the room again. Turning on his heel, he let all the anger, the desperation rise up as a scream trapped in his throat. Without the rest of his magic, he couldn't fight Egan, fight the plan he had for Griff. He picked up a cracked vase and threw it at the door. It shattered, raining shards of glass onto the floor.

"That's one way to greet someone." Riona's eyes widened as she examined the vase. "You must get your anger under control before we leave."

"We?" He snapped his eyes to her.

Riona shrugged, running a hand over the narrow braids creating an intricate design on the top of her head. The tattoos peeking out the sleeves of her shirt seemed even more pronounced on her dark skin, like they had a mind of their own. "The king has graciously allowed me to go on an adventure with you."

Griffin snorted. Graciously. The king's people were more loyal than Griffin thought because Riona voiced the words with a straight face.

"You mean he's sending you to watch me." He crossed his arms, glaring at her and wishing Egan had sent anyone but *her*.

The woman who'd tried to kill him in the pits.

The soldier who'd let him escape Kvek's stronghold.

The loyalist who oversaw the burning of Fela and the eventual trap for Griffin.

To say their relationship was complicated would be an understatement.

"If you're done gawking at me, we have to prepare. We leave tonight." She turned and walked out of the room, her steps measured like that of a soldier always marching to the beat of their master's drum.

Griffin chased after her, her white wings fluttering in his face. "We can't leave for the human realm tonight. The king made me a deal."

Riona's posture stiffened, and she didn't stop walking. "One thing you must learn, Griffin O'Shea, is that the king does not owe you anything, and he does not make deals."

But he had. He'd promised... Griffin shook his head at his own stupidity. Egan only told him what he wanted to hear. There was never an intention of letting Griffin bring one of his own men along. He didn't need a deal when he had Shauna and Nessa in his clutches, knowing Griffin would do whatever it took to see them safe.

"Come." Riona ducked through a doorway into a long corridor with no decoration, only an endless monotony of crumbling gray stone.

"Quaint," Griffin muttered, kicking a pebble out of his way.

Riona shot him a glare over her shoulder. "Myrkur Castle is the greatest castle in all the fae realms." She spoke with a monotone voice as if the words had been programed into her.

But she'd never seen the high waterfalls of Fargelsi or the magnificent sandstone structures of Eldur.

And Iskalt... he had an image in his mind of what the ice palace looked like, but he hadn't been back there since he was a small child. He shut down that train of thought. Missing people who wouldn't know him was useless.

The king was sending him to Fargelsi, a place that held so much pain, so much regret.

Riona led him out into another courtyard before stopping and turning to him. Torches hung along the wall, casting them in an orange glow. For a moment, Griffin pictured what Riona would look like with sunlight reflecting off her dark skin and through her translucent wings.

She crossed her arms and dropped her voice. "What deal did the king make with you?" Concern flickered across her face.

"Why are you asking if it won't be allowed?"

"Because I've known many like you, men who thought they could challenge the king. And you know what happens to them?"

He could guess.

"They die. And their families die. And their associates

die. The king will not hesitate to hurt the girls he is holding captive. That's the first lesson I will teach you. He is ruthless, and he is powerful. Do not cross him. If you do what he asks, he will keep his word. They will be safe in his household."

Griffin curled his fingers in. "And he has just returned my power to me. At least a portion of it."

Riona frowned. "Don't be fooled. I know what he returned to you, the single aspect of your magic. It will do you little good once we are where we need to be."

Griffin leaned against the wall. He wanted to ask where it was Riona thought they needed to be, but he pushed the question away. She'd only lie. "And what is the next lesson you need to teach me?"

"Not all who do the king's bidding are without honor." She started walking again.

Griffin didn't know where they were going until they reached the stables right inside the rusted castle gates. A few soldiers lingered nearby, and the stable boys rushed to and from stalls where dozens of ragged old beasts with dull coats looked out at them. They were the finest horses he'd seen in all of Myrkur, but nothing flourished in a land where it was always night.

Griffin once owned beautiful, strong horses, but since coming to the prison realm, he'd only seen malnourished nags and old mules.

But just like the king's people, these horses were taken care of in ways the villagers could only dream about. And still, it was nothing like the bounty that awaited them when they returned to Fargelsi.

A boy walked toward them, leading two horses by the reins.

"Why do we need horses?" Griffin reached out, running a hand along the coarse black hair of the horse's scraggly mane. "I can portal from the castle."

"Like I said." Riona mounted a gray horse and patted its neck. "Some of us have honor. We make sure deals are kept." Giving a click of her tongue, Riona nudged her horse through the gates.

Griffin scrambled to mount his horse and catch up to her. *Some of us have honor?* Was the loyal Riona questioning her king?

Something like that could be useful in the future.

Home. It was a feeling Griffin had only felt in one place before. The cottage he'd left behind in Fargelsi. If he'd been smart, he'd have kept to the rolling hills rather than becoming someone he never wanted to be at the palace.

But now, as they neared Fela after hours of hard riding, his heart ached with the knowledge that his new home was destroyed. A few structures stood tall, black marks snaking up the wood. But that was it.

The community he'd helped build for the last ten years was gone, turned to ash.

He couldn't look at Riona, refused to see if there was an ounce of regret in her eyes. "You stay here." He couldn't reveal the caverns to her, not for anything.

To his surprise, she didn't argue. He squeezed his thighs and urged his horse toward the orchards, thankful when the trees hid him from Riona's sight. Sliding down off his horse, he felt along the cliff face at the far side of the orchard, leading his horse through the vines covering the opening. Griffin left his horse in the cave entrance and stepped to the false wall concealing the caverns from potential foes. Hefting his weight against the stone, the wall moved and silence echoed from within.

"It's just me." Griffin called as he stepped into the chamber, pushing the wall back in place in case Riona came looking for him.

A cacophony of sounds and voices echoed off the ceiling as the inhabitants came out of their hiding spots.

His eyes scanned the gathering, trying to get a read on how many people took to hiding here. It was less than half of Fela's numbers.

Hector saw him first, his eyes lighting up in surprise. In three long strides, he reached Griffin and pulled him in to a hug, squeezing the air from his lungs. "We thought you were dead." Griffin pulled away as all chatter ceased and eyes fell on him.

"Where is everyone else?"

Hector's gaze turned sad. "They left."

No, his people wouldn't do that. They wouldn't abandon their community instead of rebuilding. "Not possible." Griffin wanted to search the entire cave system, he wanted to make himself believe the family that had become his life wasn't broken.

That Shauna and Nessa weren't being held by the crown.

That their village was not full of ghosts and ashes.

But this place, this prison realm, was meant to beat fae down, to strip them of everything they loved until there was nothing left. And it was all Egan's design. Not for the first time he wondered what Myrkur could become under a benevolent ruler. But he suppressed thoughts like that. It only led to wonderings of how he would do things if he were that benevolent ruler. A slippery slope for one like Griffin O'Shea.

Griffin tried to call on his magic again, finding only a single strand with a single purpose. The portal. Yet, power was no substitute for family. It couldn't erase pain that came from the very soul.

Guilt washed over him. This was all his fault. He looked to the people huddling around the smoldering fire in the hearth meant to warm only a few. They looked to him like a leader come to tell them how to get their homes back. He'd failed them, and they knew it, yet still they trusted him. He didn't deserve such loyalty.

And now the woman responsible for so much waited for him back among the ghosts of Fela.

Looking to Hector, he sighed. "I've brought two horses with me. Sell them to pay the village taxes and then rebuild. We can be what we once were, working together to keep our community whole and cared for. But we will have to pay the king's taxes each quarter now that he knows about us."

The villagers murmured in worried tones. It would be a difficult, if not impossible task, and they all knew it. But what choice did they have?

"Hector, these are your people now. You must lead them."

Hector narrowed his eyes. "That sounds ominously similar to goodbye."

Griffin couldn't explain his mission to people who had little knowledge of the outside world. His eyes caught on two sleeping figures near the back of the cave. One, a woman whose pale skin was slick with sweat. Sinead. He walked toward them, giving nods to the others lingering about.

"She's why they left." Gulliver didn't open his eyes as he spoke.

"What do you mean?"

His eyes slid open—well, as much as they could with the bruises. "Some people worry it's a plague. Every ache and pain they blame on Sinead. Only Hector will touch her and help her now that Shauna is gone."

Griffin slid down the wall to sit next to Gulliver. "She's going to be all right."

Gulliver snorted. "That's a lie."

"Yes, it probably is." He leaned his head back against the cool stone.

"The king's men came. They didn't find most of us, but Shauna and Nessa were collecting herbs to help Sinead. They took them, Griff. They let me go to get to you, but they truly do have you now, so what's the point of keeping them alive?" His gaze settled on the ground. Gulliver was a smart kid, he knew when there was no hope. "They offered you your magic back, didn't they?"

"How—"

"Your eyes. They flashed violet when you came in, but then the color disappeared. You're the one who taught me all about the magic of the three kingdoms, yet, I think the color is supposed to last longer. The king did not give you everything."

Griffin didn't know how the kid was so perceptive. "I'm not the king's man, Gullie. I made a deal to keep Shauna and Nessa safe."

"A deal with the king is never a good thing, even when protecting the people you care about. He will always twist it. Want to know who taught me that?"

He nodded.

"Shauna."

Shauna and Nessa were born in the prison realm. Their grandfather was a criminal sent to Myrkur ages ago. That was their only crime—the crime of their birth to a daughter of a criminal. A daughter who'd died giving birth to Nessa. There was no before for them, not like so many others. Like Griffin. They didn't know anything but struggle.

Shauna wouldn't want him to help the king.

But he refused to lose another friend.

Griffin leaned in real close and dropped his voice. "I'm going to the human realm."

Gulliver's eyes widened. "But... how?"

"The magic you told the king my family possessed."

Gulliver looked away and swallowed. "I didn't want to give you up. You told me before that no one could learn you're descended from a royal line, let alone the royal line of Iskalt. I'm sorry." Tears welled in his eyes.

"Gullie." Griffin bumped his shoulder. "One day, the king or maybe Kvek will come for you again, and I won't be here to protect you."

"I can protect myself."

One corner of Griffin's mouth curled up. "I know you can. But this realm has become too dangerous for you. You're coming with me."

Gulliver stared at Griffin like he didn't believe the words. "You want..." He shook his head, wincing at the movement that caused him pain. "But I'm... I don't belong." He took a deep breath, and it shook on the way out. His eyes glassed over, but Griffin didn't know if it was from the pain of his missing tail or the shock.

"Gulliver, if you stay here... I'm afraid what will happen to you when I'm gone. I can't protect you when I'm not in this realm."

"But..." He wiped away a tear, probably hoping no one saw it. When he spoke again, his voice was nothing more than a whisper. "I'm not someone who gets chosen. You can't risk whatever it is you have to do by taking the orphan kid with half a tail and nothing else to call his own."

Griffin understood his hesitation then. Gulliver wasn't scared of venturing outside the kingdom he'd known his entire life. He didn't think he deserved to go.

This kid... he had a way of breaking Griffin's heart.

Griffin turned to face him fully and completely, not letting Gulliver look away. "You haven't been an orphan for almost ten years, not since I found you. You and me, Gulliver, we're a family. And I'm not leaving you behind." He had no choice but to leave Shauna and Nessa. But this, right here, was his choice, the one the king tried to take from him by going back on his word.

He groaned, thinking of Riona. He was going to have to thank her, wasn't he?

A commotion at the mouth of the cave drew his attention as Riona herself walked in, her steps echoing off stone walls. She stood at the opening that should have thwarted her, a permanent scowl on her face.

The reeling people of Fela jumped to their feet, but they didn't yell or confront Riona. They would never forget the king's warrior who destroyed their home.

And now, her eyes took in the cavern, probably noting the meager stores, the malnourished fae backing away from her. Her gaze settled on Griffin. "We must leave."

She was right. They'd been here too long. Griffin stood and held a hand down to Gulliver. He took it and let Griffin pull him up.

Hector stood behind Riona, one hand on the hilt of his rusted sword. Griffin didn't have the heart to tell him Riona could kill him before he even drew his weapon.

What if this entire mission was wrong? He was supposed to lead a dangerous person into the three realms who'd won their peace ten years ago when they defeated Regan and the people who served her—people like Griffin.

But he'd heard no news since then. Had the peace lasted?

Was he searching for something that would divide them once again?

Griffin approached Riona, towering over her. It wasn't fear racing through him necessarily, but more of a wariness. He had to keep his guard up around her. "We leave the horses here. Hector will see to them."

"But—"

Griffin cut her off with a snarl. "We are not taking horses into the human realm. We'll have no need of them there." He reached a hand back, snatching a handful of Gulliver's threadbare shirt that was once blue but had faded to a dull gray. "And this is my man you so honorably said I could bring."

"Man?" Riona didn't bother stopping Hector from leaving to gather the horses outside the cavern. "This thief-child?" Her cold eyes slid over Gulliver's bruised face, her distaste evident. "He can barely hold himself up. No, Griffin O'Shea, we will be better off just the two of us."

A few of the villagers neared, their anger plain. "Griff." Hector's mother, Kiaran clenched her jaw. "You've led one of the king's soldiers to the only place we are safe right now?"

He put a hand on her shoulder. "We are leaving." It was time to give all his fae an explanation. He pulled back his hand and sighed. "The king has tasked me with a mission."

"Since when do you do missions for the crown?" Daniel, a Dark Fae not much older than Griffin, spat.

These people knew so little about him. There was a time when everything he did was for a crown. If his community, his family learned of his past deeds, they'd never forgive him.

"King Egan thinks it's time the world was reminded we are here." He wished he believed his own words. "He is sending us through a portal to the human realm, and eventually into Fargelsi where I will search for a way to end the magic keeping us trapped in this land of perpetual night."

And what would they learn of the other kingdoms? War? Egan was anxious for it. And his armies were ready.

The villagers talked over one another, trying to make sense of this news. If they ever did, he hoped they'd tell him because he didn't know anything. Most of all, he didn't know what would happen if he actually managed to bring down the magic—which he very much doubted he could do without the full use of his own magic.

Riona tapped her foot. "We must leave." She turned on her heel. "The thief can come, but if he passes out or slows us down, you're carrying him."

Gulliver gripped Griffin's arm. "I won't let you down. Not ever again."

Griffin didn't blame Gulliver for revealing his family's magic to Egan. He put a hand on his shoulder and urged him to the opening. "I know you won't."

Hector stopped them. "This mission is dangerous, right?"

"What? Going into a realm where no one knows who I am and asking around about the prison magic?" He shrugged. "Easy."

It was a lie, and they both knew it.

Griffin never imagined he'd set foot in Fargelsi again, but now that the opportunity was there, he longed to lie in the grass and look at the puffy white clouds. He longed to feel the heat of the sun beating down on him.

But mostly, he couldn't shake the hope that he'd see the

people he'd wronged again, that he'd find some sort of redemption.

But that was a dream from another lifetime.

Riona waited for them where the road wound along the outer edge of the orchard. The silver light of the moon guarded their steps. Griffin stopped beside her. "Not here." Not where any of those in the cavern could sneak out to watch. He didn't need them to see he was the one with the magic to open portals.

He made sure Gulliver was following before returning to the ruins of their village. Here, there was much better shelter, much more privacy.

"You're going to use magic, aren't you?" Gulliver's amber eyes lit with excitement, which made an odd contrast against his bruises.

It was hard for Griffin to remember sometimes that the Dark Fae living here had never seen magic. When prisoners arrived, the first thing they experienced upon entering the darkness of Myrkur was the absence of their magic.

Magic was the stuff of bedtime tales to fae like Gulliver.

Griffin nodded. "I need to create a portal." He needed a familiar place in his mind. He'd been to the human realm many times, and he loved every bit of it. His favorite place was somewhere called Ireland, a land of rocky crags and welcoming people. There were many places that looked out over the ocean. He could sit there for hours. Sometimes, he had. When he wasn't sent there on missions for Regan, he enjoyed exploring the human realm on his own.

"Get ready to step through the portal, I'm not sure how long I can keep it open."

Gulliver wasted no time in stepping up beside him, but Riona's scowl never left her face.

"I'm not diseased." His mind went back to Sinead, but the prison realm couldn't be his worry when he left. He had to focus on one problem at a time, and right now, that meant keeping himself and Gulliver alive.

Riona stepped to his other side. He shot her the kind of smile the old Griffin would have worn. Sometimes, he was able to catch glimpses of the man he was, the one that hadn't yet been hardened by this place.

Was there an old version of Riona?

His magic made the hairs on his arm stand on end as it gathered and pooled in his belly. He kept a firm image of Ireland in his mind. Gulliver would love it, but they couldn't stick around long enough for anyone to see his tail.

He counted backward in his head before the magic exploded from him in a flash of violet.

The blast sent Gulliver and Riona tumbling to the ground.

"Did it work?" Gulliver asked, looking around, excitement in his eyes. "Or does the human world look identical to ours?"

Riona pushed to her feet. "No, it doesn't. Griffin failed." Her accusatory glare cut through him, but he wouldn't back down.

"I've been without magic for ten years, so excuse me if it takes a while to get used to it again." Maybe this was a mistake.

Maybe the king put faith in the wrong man.

Or maybe, Griffin's magic knew something he didn't.

"Let's try again."

This time Gulliver hesitated, standing farther back from Griffin's side. Riona didn't move. Griffin let the magic free, but it didn't blast out of him like before. This was more of a slow trickle. One that, again, produced no portal.

"Maybe you're thinking of the wrong place." Gulliver shrugged.

"Gullie." Griffin's grin stretched wide. "You're a genius." If he was going to create a portal for the first time in ten years, one strong enough to breach the magic of the prison realm, he needed to choose a place that had more meaning to it. A place he'd visited more times than he could count.

Gripping Gulliver and Riona's hands, Griffin closed his eyes, picturing green pastures just outside a small town. And a broken-down barn where the girl he would forever love used to play. A smile curved his lips, and when the magic rose up in answer, it felt right.

A gust of wind blew the hair from his forehead. He stepped forward without opening his eyes. Dry and cracked dirt turned to fresh grass beneath his feet. The cool night breeze stilled, and Griffin's magic stuttered and faded as the bright sun greeted them.

When he opened his eyes, pain surged through his head at the brightness of the sun. Shielding his eyes, the first thing he saw was the small white house that needed more than a few repairs, and the unused barn.

The lawn hadn't been cut recently, and it curled around his feet. He'd let go of his companions and turned to watch the two Dark Fae revel in the first sunlight they'd ever felt.

Both stood, clutching their hands to their eyes.

Ten years of hard living in a realm without light was difficult for him, but they'd never seen the sun before, and it was too much.

Still, even Riona smiled as she squinted into the sun. Mimicking Griffin and lifting a hand to shield her eyes, her entire posture relaxed.

"You did it." Gulliver beamed a proud smile. "We're... free."

Griffin pulled him into a side hug, not wanting to ruin this moment with thoughts of all those they'd left behind. This wasn't a trip of joy.

They had a purpose, people to save.

A peace to destroy by opening the borders of the prison realm. Likely, Griffin had just taken his first steps to bringing war to his world.

And once again, he was on the wrong side, because someone who didn't deserve his loyalty pulled the strings he had to dance to.

He chanced a glance at Riona, knowing she was here to keep him in line.

First, he had to survive. Do what he could to free Nessa and Shauna and all the others.

Then, maybe he could change his fate.

He could be a good man, choosing for himself where his loyalties would lie.

There was nothing to be done about that from the human realm. "Come on." He took off toward the barn, already knowing there'd be no animals inside. "We need to stay hidden until the sun goes down and I can portal us into Fargelsi."

Gulliver matched his stride despite the obvious pain it

caused him. Griffin would make sure he saw a healer in Fargelsi.

"So." Gulliver grinned, his tail showing no signs of life. "Why does a human farm mean so much to you?"

Griffin opened the door and ushered them through. Riona collapsed onto a hay bale. "I miss the dark."

Of course she did.

"The sun is intense. Am I supposed to see black spots in my eyes?" Gulliver asked.

Griffin grunted. "What you're supposed to do is not look directly into it. Trust me, you'll feel a lot better once you've adjusted."

Gulliver climbed onto a stack of hay bales and grinned down at Griffin. With his bruising, it looked sort of menacing instead of happy. "You didn't answer my first question."

Griffin sat and rubbed a hand along the back of his neck. "The woman I once loved used to live here."

"You fell in love with a human?"

He shook his head. "Brea Robinson doesn't have a human bone in her body. She was a changeling."

Riona scoffed. "Changelings are myths. Don't listen to him, boy. He'll have you believing nonsense."

Griffin shrugged. They'd learn for themselves, eventually. The story of Brea Robinson and the human she'd been exchanged with at birth—Alona Cahill—was told far and wide in the fae realm.

Because the girls in question sat on thrones in two of the three kingdoms—and Brea's half-sister sat on a third.

But that history was for another time.

Griffin leaned his head back and closed his eyes.

This time, the image that filled his mind was one he'd tried to erase from his subconscious.

He'd lost that battle, because all he saw was Brea walking toward him and accepting Griffin as her husband.

She hadn't known how fae marriages intertwine magic and love.

Fae marriage bonds lasted forever. And the only way to break them was through death or a trip to the prison realm.

It had been ten years since he felt their marriage bond snap. But time did not erase all feelings.

Gulliver looked down on him and lowered his voice. "Don't worry, Griff. I believe you. That's what matters."

In that moment, as he pushed memories of Brea away, it was.

No matter who he spoke to or came across, they wouldn't remember him, and it had to stay that way for him to survive it.

Griffin leaned back, letting the sunlight warm his face. He couldn't get enough of it. Yet, Gulliver sat in the shadows of the barn, shielding his face from the sun's rays streaming in through the window. His cat-like eyes ran with tears from the brightness of the late afternoon light, but he couldn't stop himself from looking at everything he could see.

"When will this misery end?" Riona's voice sounded muffled under her wings she'd shielded herself with.

"A few more hours, but it's fading. You'll be fine once the sun begins to set, and then we'll go into town for provisions."

"Do it again, Griff." Gulliver begged. "Open a portal."

"I can't right now, I must rest for a while and wait until night." He glanced at Riona, wondering if she understood the limitations of his power.

"Stop your endless chatter," Riona grumbled, burrowing deeper into the last moldy bits of hay they could find in the abandoned barn. Sometime over the last decade, Brea's parents had moved away. A foreclosure sign faded with age sat in the front yard where Brea used to play as a little girl.

"We should let Riona rest. Let's go for a walk in the shade." Griffin tilted his head toward the door. "Keep the hood pulled down low over your face, and you'll be fine."

"Don't go far," Riona warned.

"Where would we even go, Riona? We'll be just across the yard." Griffin led Gulliver toward the house, guiding him with a steady hand until they entered the shade of the house.

"Will we get to see any humans, do you think?" Gulliver asked, searching the yard as if a human might appear at any moment. He held a hand up to shield his eyes and stumbled over his own feet—which was unlike the steady thief.

"We will when we go into town this afternoon." Griffin chuckled at his eagerness. He reminded him of Brea and her certainty that dragons had to be a thing in Eldur—the land of fire. "But I need you to be very careful while we are there. Humans don't have things like tails and wings or cat eyes. You must promise to listen to me and do exactly as I say."

"Promise."

Griffin moved to sit on the back porch steps, gently pulling Gulliver down to sit beside him. His tail was bandaged, and the poor kid couldn't get comfortable anywhere.

"Tell me more about magic," Gulliver pleaded. Where the boy was delighted with what little magic he had seen so far, Riona seemed terrified of it. A fact Griffin tucked away for the future.

"There are three fae realms," Griffin began.

"I know that already," Gulliver interrupted. "In Fargelsi, it is always spring. The lands of Eldur are dangerous with hot deserts and beautiful oasis. And Iskalt is cold and dark, but not as dark as Myrkur. I want to know about the magic."

"Well, fae magic is as different as the people who wield it," Griffin said. "In Fargelsi, the people draw their magic from nature. They must speak the spells to bring forth their power. They can grow buildings right out of the ground and light fires with a single word. And in Eldur, where the fire fae live, they draw their magic from the sun. During the day they are far more powerful than Fargelsians who have use of their magic at all times. But at night, when the sun fades, so does Eldurian magic, leaving its people powerless until the sun rises again. And in Iskalt, where I was born, we draw our magic from the moon, which is why we're stuck here until night falls."

"Wow, I bet Eldur and Iskalt hate each other," Gulliver said.

"We did for a long time. But my brother is king of Iskalt now, and he grew up in the Eldur queen's court. The new Eldur queen was like a sister to him. And my wife, Brea... I guess she's my ex-wife now—such a human thing—is a princess of Eldur *and* Fargelsi, and she's probably the Iskalt queen too. Brea's half-sister is the queen of Fargelsi now, so they are all friends. These are things I need you to know so you're prepared for whatever we might face, but let's keep that knowledge between us. The less our traveling companion knows, the better."

"I don't think she likes magic." Gulliver nodded toward the barn where Riona stood in the doorway with her jacket draped over her head and her wings tucked under her long shirt in case any humans happened by. "She definitely doesn't like the sun."

"Is it this bright every day?" Riona walked toward them, shielding her eyes.

"You'll get used to it."

She looked up at the run down two-story house with a frown. "Do all humans live in such nice houses?"

"This is actually an old abandoned house." Griffin wasn't sure how to explain the things she would see on this trip. To someone who'd grown up in Myrkur, Brea's old home looked like a mansion.

"Abandoned?" She scowled. "Two families could live here and never see each other. Ugh, how do the humans not burn up here?" She moved back into the shade, tying a strip of fabric around her long braids to lift them off her neck. "It's so hot here." She fanned her face. "It is like this in Fargelsi?"

"I'm afraid the sun is brighter and hotter in Gelsi." Griffin elbowed Gulliver, letting a small smile cross his face. It was bad parenting to so obviously enjoy her discomfort, but it wasn't like she hadn't earned it.

Her shoulders fell. "I can't do this." She shook her head. "My eyes won't stop running, and it's like a sword stabbing into my head every time I open them."

"That's why we're going into town soon. We need some supplies before we leave for Gelsi."

"And how do you intend to pay for these supplies?" Riona frowned.

"The king said he would give you enough money for the journey." But Griffin sighed. Of course that promise was just another lie. He wondered how Egan expected loyalty when he gave none.

"I brought some small gemstones with me, but I don't know if they will be worth much to humans."

"Surely we have something of value to trade. Something that wouldn't be suspicious to a human." Griffin began to feel the futility of this mission. They would never get anywhere without the means to purchase what they needed.

"I stole this from the man who took my tail." Gulliver held up a gold ring with a stone the size of a fire nut.

A triumphant smile lit Griffin's face. "That's my boy." He took the ring, thinking he wasn't so great at this parenting thing. "Stealing is wrong, but in this case, I will allow it. We will fetch a fine price for this at the pawn shop in town. It won't bring back your tail, but it's the least you deserve for what that man did to you. Today, you're going to learn what a cheeseburger is."

Griffin held his breath as the human peered through a thick lens at the stone in Gulliver's ring. Griffin kept a hand on Gulliver's shoulder to keep him from wandering around. In his current state, he was like a nervous horse in a house, knocking things over and tripping on his own feet.

"Beautiful opal, and the gold is twenty-four karat. I can offer you two hundred store credit and two hundred cash." The man set the ring down.

"Deal." Griffin nodded and went to look around, grateful to see a large selection of sunglasses.

The man behind the counter gave them odd looks as Gulliver pulled the hat down to further conceal himself. It only sort of did the trick but if the man noticed anything different about them, he didn't say.

Riona hadn't taken her eyes off the human yet. "Stop

staring," Griffin whispered. She looked uncomfortable with her wings stuffed inside her jacket. All her clothes were made to accommodate her wings with slits in the back. She would need a better disguise.

Griffin searched through the sunglasses for styles that wouldn't stand out. Something that looked like it came from an apothecary or a smithy. And the lenses couldn't be too dark. Just enough to conceal Gulliver's eyes and give them both some comfort from the sun's bright light. He even grabbed a pair for himself.

Riona and Gulliver watched as Griffin searched for clothes that wouldn't be too conspicuous in the fae world. He gathered an outfit for each of them and let them choose a backpack to carry them in. He spent about half of their credit. The other half he used to buy some extra supplies. It was the best he could do given that their "king" hadn't provided them with the means to do the job he'd sent them to do.

"Thank you, sir." Griffin ignored the way the man eyed them suspiciously and accepted the money that would buy them one of the best meals they would ever eat. "I must warn you of something before we get to the tavern. McDonald's has what I can only describe as a torture park. I went to examine it many years ago, climbing into this structure where children hit me on their way by. There was an entire area with little balls they threw at me. And then a group of human females started screaming at me that I wasn't supposed to be there. It was my first experience with human torture. I will protect you from it."

Gulliver gave him a relieved smile. "Thank you."

"Here, put these on." Griffin passed the sunglasses to

each of them as they left the store in their new clothes. He tucked his into his shirt pocket.

"What is this contraption?" Riona stared at the glasses. "I don't need spectacles."

"Put them on." Griffin insisted.

"Ohh." Riona sighed in relief as she slid the glasses in place. "That's so much better."

"Hey, I can see!" Gulliver's eyes stopped watering almost immediately.

"These should make it easier for you until you adjust to the sun." He passed them each a backpack with their old clothes and a few tools that might come in handy later.

As they walked along the sidewalk, Griffin kept a close eye on Riona. He still didn't trust her, but she was clearly unnerved by the human world.

"I always heard they didn't have magic." She eyed the cars coming and going along the street, and he imagined none of it made any sense to her.

"I guess in a way they do have magic, but they call it science and technology."

"They just ride around in their metal beasts like it's nothing." She shook her head in wonder.

"I think you're going to need to learn to just go with it, Riona," Gulliver said as they crossed the street to McDonald's, his eyes wide and unblinking trying to take it in all at once.

"The kid is right. The human world is overwhelming in its own way," Griffin said. "But when you're faced with magic, real magic, you're not going to have time to react with fear and distrust."

"I'm starting to see that," she murmured, following

Griffin into the too bright fluorescents of McDonald's. "I just don't like it."

Griffin glared at the bright blue torture structure across the restaurant. Once he ordered their food, he made them sit as far as possible away from it, casting suspicious glances whenever he saw someone enter the area with the torture balls.

In the end, Gulliver ate four cheeseburgers and two apple pies before he was finally full and sleepy.

They managed to avoid the human torture balls and made their way back to the farm just as darkness fell, and Griffin's magic came alive inside him once again.

"Do it again, Griff." Gulliver giggled, actually giggled. It was the most child-like sound Griffin had ever heard from the boy.

Griffin couldn't help his answering smile as he began to open a portal between his hands, squeezing it down to a pinprick of light and letting it swell into a sphere the size of his head.

"Stop your horsing around." Riona stepped away from Griffin, the violet light of his magic reflecting in her dark lenses.

"You can take those off now, you know. It's dark."

"Not dark enough with all your flashing lights," Riona muttered as she tucked her glasses into her bag.

"I'm practicing." Griff pulled on his magic, feeding more into the beginnings of a portal in his hands. "It's been a decade since I last held my magic, and portaling into Fargelsi is going to be difficult. My magic requires that we return to the place where we last were in Myrkur. I'm counting on the border magic not allowing that. Otherwise, this mission is doomed before it truly begins."

"Might as well give it a shot here," Gulliver said, looking around the Robinson's overgrown drive.

Griffin guided them to the open field where the moonlight shone brightest. Chills ran down his spine when he realized it was the exact spot he'd portaled to when he first came looking for Brea Robinson all those years ago. It felt like another lifetime. A time when he was just a young kid with a head full of all the wrong ideas.

"Wait!" Riona took another step away from Griffin. "I need a second." Her voice shook with anxiety.

"It's okay." Gulliver took her hand in his. "It's just like stepping through a doorway."

"Right." She lifted her chin but stayed where she was. Probably not a bad idea for them to keep their distance since he had little confidence this would even work.

He lifted his face to the moonlight, letting it revive the magic within. It felt good. Like he'd found a missing piece of his soul. With a deep breath, Griffin called on his O'Shea magic, the violet light sparking at his fingertips as he pulled his hands apart, opening a dark black portal... to Fela. His hands trembled as the magic rebelled against him, and the portal collapsed.

Riona gave a startled gasp, and Gulliver groaned, kicking a clump of grass in frustration.

"No, that was good." Griffin wiped a clammy hand across his brow, feeling faint from the effort. "The magic around Myrkur won't let me in. That's what we want."

"So, what now?" Riona asked.

"Now, I need to focus." Griffin rubbed his hands

together, clearing his mind of thoughts of Myrkur. For years, he never let himself think about Fargelsi. About the home he'd left behind. Not the palace where his adopted mother reigned, but the small cottage on the shores of Loch Villandi. How might his life have played out there if he could have contented himself with the simple life of a farmer?

He couldn't dwell on what ifs now. He let his mind recall the days he'd spent with Brea when she first came to Fargelsi. Their time at the cottage were among the happiest memories of his life.

Violet light crackled under his skin, sparking at his fingertips as he once again pulled his hands apart, creating an opening in the atmosphere, like a tear in the fabric of the human world. Late afternoon sunlight spilled through the opening, and the scent of home filled his senses.

Riona groaned, scrambling for her sunglasses.

"You first, Gullie." Griffin nodded for him to step through the portal. Riona followed.

With a last look at Brea's childhood home, Griffin returned to his.

CHAPTER TWELVE

No air smelled as sweet to Griffin O'Shea as that of the Fargelsi countryside. As the portal closed behind him and his magic faded once again, Griffin took a deep breath. He was home. He could see the hillside cottage Queen Regan had given him when he was still only a young man. She'd recognized his need for his own space away from the chaos of palace life. In those moments, she had been good to him. A true mother who cared for the young Iskaltian prince she'd taken as her charge when he was just two years old. Those moments made it difficult to think poorly of her even now.

Griffin turned away from the cottage to find Gulliver running in circles in the thick green grass of the open pasture, a huge smile on his face, and the first flicker of movement in the remnant of his tail.

"Slow down, Gullie, you're going to—" Griffin shook his head when Gulliver tripped over his own feet. Losing his balance, he stumbled head over heels down the hillside.

Griffin jogged to catch up with the boy when Gulliver fell over again trying to stand.

"You all right?" Griffin leaned down to help him up.

"I'm fine." Gulliver dusted himself off. "Everything's just off kilter without my tail. I don't feel like me. You think I'll always be this clumsy oaf now?" His slim shoulders drooped. "I feel so useless."

"You are going to be fine, Gullie." Griffin bent down to his level. "It'll take some time to heal, but you'll be okay, I promise. Now, come help me make camp in the woods. It's been a long day for us already, but sunset's not far off. We'll rest up tonight, and then, in the morning, we'll see if we can buy some horses from one of the farms in the area." He turned to see Riona standing with her arms crossed over her chest and her sunglasses perched on her nose.

"You all right?"

She nodded. "Just tired. I don't know how I'll manage in this cursed daylight." She followed Griffin and Gulliver along the trail and into the forest.

"Loch Villandi is just ahead. We'll camp there where it's cooler, but do not touch the water. You hear me, Gullie?" Griffin raised his voice. "No matter what, you don't go near the water. I don't want you falling in. Loch Villandi's waters are deceptively beautiful, but dangerous. Stay away."

"Yes, sir." Gulliver said over a huge yawn as he rubbed his belly. "We have any leftover cheeseburgers?"

"Why can't we just portal to the palace?" Riona stomped through the underbrush early the next morning as they made their way up to the cottage. Griffin had scouted ahead to find a young family lived there now.

"Griff has O'Shea magic," Gulliver explained. "He can open portals to the human world but not from place to place inside the fae realms, right, Griff?"

"That's right, buddy. Besides, it's only a few hours to the palace. If we leave soon, we can start making inquiries in the Dragur Village this afternoon." He had no idea how he was supposed to get an audience with the former king when no one knew Griffin used to be a royal himself, but he'd have to think of something soon.

"Very well." Riona rooted around in her bag. "Use these." She handed him three small dark gemstones. They glittered in the morning light. At first, they appeared black and then a deep garnet and purple.

"Myr opals. They're worth enough to purchase horses and whatever else we might need for travel. That is, if you can even find anything worth purchasing out here in the middle of nowhere."

They reminded Griffin of fire rubies from Eldur. They would fetch a good price well beyond the cost of horses and provisions.

"You two stay here while I go talk to the farmer and his wife."

"Not going to happen." Riona shook her head. "I don't trust you."

"If you think I'm going to leave Gullie behind just to ditch you, then you haven't been paying attention." Griffin set off along the path to the cottage.

The farmer met him along the way.

"Saw your campfire this morning." The young fae man tilted his hat in greeting. "Where you headed?"

"Vindur City. We have need of horses and provisions if you or any of your neighbors have any to sell." Griffin fished the gemstones from his pocket, letting them catch the light so they sparkled like fire in his hand. The farmer's eyes widened at the sight. He could trade the stones for enough coin to plant his crops for the coming season and line his pockets with the rest.

"Aye, I have a couple of horses I can spare. Come with me to the barn, and I'll see you properly outfitted for your journey." The man was kind and chatted easily with Griffin about the way to Vindur. The ease with which the man trusted caught Griffin by surprise. The Fargelsi of his past was not a land where neighbor trusted neighbor, much less a veritable stranger.

After a drink of fresh cider at the farmer's wife's insistence, Griffin made his way back to camp with two saddled horses and plenty of food and cider to fill even Gulliver's belly.

Griffin smiled at the parcel of silver figs the farmer's wife brought him. He'd planted the fig trees himself when he lived here. They were his favorite fruit. He liked them fresh from the tree, warmed by the Gelsi sun.

"Griff!" Gulliver called when he returned to their camp. "Look what I found!" He ran up to Griffin, his cap full of ripe Gelsi berries.

"You didn't eat any of these, did you?" Griffin asked in alarm. The magic-blocking berries were Regan's favorite weapon. She'd used them to subdue her people and stifle their magic.

"No, Riona said we should ask you about them first, but there are hundreds of them, Griff. I've never seen so much fruit. There's not a dead bush among them."

"Riona was right. You can't eat these." Griffin dumped the contents of Gulliver's hat onto the ground. He wasn't sure what they might do to Dark Fae. Gulliver and Riona didn't have magic, but they were magical beings. "New rule. Don't eat anything in Fargelsi without checking with me first. Actually, scratch that. Don't *eat* anything or *touch* anything in Fargelsi without asking if it's safe. The prettier a thing is, the more likely it's dangerous."

"I was hoping we could feast on berries for breakfast."

"How about sun warmed figs and fresh cheese instead?" Griffin handed him the package from the farmer's wife.

"You got food *and* horses?" Gulliver's tail gave an awkward flick behind him causing him to leap back like something goosed him on the rear.

"Settle down there, kid. That tail of yours seems to be waking up. How's it feel? You need fresh bandages?" Griffin checked over his various bruises and cuts, glad to see they were healing.

"It's kind of numb." He sighed. "Like it's not quite there, so it surprises me when the feeling comes back."

"We'll find a healer we can trust and see what they can do for you." Griffin popped a silver fig into his mouth. He'd have to do some creative lying to explain the presence of the kid's tail to a fae who'd never seen such a thing before.

"Is everyone in this land so rich they can afford to sell their best horses and provisions on a whim?" Riona examined the fine pair of geldings and their sleek leather saddles.

Griffin offered her some fresh fruit and cheese and went

to retrieve his bag from their camp. "I think, Riona, you will soon learn a hard lesson. It's not wealth you see here, but you have seen so much extreme poverty you don't know the kind of lives average fae can live here."

She scowled at him. "You forget I live in the king's fortress and want for nothing."

"The king's castle is a hovel. Just wait. I'll show you a true palace." Griffin left her to mount her horse. "Gullie, tuck your tail in and keep your glasses on. If we meet anyone along the way, remember, the fae here have never seen the likes of you."

"Am I that strange looking?" Gulliver asked over a mouthful of cheese.

Griffin pulled himself up into the saddle and reached to haul Gulliver up behind him. "You're a handsome lad, but in this land, people look like me. Boring and plain with only pointed ears and shining eyes to set us apart from the humans. You are far more interesting."

He turned to Riona. "That goes for you too. Keep your wings hidden, and if we run into anyone on the road, let me do the talking."

"Very well, but don't forget for a moment, I am in charge of this mission."

"I sincerely doubt you will ever let me forget it." Griffin nudged his horse along the trail toward the road to Vindur City.

"The heat is insufferable here." Riona dabbed at the sweat running down her face as the cool Gelsi breeze stirred the tall grasses along the rolling green hills around them.

"It feels quite cool to me," Gulliver said, munching on a snack of hard tack and nuts. The boy hadn't stopped eating since they left Myrkur. "You sure you're not just complaining to have something to talk about?"

Griffin chuckled at his honest assessment of her constant grumbling. "I think maybe she's having a harder time because she's a Slyph and you are Tuatha De Danann." The Tuatha De Danann were Dark Fae of the land, and Griffin long suspected they were among the oldest fae creatures in all the realms.

"My mother was a Slyph, but I am not," Riona said, matter of fact.

"I thought all fae who fly were Slyph," Gulliver said.

"How many Slyph have you seen with white wings and dark skin?" Riona raised a brow at Gulliver.

"None." Gulliver shrugged and fished around Griffin's bag for more figs.

"Will you stop eating? Save some for the rest of us." Griffin swatted his hand away.

"So, what kind of fae was your father?" Gulliver asked in that way kids could get away with but adults never could.

"Gullie, that's rude."

"What? She's pretty, I just want to know how she got white wings."

"My father was Asrai," Riona said. "My mother was of the sky, and my father, the sea. There used to be many with such origins all living together." Her smile turned sad.

Griffin found himself studying her face for any sign of

Asrai features, but he didn't know what to look for. He suspected her Asrai blood was the cause of her discomfort in the sunny climate of Gelsi. Asrai blood ran cold, and they preferred the depths of the seas and lakes they inhabited.

"We will reach the Dragur Forest soon. You'll be more comfortable in the shade." Griffin picked up their pace.

"Remind me of our new rule, Gullie?" He cast a glance over his shoulder at the boy.

"Don't touch anything or eat anything. I got it, Griff. I am twelve, you know."

"Well, that rule is extra important in the Dragur. It's an ancient place filled with dangerous creatures and poisonous plants. Once we reach the village on the other side, we'll find a room for the night and inquire at the palace to see if the queen takes audience with her subjects the way the Eldur queens do. That's our best hope of getting in to see Brandon. And if that goes well, we'll see about finding a healer to look at your tail."

"It's throbbing something fierce after sitting in this saddle all day." Gulliver fidgeted behind him.

As the afternoon wore on, Gulliver dozed against Griffin's back, and Riona fell silent, leaving Griffin to enjoy his homecoming. As much as he'd missed the sun, he welcomed the cool shade of the Dragur Forest.

"I don't think I like this place." Riona rubbed her hands over her arms. "It feels... wrong."

"They say the forest was once haunted," Griffin said, giving her a sympathetic look. "It's always rubbed me the wrong way too. But if we keep to the road and reach the other side before nightfall, we will be fine. You don't want to let the sun go down on you in the Dragur."

"I don't think I like Fargelsi. It is beautiful and so green and lovely. I just can't quite decide what it is that I don't like —besides the sun. The glasses help, but it's just so infernally bright. I'll never get used to it."

"I used to say that about Myr," Griffin said. "In those first few years, the darkness haunted me. I found it deeply depressing until I began to see the beauty in it. It's never felt quite right to me, but I adjusted. I still missed the sun and the vivid colors though."

"Well, I don't plan to be here long enough to adjust." Riona shifted in her saddle. "But I can see how much you've missed this place." She scowled down at a row of bushes along the side of the road. The blood-red flowers bobbed in the breeze. "I think it's the colors that bother me. Everything looks so unnatural it hurts my eyes."

"Open your mind, Riona." Griffin laughed, stretching his arms out wide. "Take a moment to experience the land and culture that is not your own. Yes, it's different and very foreign to you, but maybe you can find a way to enjoy this adventure. You can still think the colors are weird and the smells strange. That doesn't make them wrong."

"Perhaps you have a point." Riona lips twisted into something resembling a smile.

Familiar landmarks sent Griffin's heart racing as they approached the outskirts of Dragur Village. It had grown in the years of his absence. The trees were taller, thicker. There was an abundance here that wasn't here before. The inhabitants of the village lived in the trees, using their magic to grow their houses from the trees themselves.

Griffin watched the wonder cross Gulliver's face as he saw the villagers come and go from their tree houses, using the winding stairs made of bark and vines to reach the heights of the village in the canopy overhead. That was where most of them lived, while the businesses flourished beneath them on the forest floor. Rock buildings rising from the ground now stood between massive tree trunks with open doors, welcoming weary travelers into taverns and inns that had grown prosperous in the intervening years.

As they approached the palace, Griffin experienced a moment of extreme confusion. Everything was so different. But of course it would be. The Gelsi Palace he knew as a child was destroyed in the battle between Regan and Brea. His wife had turned the palace to rubble. Of course the new queen would have built a new one in its place.

"Woah." Gulliver gazed up at the twin waterfalls. That detail hadn't changed. Nor had the vine bridge that stretched from the forest across the Villandi River, though it wasn't quite the same either. These vines were white with the palest blue flowers.

Riona reined her horse to a stop as she stared in awe at the towering ivory structure. The new palace held hints of the old, but it was lighter… somehow happier than the palace of his memory.

"It looks as if it grew from the ground," Gulliver said in wonder.

"It did." Griffin smiled at his open-mouthed stare. "That is how the magic of Gelsi works. The people of this land speak an ancient language of power that can call forth anything they want from the land itself. They have only to learn how to ask."

"I never knew such riches existed," Riona murmured.

"You were right, my king's fortress is a hovel in comparison to this sheer beauty."

Griffin couldn't take his eyes from the place that was so like the one he'd once called home. Pale ivory towers seemed to reach for the clouds, taller and stronger than the ones that stood there before. Bright blue tiles gleamed from the domed roof of the central structure. Hundreds of crystal clear windows glinted in the sunlight, letting the fresh Gelsi sunshine sweep the halls inside. White vines with bright green leaves crept up the sides of the towers to wrap around the spires. The twin waterfalls fell at each side of the palace, crashing to the river below.

"Time to go see if we can bluff our way inside." Griffin nudged his horse forward.

"You grew up here?" Gulliver whispered.

"This palace is new. The one that was here when I was young was similar and every bit as grand as this one."

"You think they'll let us inside?"

"Somehow I doubt that." Anxiety gripped his chest as they made their way across the bridge. Part of Griffin expected Regan to show up any moment, screaming at him for his absence all these years. But somewhere behind those walls, beyond the palace to the gardens, lay the grave of the woman who'd raised him. Against his better judgment, love for that woman still stirred in his heart.

"State your business at the palace." The guards at the open gates halted their approach, staring wide eyed at Riona and her unusual tattoos that never seemed to still along the surface of her dark skin. He should have known hiding her wings wasn't enough.

"We are here to speak with your queen and her father,

Brandon O'Rourke. You will let us pass." Riona spoke with authority as she reached for her sword and unfurled her wings.

Blast that woman for not listening to him.

Her white wings spanned the width of the bridge, blocking the guards on the palace side from those on the village side of the river. Delicate like lace, the filmy membranes of her wings seemed as if the slightest pressure would tear right through them. But a Slyph's wings were like armor, and Riona was prepared to wrap them around Griffin and Gulliver and force her way past the guards.

"Riona, no!" Griffin stepped in front of her. "This is not the way. These people are not our enemies."

"What is she?" the queen's guards murmured, drawing their weapons. Uncertainty and fear spurned their actions, and Griffin knew they were about to find themselves in a dark cell far beneath the palace. Maybe then, Riona would stop complaining about the sunlight long enough to realize she'd ruined everything.

"Griffin O'Shea." A familiar voice cut through the tension as the guards parted for the last person Griffin ever expected to see again.

"Myles?" Griffin shook his head in confusion. Ten years, and the boy he'd once abducted from the human realm still wore that stupid smirk on his face.

"It's been a while, Griff." Myles shrugged, waving the guards away. "I see you've made some interesting new friends." He eyed Riona with curiosity before turning to Griffin with a smile. "Do you have any idea how weird it is to be the only person in the whole fracking fae world who remembers you?"

Griffin had no words, no actions as he stood frozen on the vine bridge that was once destroyed in an epic battle between his wife and his surrogate mother.

Their family was... complicated.

Especially because he assumed said wife was now married to his brother.

Complicated indeed.

But... no one was supposed to know who he was. He'd come to terms with the three realms not knowing he ever existed, to being a stranger in their midst.

And yet, the smirking human gave him hope.

Griffin stayed quiet as Myles ordered the guards to take Griffin and Riona's horses to the palace stables and turned to walk back into the palace.

Myles threw a look over his shoulder. "Well, come on then. The day Griffin O'Shea shows up is a special one." He looked to Gulliver. "Do you know why?"

Gulliver shook his head, not taking his eyes from the human.

A smiled widened Myles' lips. "Because, dear boy, it means I get to prove to my wife I was right. That there really was a red-headed dude who abducted me and then married by best friend, trying to trap her with wonky fae vows that don't allow for divorce. I mean, seriously Griff, it's the twenty-first century." He skipped, literally skipped, down the gleaming marble hallway.

Next to Griffin, Riona kept a hand on the hilt of her sword. She'd pulled her wings in, but they were still visible, causing every servant they passed to stop and stare.

Myles pushed open a heavy oak door, held in place by a series of flowering vines. Griffin had never forgotten how beautiful Fargelsi was, how full of life.

But he had forgotten how it made him feel. Here in this kingdom, he could breathe.

Riona hesitated on the threshold. "I don't like it here. Why is he smiling so much?" She paused. "And singing? Something isn't right with this man."

Griffin peeked into the sitting room where Myles hummed a song as he poured goblets of wine at a table in the back. "There are many, many things wrong with Myles." He shook his head with a hint of a smile. "But right now he is our best hope." He was their way in, their way to an audience with Brandon.

Gullie pushed past Griffin and flopped onto the couch. "Oh." He sighed. "This is comfortable."

Sometimes Griffin forgot people like Gulliver that had never been outside the prison realm didn't know there was anything better than the squalor they'd always known.

And Griffin wasn't sure if that ignorance was a gift or a curse.

"What are you singing?" Gulliver sat up.

Myles looked to him and grinned. Riona was right. He smiled too much. But then, Griffin had once been a man liberal with his smiles.

"Just a little Beatles."

Gulliver removed his sunglasses, oblivious to the gawking that came from Myles. "Beatles? Like a bug? You're singing about bugs?"

A laugh burst free of Myles. "I like you, cat man."

"Cat man?"

Myles joined him on the couch. "Like a superhero. Someone who saves the day. They're always different from anyone else, but that's what makes them special."

"But I'm not different. In Myrkur, all the Dark Fae have distinguishing features. Horns, tales, wings..."

"Myrkur?"

"We don't have time to tell each other everything we don't know." Griffin snagged a cup of wine. "Because with Myles, that's a lot."

Myles opened his mouth to protest but shut it and shrugged. "Here's my order of knowledge importance. One, will knowing something make my wife mad? Two, will not knowing something make my wife mad? Three, will—never mind, let's just say I want to keep her happy."

"So, that's how you came to be here? You married a fae woman?" Griffin still couldn't fathom how the human came to be here in Gelsi.

Myles jumped from the couch. "Oh yeah." He walked toward a bookshelf. "I was in here earlier and forgot it."

A golden circlet made to look like a ring of vines rested on the shelf. Myles picked it up and set it on his head. "I'm sort of King of Fargelsi. Sometimes, I forget."

Riona scowled. "How does one forget they're king?"

But Griffin knew how. He was Myles.

Myles shrugged. "I mean, the queen is ruler of Gelsi. She handles the diplomacy stuff. The last time I tried to help, I accidentally gave the farming rights of the same plot of land to three people. Before that, I organized the solstice party and ordered the wrong kind of wine. The queen usually waters it down for that night to keep it somewhat classy. Well, I didn't do that, and let's just say pandemonium ensued."

"We sure this guy is a king?" Riona gave him an incredulous stare.

Myles lifted one shoulder in a shrug. "King Consort. I have duties of state, and I assist my wife in making decisions. Though, I prefer to sit on the throne and look pretty while she rules the kingdom."

"That doesn't seem fair." Gulliver gave him a thoughtful look.

"That's my specialty." Myles smiled. "I'm really good at doing nothing and looking pretty. Though, I do dabble in mediation between tenants and landowners from time to time."

Griffin had a feeling Myles was very good at that. Hearing him speak made Griffin long for better times. When he wasn't beholden to a cruel king who held Shauna and Nessa captive. He couldn't take a moment of relief being back in Gelsi because he knew the conditions his people were living in back in Myrkur.

Griffin drained the rest of his wine and advanced on Myles. Myles scrambled away from him.

"Hey, remember when you kidnapped me?" Myles' voice shook. "That was fun, right? We don't want to spoil it with a repeat."

Gulliver's brow creased. "Griffin wouldn't do that."

Griffin could feel Riona's eyes burning into him, seeing him in a new light. "Gulliver," she started. "I think you'd be surprised what people do when they have no other choice."

Was that about Griffin or her? It was the first crack in Riona's armor, and he couldn't help wondering what King Egan held over her.

Turning his attention back to Myles, Griffin ran a hand through his hair and sighed. "You aren't supposed to remember me, Myles. That's what I signed up for. The prison realm erases people from the three kingdoms as though they'd never existed."

But one person remembering him meant others had been told of Griffin the traitor, the abductor. The man who'd loved a girl so completely, he'd paid the price of her freedom, entering the prison world of his own accord to break their marriage bond and let her go.

Myles' eyes darted from Griffin to Riona and back to Gulliver. "Why have you returned? More importantly *how* have you returned?"

Griffin scowled. "King or not, you will answer me when I ask a question."

"I didn't hear a question."

He pushed out another sigh. Myles had always been difficult. "How do you know who I am?"

Myles put a hand on the back of the couch as if to steady

himself. "We don't know for sure. For the longest time, everyone thought I made you up as a joke. Once I managed to convince a few people I was actually serious, Brandon went through his books. It took months, but he found a bit of buried information. We knew it wasn't because I'm human. If that was the case, Queen Alona would remember you too. And she doesn't. I've asked."

Griffin didn't interrupt him, instead nodding for him to continue.

"There was one difference between me and Alona. When you went into the prison realm and crossed the magical barrier, I was already back in the human realm."

Griffin took a step back, not meeting anyone's eyes as the thought rolled through his mind.

The prison magic, as powerful as it was, didn't reach into the human realm. A smile slid across his lips. "Myles, I think I love you."

Myles smirked. "Well, whatever floats your boat. But I do have to warn you I'm married to a queen, so it's going to take a lot of presents to win my heart."

Riona looked accusingly as Griffin. "This human is an idiot. You couldn't have found *anyone else* to help us on our quest?"

"Don't you get it?" Griffin asked. "This is the first piece of the puzzle, the first chink in the magic. No magic is infinite and all powerful. And if the barrier magic around Myrkur, the same magic that steals memories and magic alike, can't penetrate the human realm, it means it has a weakness, two weaknesses since we were able to portal into the human realm through the barrier magic. And when there are two, there are more."

Riona pursed her lips. "You're talking to two fae and one human who have no magic. At least, I hope the human doesn't have magic because he'd probably light the entire world on fire. Explain what you mean."

Griffin couldn't contain his excitement. He smiled as he spoke. "Think of chain mail. You're used to that, yes?"

She nodded.

"Good. Each link is connected to another, to many more. And it's strong." He demonstrated with his hands. "So, think about the links and what would happen if a handful of them failed, if they didn't stay linked. What would you get?"

Understanding lit in her eyes. "A vulnerability."

"Exactly." He paced the length of the room and back again. "Exactly." His feet stopped moving. "We need to find the next vulnerability."

Myles' eyes widened as he looked at them. "You did break out, didn't you?"

Riona straightened her spine. "I am one of King Egan's trusted soldiers. We have no need to break out."

Griffin thought for a moment. "We didn't escape from Egan, but we did break out through the magic."

"King... you mean the prison realm has a king?" Myles turned to Griffin in surprise

"Of course." She scowled. "How else would we survive?"

Griffin held his tongue, trying to keep his ideas of surviving from ending this quest before it really began. Riona lived in Myrkur, truly lived. She had everything she needed while the people of Fela and other villages barely had enough to eat. It was something she'd never understand. He knew that because the old Griffin wouldn't have known.

He was blind to the hardships of the people Regan trapped in Fargelsi with a border magic that...

Gulliver's eyes narrowed. Riona stopped moving.

And Myles, well, he watched them with a new distrust in his eyes. "You're trying to bring the prison magic down, looking for its weak points like Brea did with the Fargelsi magic. Only this time... you want to release all the criminals."

It was a statement more than a question. Griffin saw it in his eyes. Myles knew the truth. Well, not the entire truth. He thought Myrkur was a land of criminals, not the Dark Fae.

"You don't understand." Griffin pointed to Gulliver and then to Riona. "Have you ever heard of Dark Fae?"

"Of course."

Griffin leveled him with a glare. "Outside of the children's stories."

"Fine. No. But they're not real."

"Aren't they? Try telling Gulliver his tail is a fake. Don't let Riona know you think those wings are a trick of the light. The Dark Fae are fae just like me and that wife of yours. And they too have been forgotten by the world. Yet, unlike me, they never deserved their fate." He had so much more he wanted to say, but Myles wasn't the right person to tell of the king who was dying to start a war once the magic was gone. And he certainly wouldn't say it in front of Riona.

"All of them?" Myles rubbed the back of his neck. "They're all real?"

Before Griffin could answer, the door burst open, and four children ran in, the last of which stumbled with each step.

"Papa." One of them lunged for Myles.

The tension vanished from his posture as he picked up two squealing girls and threw them on the couch. "Now, girls, Papa has to talk to these nice people."

Griffin couldn't wrap his head around Myles being a father, something Griff wouldn't get to do if he couldn't bring the magic down. There was no way he'd ever bring a kid into the prison realm.

But this... the excited chatter, constant babbling, and endless smiles... it fit the joyous human.

"Papa." A tiny girl with thick ebony hair tugged on his sleeve. "We heard there was someone with wings in the palace." She stared at Riona in awe.

One of the other girls walked to Riona and reached up to touch her tattoos. "These are pretty."

Even Riona softened at that and gave the kid a smile.

"All right, girls, how about you go find the triplets? I do believe they might have a snack ready for you."

Wings forgotten, their high-pitched voices talked of cookies and cakes as they ran from the room.

Myles closed the door after them, his casual smile fading from his lips. He took a deep breath. "I don't only remember you, Griff. I remember everything you did. They're not actions I will ever forget. I was locked in a dungeon because of you. My best friend almost traded her life for mine because of you. I'm glad Brea and Lochlan don't remember. It would only bring them pain."

Griffin couldn't respond because every word he said was the truth.

That was the problem with truths.

They cut deeper than any sword.

Gone was the Myles of a few moments ago. In his place stood a man version of the boy he'd once known.

"None of us are the people we were ten years ago."

Myles shook his head. "Our appearances might be different, we might have new goals, but our souls, Griff, who we are inside doesn't change."

Griffin hoped he was wrong, that a yearning for power could be washed away.

But who was he kidding? Here he was in Fargelsi trying to bring down magic at the behest of a king just as bad as Regan. Possibly even worse.

It seemed history was repeating itself.

But this time, Griffin wouldn't let his mistakes define him.

He stepped closer to Myles and looked down on him. "You're wrong." His voice came out gravelly, raspy.

"For the sake of the three kingdoms, I sure hope I am, Griff. The next time you betray someone I love, I'm going to kill you."

He'd try, at least. But if Griffin did lose his way again, he might sharpen Myles' blade himself.

CHAPTER FOURTEEN

Griffin followed Myles to his wife's throne room. What a strange thought that was. Myles Merrick. A human of little importance was now the king of Fargelsi—a title Griffin once aspired to. One he thought was owed to him as the son of a king. Nephew of a king. Brother of a king. It was in his blood.

But ten years in a prison realm had chased away all ambition. In Griffin O'Shea's world, the most he aspired to was his next meal. A safe place to sleep at night. And a better future for the boy who was as much a son to him as any born of his flesh. He was not that man anymore. At least he hoped not.

"Wait here." Myles nodded as he approached the queen, busy in a meeting with her nobles. They sat around a table together, the queen's throne across the room on a raised dais —seemingly there for tradition's sake as a symbol of her power.

"What is it, Myles?" Queen Neeve asked as Myles bent

to deliver the news. "What? Lochlan doesn't have a brother." Neeve frowned as her gaze wandered into the shadows where Griffin stood between Riona and Gulliver—tails and wings secreted away under their clothes.

"She has what? Myles have you fallen asleep while reading one of your fantasy books again?"

"Not lately, darling," Myles said, his good humor as rock solid as ever. He murmured some additional information for her ears alone.

"Oh, I see," the queen said as she stood at the head of her table. The other nobles rose to their feet out of respect. "Everyone, I must ask for your patience." She smoothed an ink stained hand down the length of her simple ivory gown. "It seems an important matter needs my immediate attention. Might we adjourn until tomorrow?"

"Of course, your Majesty," one of her nobles replied as they each gathered their documents and maps and matters of diplomacy for discussion. The governing of Fargelsi had changed dramatically since Regan was in charge.

"Father, please stay. I think—I hope you'll bring some sense to this conversation," she muttered, her gaze drifting to Riona.

"Of course." Brandon crossed to the door to see the others out.

Griffin hardly recognized the man who looked so much like his sister. Brandon had aged over the last ten years, but he was no longer the malnourished, beaten down version of himself he had become during the years of his imprisonment. This man had a fire in his eyes—a fire Griffin found startlingly familiar. There was much of Regan's countenance in her older brother.

The queen waited until the room was cleared before she spoke again. "Myles." She paced the room. "Seriously... what?" She placed her hands on her hips. "I'm going to need more information than 'we have visitors from the prison realm.'"

"Griffin O'Shea has returned, and he has need of an audience with you and your father." Myles nodded in respect toward his father-in-law.

"And I'm supposed to know who this Griffin O'Shea is?" She tapped her foot in irritation.

"No, you've forgotten him, darling." Myles flashed a brilliant smile at his wife. Clearly, he was enjoying himself. "But I've told you about him before. You just choose not to listen to my 'humantales' as you call them."

"Myles."

"Oh, fine. Ruin my fun." Myles dropped to an empty seat at the table. "Griff is Loch's brother. Everyone has forgotten him but me because I was in the human world failing to learn to live without you when he was sentenced to the prison realm for his crimes. Griffin was Queen Regan's foster son in the way that Lochlan was Queen Faolan's."

"Skip to the important part, Myles." Griffin stepped forward.

"Right." Myles scratched his jaw, taking an insufferable moment to think before he continued. "Let's just focus on the fact that we have three visitors from the prison realm, and one of them has a spectacular set of wings, and the other, I hear, has a tail in need of some medical attention." Myles winked at Gulliver, and the boy blushed to the roots of his hair. He seemed unable to take his eyes off Neeve. She was beautiful, and Griffin realized Gulliver had probably never seen a woman quite like her before.

"She has wings, really?" Neeve quirked a smile at her husband. "Or are you just fooling me?"

"She has wings." Riona stepped forward. Slipping her long coat from her shoulders, she unfurled her delicate white wings, letting them shimmer in the candlelight from the chandelier overhead.

"Oh my." Neeve stumbled back, falling into the chair she'd just vacated. "You're Dark Fae?"

"Yes, your Majesty," Riona said, surprised. "I had not expected to find those who knew of us outside of Myrkur."

"I-I've read of such fae from histories and mythologies, but I never anticipated seeing one with my own eyes. You said you are from Myrkur? Where is that... I apologize, where are my manners? What is your name, dear? And, oh my, your wings are just so beautiful." She leaned forward, a glint of mischief in her eyes. "Can you really fly?"

Riona cast a wary glance at Griffin, unsure what to make of the queen's ramblings.

"I am Riona... Majesty," Riona stuttered. "Myrkur is the night realm of the Dark Fae, you know it only as the prison realm. And yes, all Slyph fly... ma'am."

"Slyph? Fascinating." Neeve's eyes sparkled with interest.

"And you are?" Neeve's attention turned to Gulliver, and Griffin nudged him forward.

"Take off your glasses," Griffin whispered.

Gulliver took a clumsy step forward and whipped his sunglasses off so she could see his cat-like eyes. "Gu-Gullie, your Majesty." Gulliver tried to dip into a courtly bow, but he over-corrected and face planted on the rug in front of her.

"Oh my, are you okay?" Neeve shot out of her seat to help him up. "Myles you said this child was injured?"

"It's nothing, my lady." Gulliver leaped back to his feet. "Just my tail is all."

"Your tail?"

"Yes, ma'am. I am Tuatha De Dannan. Dark Fae of the land." He lifted his chin with pride.

Griffin stepped forward, placing a hand on Gulliver's shoulder. "He was captured by some men from the prison realm, and they tortured him for information, your Majesty. They cut off part of his tail."

"What? When was this?" Queen Neeve put a motherly hand to Gulliver's face, checking over his faded bruises.

"A week ago, but it still pains me something terrible," Gulliver said, his bottom lip trembling for effect.

"Of course it does, you poor dear." Neeve folded him into her arms. "Myles will take you to see my personal healers right away. Are you hungry, darling?" Neeve steered Gulliver to the table of refreshments set for the nobles and made him a plate herself.

"It *has* been a while since we last ate," Gulliver said. Griffin chuffed the little liar on the back of the head.

"Myles why don't you take Gullie to the healers and help Riona get settled in her rooms for the night."

"That is not necessary, Majesty," Riona tried to protest. "We planned to find a room in an inn."

"Nonsense. You must be exhausted. I will speak with Griffin this evening, but we will see you both at breakfast in the morning."

"I am afraid I am here as my king's envoy." Riona stood unmoving, her arms braced behind her back. "I must insist I stay."

"And I am afraid I do not know your king, Riona. This is Fargelsi, I am queen here. We will speak further tomorrow."

Riona seemed ready for a fight, but Griffin shook his head, trying to reassure her without words that this was how it needed to be. This was the chance he'd hoped for, and he wasn't going to let her screw it up. He needed to speak with Neeve and Brandon alone.

"This way, Riona." Myles guided her toward the door, not giving her a chance to defy the queen any further. "Gullie, bring your snacks, and let's go see a man about a tail."

With a sigh of frustration, Riona did the only thing she could, she followed Myles from the room.

"You really are Griffin? O'Shea?" Neeve studied his face. "I don't see much of a family resemblance with Lochlan. All these years, Myles has talked of you, and we've all thought it was just one of his elaborate pranks."

"I never expected to return to find anyone had remembered me." Griffin finally found his voice. "I expect it will make all of this more difficult. But I have much to explain—preferably while we are alone." He glanced over his shoulder to make sure Riona was gone.

"Please, have a seat." Neeve offered him a chair at her table. "Why have you come? Actually." She frowned as Brandon moved to join them at the table. "*How* have you come here from the prison realm?"

"It is a very long story." Griffin sighed. "But I desperately need your help." He launched into an explanation of the events that had led him here, taking a grateful sip of wine when the queen served him herself.

"This King Egan seeks to bring down the barrier around Myrkur?" Brandon frowned. "And he's sent you to find out how it was created?"

"I know how this must seem," Griffin began. "I'm a stranger to you, come to tell you an outlandish story, and I can't assume you will help me accomplish this impossible task I've been sent to do. But the lives of two people who are everything to me are at stake. Egan will make Shauna and Nessa wish for death if I fail. I don't intend to give Egan what he wants." He glanced at the door again, expecting to see Riona's shadow on the other side.

"You are safe here, Griffin," the queen said. "Myles will not let her out of his sight. Ask me what you must, and I will do what I can to help you."

"Help me free the innocent people of Myrkur who do not deserve the prison sentence they have been dealt simply because an O'Rourke ancestor decided the Dark Fae must be removed from your world. Help me find a way to save my family from a terrible fate. Once they are safe, I will not rest until Egan and those like him are brought to justice. I do not want to bring the barrier down—that is not my goal, though my traveling companion must think otherwise—I only want to free those who deserve a better life." He didn't tell them of Egan's vast army. Right now, all that mattered was Shauna and Nessa and the people of Fela.

"And you believe I can help you?" Brandon asked. "That is why you came to Gelsi, is it not?"

"I hoped you would be able to point me in the right direction." Griffin felt the futility of this request. Brandon spent twenty years as a prisoner. What could he know about any of this?

"I don't know much of my grandmother's history. She died long before I was born and her deeds were... frowned upon by those who came after her. I can only imagine the barrier around Myrkur is similar to the one that once stood around Fargelsi. Regan learned the barrier spell from somewhere, and I imagine that had something to do with Queen Sorcha. They were close when she was a child."

"Regan kept her spellwork private," Griffin said. "She didn't share it with me except to teach me simple things."

"She truly was like a mother to you, wasn't she?" Brandon shook his head, baffled by the magic that had removed Griffin from their minds.

"She was the only mother I ever knew. My mother, the Queen of Iskalt, and my father were killed when I was only two years old. The arms that held me when I was scared... the hands that dried my tears and nursed me when I was sick... they were Regan's."

"And Lochlan sentenced his own brother to the prison realm for remaining loyal to the woman who raised him?" Neeve frowned, a look of sympathy on her face. "It just doesn't sound like something he would do."

It was strange how they saw things differently now. No one had sympathy for Griffin when Regan's crimes were still fresh and raw in their minds.

"I chose to go to the prison realm as my punishment for working against Iskalt and Eldur. I had my reasons for making such a choice." But none of that was important now. "Regan's grimoire may have had answers, but it would have been destroyed when Brea brought down the palace—I'm sorry, I've forgotten myself—Queen Brea."

"Don't call her that to her face." Neeve grimaced. "My sister has never wanted to be queen of anything."

"That sounds like Brea." Griffin smiled.

"I do not know if she was in possession of any of Sorcha's spells or where she'd have gotten them," Brandon said. "And you are right, everything was destroyed after my sister died. Whatever she learned of barrier magic likely came from somewhere dark. It took Brea's magic to destroy the barrier around Fargelsi. Someone with both Eldurian and Fargelsian power. But she still needed the help of many magic wielders." Brandon paused to refill their wine glasses.

"We have precious few records about the origin of the prison realm," he continued. "Perhaps that is because those who were present at its creation forgot everything they knew about it when it was completed?"

"From what I understand, that was not something that was supposed to happen," Griffin said, taking a long sip of wine. "Egan believes it took the magic of all three realms to create the barrier, but the magic that made everyone forget, that was Sorcha's doing."

"So, it stands to reason that it would take the magic of all three realms to see it destroyed," Brandon added, sharing a wary look with his daughter.

"You don't think it's as easy as that?" Neeve glanced at her father.

"I wouldn't call what we did to end Regan's rule easy," Brandon said.

"Of course not, but it can't be as simple as doing the same thing all over again?"

"No." Brandon frowned. "We are dealing with older, much more complex magic this time. A spell like that grows stronger with time, and three generations is a very long time for this barrier to take on a life of its own. It's evolved. It will not be easy to breach this magic—if that is even possible."

Neeve shared a nod of agreement with her father before she turned to face Griffin. "This King Egan likely hasn't put all his trust in you," Neeve said. "That is why he's sent his envoy with you. We cannot allow an unknown king to flood our borders with the criminals we have so ignorantly sent to Myrkur. And Griffin is right, we owe it to the innocents to help them in any way we can."

"Thank you." Griffin let out a strangled breath, and his body relaxed for the first time since he'd left Myrkur. He hadn't realized how much he'd anticipated their refusal to help.

"You have Fargelsi in your corner," Neeve continued. "But you will need Iskalt too. This will take the combined effort of all our strongest magic wielders across the three kingdoms. You must go to Iskalt and tell the king and queen everything you've told us," Neeve said. "In this matter of magic, Lochlan will stand for Iskalt and Brea will stand for her sister, Alona, Queen of Eldur."

"Thank you, your Majesty." Griffin dipped his head, surprised at how quickly she trusted him, and knowing if her memories were intact, she'd have him thrown from the palace.

"We will all work together to find a solution, Griffin. That is what we do now." She placed a cool hand over his, but Griffin couldn't hear anything she said over the beating of his heart. She was sending him to Brea. To the woman who was once his wife—now married to his brother.

Returning home was hard enough, but he wasn't sure he had the strength to face Brea, knowing she would never recall the memories of the life they'd once shared.

Griffin had never spent much time with Brandon O'Rourke, the king who'd been locked away in the palace dungeons the entire time Griffin had grown up.

Regan hadn't let anyone in on that secret, the fact she'd captured her own brother, the rightful Fargelsian king, the only person who could have defeated her until Brea Robinson came along, prepared to burn everything to the ground to end her aunt's rule.

Brandon led Griffin from the throne room and down a long hall. It was strange to be in a completely different palace where Regan's had once stood. Griffin's gaze slid to the tapestries hanging along the walls, the wood underneath his feet. This palace suited Neeve, the woman who'd grown up as a servant in the very kingdom she now ruled.

"It's strange, isn't it?" Brandon didn't look at Griff, keeping his eyes trained on the hall ahead.

Griffin released a long sigh. "I used to run through

Regan's palace, dodging servants and guards." He'd only seen a few such servants since stepping inside this palace.

Brandon was quiet for a long moment. "My daughter doesn't like others to serve her. She pours her own wine, keeps her rooms tidy, and even makes Myles carry water from the well to their rooms."

Griffin pictured the Neeve he'd known. She would have been intimidating with her height if she hadn't kept her eyes trained on the ground. She'd barely spoken except to Brea. But this queen version of her met every one of his looks with one of confidence. "She's a good queen, isn't she?" Somehow, he knew she couldn't be anything less.

Brandon stopped walking and turned to Griffin, the smile fading from his face. "She is. I don't know you, Griffin, but I trust Myles, and I probably know more about the prison realm than anyone in this world. Even if I didn't believe you, that woman with wings and the kid with a tail are proof enough. So, I'll say this, my trust lasts up to the point you betray either of my daughters. If that happens, I will make sure there's no prison realm for you, only death. Do you understand me?"

Griffin stared at him, wondering just how much Myles had told them of his past transgressions. It was enough for Brandon to feel the need to protect Neeve and Brea—both daughters he hadn't known until they rescued him more than ten years ago. "I don't intend to betray them." He'd never intended for any of his betrayals to happen, but that hadn't stopped them before. He kept that part to himself. "I also don't expect you to remember my relationship with your sister, but you have to know one thing. I betrayed Regan when I helped Brea, Neeve, and you escape Fargelsi through the swamps of the Southern Vatlands. I let you through the queen's barrier."

"Even if that is true, Griffin, one heroic act does not forgive a hundred cowardly ones." He started walking again, leading Griffin up a spiral staircase. He didn't knock as he pushed open a door. "We will talk more in the morning." And then, he was gone, leaving Griffin on the threshold of a sitting room. This was no ordinary sitting room though. It looked... human? An overstuffed leather couch sat next to a reclining chair.

Gulliver was on the couch, and Riona had taken the chair. Myles stood in front of them like he was telling them a story. Griffin inched closer, trying to hear what he was saying.

"Then, there was a battle, and none of us knew what side he was on. He sort of fought for us, but then, he tried to save Queen Regan when my bestie was tearing her palace apart stone by stone with her magic."

Riona pursed her lips. "What is a bestie?"

"A friend." Myles laughed. "A best friend. She once thought she'd killed me because Griffin told her I was dead."

"Myles," Griffin growled, stepping farther into the room. "What have you told them?"

Myles turned slowly as if wishing Griffin weren't standing right behind him. "Oh, erm, nothing much. Just how glorious we all thought your red hair was. It really matches your... er... pale skin tone."

Neither Gulliver nor Riona laughed at that. By the way Gulliver stared down at his hands, not talking, Griffin knew what tales Myles was spinning. Tales of a man who'd betrayed everyone who ever loved him. Lochlan. Brea. Even Regan in the end.

Myles kept talking as if he hadn't just shattered the fragile bonds between the three of them. "So, these are Brea and Lochlan's rooms when they come."

Griffin's eyes widened. No wonder everything looked so human. Brea would never fully leave her upbringing behind.

"We would have put you in guest quarters, but with the minimal staff we keep here, Neeve wanted you in rooms that were already made up. I'll play tour guide."

Griffin followed the human to the hall where the bedrooms branched off from the sitting room.

"Make yourselves at home. Just don't... break anything, yeah?" He turned away from Griffin and walked toward the door into the hall. "We will talk again in the morning, Griff."

Once he was gone and the door shut behind him, Gulliver stood and walked toward one of the bedrooms without saying a word.

"Gullie," Griffin called after him.

"Give him some space." Riona walked to the hearth, the wood had grown up from the floor, complete with flowering vines. Inside, a fire struggled to gain momentum. She crouched down to stoke the embers back to life.

"This castle is cold." Her wings fluttered as she stood and backed away from the fire.

To Griffin's surprise, she didn't go in search of her bed. Instead, she took a seat on the couch. Griffin joined her and stared into the dancing flames. He closed his eyes and leaned back against the cushion. It was odd finding comfort here. Yet another thing he had to thank Neeve and Myles for.

"I've heard stories of Queen Regan."

At Riona's words, he opened his eyes. "Most in Myrkur have. She sent a lot of people to the prison realm." He sighed. "When we cross that magical border, we know the world will forget us, but do you ever wonder if it would be better if we too forgot?"

Riona was quiet for a long moment. "No." She paused. "If we forget the evil we do, how are we ever supposed to atone for it?"

"Do you really think there's atonement for people like me?"

"I have to."

"Why?" He turned his head to look at her.

"Because you and I are the same, Griffin. And I refuse to believe I can never make things right."

"Why do you serve Egan?"

She met his gaze. "Why did you serve Regan?"

In all the years of his imprisonment, he'd tried to answer that very question. Why had he served someone he knew was evil? Why did he hold captive the very people who wanted to save the realm?

Only one answer had ever made sense to him. "Because she was all I had."

"Do you ever wonder if what makes a person good or bad is just circumstance?"

"All the time."

This was the first honest conversation he'd had with Riona, and there was small comfort in the fact he wasn't alone this time. Riona was trapped in the same cycle he'd been in most of his life.

"Tell me about your wife."

His wife. Brea. Another sigh rattled from his chest. "Brea

is Regan's niece. I captured her from the human realm where she'd lived her entire life for protection. But she saw me as her savior, not her captor. At least at first." He smiled, thinking about spending time with Brea at his cabin and riding horses.

"You loved her?"

Griffin nodded. "As much as I was able. I was raised by a woman who had expectations and conditions that came along with her love. I thought I could love Brea even when I was hurting her. She escaped once—thanks to Queen Neeve, actually. So, I was sent to retrieve the one person who could get her back to Fargelsi. Myles Merrick, the person she cared about more than anyone."

He hadn't told this story in the years he'd lived in the prison realm. No one was supposed to know about his connection to Regan. It would have put a target on his back.

"Keep going." Riona leaned forward, resting her elbows on her knees.

Griffin sucked in a deep breath. "It worked. She exchanged herself for Myles. When Regan told me I was to marry Brea, I never thought Brea would have been kept in the dark."

"About what?"

"Fae marriage."

Curiosity lit in Riona's eyes.

Griffin shoved a hand through his hair. "A fae marriage is a magical bond. It tied Brea to me whether she loved me or not. It created that love in her."

"What happened?" Riona stared at him, hanging on his every word.

"Our entire world imploded. War came to Fargelsi, a war

led by Brea herself. She was the most powerful fae I've ever seen. And she was in love with my brother. Lochlan never would have sent me to the prison realm. He hated me, but I think he loved me too."

"If he didn't send you..."

"It was my idea. My uncle sits in a cell in Iskalt so the people will never forget what he did to them. I didn't want that, but mostly, I did it for Brea. As soon as I passed through the magical barrier, our marriage bond severed. I felt it the moment it broke."

Riona sat still for a long moment, too long. Griffin was not a fae to trust, not like she'd ever have trusted him anyway.

"What does it feel like?" Riona's voice was so low he wasn't sure he heard right at first.

"What?"

"Love. What does it feel like? It seems in your previous life, you had much of it. Regan, as bad as she sounds, obviously loved you. You said yourself your brother wouldn't have sent you to the prison realm. And this wife of yours, I'll bet she cried for you. I just..." She took in a deep breath. "I'm curious. I want to know what that feels like."

"It's painful. Love has led to the most painful experiences of my life. I didn't just love Regan, I followed her down a dark path—always hoping she would make better choices, and I made excuses for her when she didn't. Loving her destroyed me. I think my brother would deny loving me. And Brea... there was a point I think she truly did feel... something for me, but I betrayed her worse than anyone. So, I guess I'm saying love is the great destroyer. But it's also the most amazing feeling in all the worlds."

Tears gathered in his eyes, but he blinked them away. He'd known coming back would be hard, that being surrounded by people who didn't remember him would crush what was left of his soul.

Riona reached over and took his hand. He turned his head to look at her. "And your king... he's going to kill my family." What was left of it. No matter what happened outside the prison realm, he couldn't lose sight of what was at stake. He was no longer Griffin O'Shea of Iskalt. This wasn't his world anymore.

"I'm sorry."

Griffin sighed. "I don't understand you, Riona."

"You're not the only one who has done evil. Egan..." She didn't finish.

Griffin turned, still not letting go of her hand. "What does he have on you?" He skimmed his gaze along the tattoos covering her arms. They told a story he couldn't decipher. "Who are you?"

She pulled her hand from his. "We all have secrets to protect, Griff. And mine would only put you in greater danger."

"Danger? Riona—"

"I'm tired, Griff. I think it's best if we all get some sleep." She didn't look at him as she walked away.

Griffin heaved himself to his feet and headed toward the third bedroom. Stopping at the door, he realized Gulliver's door was still open. He pushed it wider to find Gulliver sitting against the wall next to it, tears streaming down his face.

"Gullie? Are you hurt?" He looked to the tail that was wrapped with fresh bandages courtesy of Neeve's healers.

Gulliver shook his head. "I don't think I know you at all, Griff."

"Were you listening to our conversation?"

"I'm sorry. I just..." He released a breath.

Griffin slid to the floor next to him. "I never wanted to put you in danger."

Before Gulliver could respond, the door opened again.

"Gullie? I heard crying." Riona's gaze found Griffin's. "Oh, I'll go and let you take care of it."

"*You* came to help Gulliver?"

She shrugged.

"Please stay." Gulliver stared up at her, his eyes shining.

Riona hesitated for a moment before lowering herself to the floor in front of them. Griffin could barely see them in the dark, but they were all creatures of the darkness now.

"We shouldn't be here, Griff." Gulliver wiped a hand across his eyes. "These people... you did bad things to them, and I... I... I don't even know you."

Griffin heard Neeve promise to help, they even told him where to go next, but he wondered when it came down to releasing Myrkur from the prison magic... would they help then? Once they learned of the existence of ogres and all manner of Dark Fae, would they choose to remain in their peaceful world?

He hadn't missed the distrust in their eyes. Probably thanks to Myles' stories. Griffin put an arm around Gulliver's shoulders. But their current situation wasn't the one that had Gulliver crying.

"Hey." Griffin nudged him. "You know this version of me better than anyone."

Gulliver shook his head but didn't utter a word in response.

"I need you to trust me, Gullie. I don't want to do this without you. We have to go to Iskalt where my brother and my ex-wife will show no recognition. It's going to hurt. A lot. But our mission isn't about me. This is for Shauna and Nessa, remember?"

Gulliver nodded and wiped the tears from his eyes.

Riona studied both of them. "Iskalt? Why?"

He wasn't sure if Brea and Lochlan would help him. It seemed too simple, too familiar. Ten years ago, Brea brought down the barrier around Fargelsi. There was little chance that was all they needed to do this time. Yet, it was a start.

But he knew of one other person who also studied boundary magic with Regan. He would prove unwilling to help, but he also happened to be in Iskalt. "We must speak with my uncle."

Gulliver looked up at him. "But Myles said your uncle was a bad man."

"He is."

"He said you used to be a bad man too."

Griffin sighed. Myles needed to learn to keep his mouth shut. "Listen to me, Gullie, I will never hurt you, and I will *never* betray you. No one in the three fae kingdoms knows what we have been through in Myrkur, they do not understand what it is to live in darkness, to fight for everything we have. But we do, and that knowledge binds us."

Riona scooted forward and took their hands in hers. "The three of us against the fae realm."

Griffin didn't show his surprise as Riona dropped the

wall that had existed between them. Now that they understood each other, she seemed more real.

"These people don't remember me," Griff said. "And maybe that's a good thing. But they will feel no loyalty to me, no love. We can't trust any of them."

"Only each other." Gulliver nodded.

Griffin squeezed him tighter. "We will one day have to go back to Myrkur and resume our roles fighting one another, but out here, we fight for the same thing."

Riona didn't release their hands. "Here, we fight for each other."

CHAPTER SIXTEEN

"Griff!" Riona's scream tore through their suite of rooms, sending a spike of fear right into Griffin.

He raced from his room, across the sitting room, and slammed open Riona's door to find her standing before a looking glass in a mess of ocean blue that left her arms bare. The tattoos normally painting her dark arms were gone.

As in, vanished, leaving behind beautiful unmarked brown skin.

"How?" Griffin couldn't take his eyes from her arms. "You yelled for me? I thought you were dying."

Riona sent a scowl over one shoulder. "Someone is going to die if they don't get me out of this ridiculous dress."

Griffin's expression softened. He'd known another girl ten years ago who'd hated the Fargelsian styles when it meant she couldn't live in her riding pants.

"You look..." He couldn't finish the sentence as his eyes traced the body-hugging bodice that flared slightly at the waist before raining down in multicolored panels.

"Ridiculous?" She groaned. "I look completely and utterly ridiculous."

The door opened again, and Gulliver let out a low whistle. "Riona, you look beautiful."

Yes, that. Those were the exact words Griffin had tried to get out and failed.

She softened a little at Gulliver's praise. "How am I to wear a sword with this dress? I don't even see anywhere to hide a knife."

Griffin crossed his arms and leaned against the wall. "And who are we knifing tonight?" He couldn't look away from her tattoo-less arms.

"I don't know, Griff. You seem to have made every fae in the three kingdoms your enemy."

"Doesn't count if they don't remember they're my enemies." He woke in a much better mood today surrounded by the finery he was once accustomed to. Then, the guilt came. Nothing here should make him content. He'd wanted to leave for Iskalt right away, but Neeve asked for one day. Griffin wasn't sure why she needed the time.

Riona reached behind her, trying to tighten the laces of her backless dress, but her wings created an obstacle the dress wasn't made for.

Griffin pushed off the wall and batted her hands away. "Let me do it." His fingers brushed her skin as he began at the bottom, tightening her bodice. When he reached the top of the dress just under her wing joint, his finger brushed over a raised scar, and he froze.

He could only imagine what kind of punishment created such a scar on a Slyph. It seemed someone tried to take her wings. Anger rushed through him at the thought of such a gruesome injury that could have robbed her of the ability to fly.

Riona's wings fluttered, slapping him in the face until he backed away. "Riona... I—"

"Leave it alone, Griff."

"But—"

"It was a long time ago." She turned back to the mirror.

Gulliver, oblivious to everything, smiled. "At least they left us clothes that accommodated us." His tail had been coming back to life. The healers believed it would soon grow to the length it was before.

Griffin didn't step back from Riona. He had so many questions. "You smell like rosewater." Those words were not supposed to leave his lips.

Riona's face flushed. "I had a bath this morning while you were out exploring the palace."

"Did a servant bring you water?"

"No, but the queen did."

Griffin's eyes widened. "Riona... you can't have a queen bringing you water."

"Why not?"

"She's a queen! There are rules."

Riona shrugged. "She didn't think there were rules when she showed up at my door with buckets of water." She ran a hand over the top of her tight braids. "At least they let me refuse to have my hair done for this dinner. Seriously, who dresses like this for a meal?"

Griffin had to agree. He looked down at the light blue trousers and silk shirt they'd foisted on him. When Regan ruled here, this kind of dress was required to be in her presence.

But Neeve seemed different.

At least, he'd thought so.

There was a knock at the door to the sitting room, and Gulliver ran to answer it.

Griffin couldn't take his eyes from Riona. Lifting a hand, he ran his fingers down one arm. "Where are your tattoos?"

She turned toward him. "They appear when I choose."

"You can control them?" He gripped her wrist and pulled her arm closer. She didn't free herself, instead, letting him examine every inch of skin between her fingers and her shoulder.

"The tattoos are a part of me." Her voice was low. "All my people had them."

"If they're a part of you, why would you hide them?"

She turned back to the mirror. "You should go see who is at the door."

He stepped closer to her, the woman he'd once fought with in the king's arena. They both owed each other so much. The night before, he'd told her more than he'd told anyone in the prison realm, and he knew why. They were the same.

Putting a hand on one shoulder, he leaned in. "Don't hide any part of yourself, Riona."

"Isn't that what you do with your secrets?"

It had been. "Yes. Be better than me. Do better. There's still time."

Her entire body shivered, and he turned toward the bed for her cloak, settling it over her shoulders. She closed her eyes, releasing a sigh, and the tattoos returned.

"What do they say?" He traced a pattern of lines on the back of her neck.

Her eyes opened, and she stared at him in the mirror. "I'm dangerous, Griff. I don't know what they say, but I get this feeling. Whatever it is, it's not good. These tattoos that tell my path, it's my future actions they foretell. Not my past. And I can't help thinking whatever it is I'm meant to read in them will change everything for me." She bit off the last word and sucked in a long breath, sparing one more glance for Griffin before brushing past him to walk into the sitting room.

She was dangerous. Griffin ran a hand through his hair as he followed her and found Gulliver, Riona, and Myles waiting.

"So, here's the thing." Myles clapped his hands together. "My wife doesn't trust you. I don't trust you. But for some reason my father-in-law wants to talk to you tonight. Hence the dinner. Neeve promised she would help you, but I've got to admit, Griff, I've spent the last ten years filling her ear with stories about you. When you're the only person in the world who remembers something like that, you go out of your way to make sure you never forget."

"Now, who wants a nice dinner? It's taken me a while to get used to royal food, but who is up for something that sounds just as gross as it tastes?"

Myles didn't know that Griffin and Gulliver weren't used to having many food options at all, so they'd eat whatever was put before them.

Riona shrugged, tucking in the bit of vulnerability she'd shown Griffin and instead became the stoic woman who'd fought him so expertly in the pits.

Griffin smiled to himself. He liked the fierce version of

Riona. He liked the contemplative version. And the version that was curious about him, about Brea.

And then, there was the one who'd sat on the floor of Gulliver's room the night before, accepting the truth that the three of them had to work together, had to protect each other. That Riona... he liked her the most.

"Her tattoos are back," Gulliver whispered. "I like them."

Griffin slid his arm around the young man's shoulders. "Me too, Gullie. Me too."

The dining hall wasn't what he'd expected. Instead of the long table that could seat too many people, Brandon sat behind a shorter mahogany table near a blazing hearth. Two candelabras provided light for the table. Griffin's gaze slid up to a chandelier casting flickering light across the room.

Just like everything else in this palace, the room held an easy comfort Regan's palace never had. She never wanted her guests to get too used to her palace.

All night Griffin had stayed awake in bed wondering if Regan was going to walk through his door. In those moments, he wished he'd taken Gulliver and run from Egan. They could have escaped into the human realm and lived there, far away from the people he didn't want to face.

Footsteps ran toward them like a bunch of tiny drumbeats followed by squeals from the children who weren't dressed as nice as Griffin and Riona.

Brandon stood to greet them, a reserved smile on his face. "Take your seats. The queen will be here shortly."

Myles snorted. "Eventually, she might make an appearance. It's month's end, and you know how she can't resist, Brandon."

Brandon sighed, but his smile belied his annoyance. Both men obviously adored Neeve.

Griffin took a seat and gestured for his companions to do the same. "What's month's end?"

"It's the lantern festival." One of the children—a tiny blond girl hopped onto a chair and snagged a roll.

Brandon sent her a scowl for her table manners, but it was with obvious affection.

Myles sat next to his daughter and proceeded to imitate her in taking a roll, slathering butter on it, and stuffing it into his mouth. "The lantern festival is an ancient Fargelsian custom that was abandoned in the time of Queen Sorcha." He swallowed. "You don't know how it was in Fargelsi after we defeated Regan. The people were free of the boundary spell, but they couldn't be free of everything she put them through. Many had been forced to work for her, others lived for years in the dungeons, their families never knowing where they were. So, we restarted a few old customs to bring joy into their lives again and to highlight the peace we'd fought hard for. The lantern festival was one."

Griffin tried not to let Myles' words strike him as hard as they did. He'd had a hand in keeping the Fargelsian people in line.

The kids around the table chattered about going to watch the lanterns rise after supper.

Gulliver asked the question Griffin wanted an answer to. "What happens at this festival?"

A festival was something Gulliver would never have

seen before, Riona either. But Griffin remembered the many parties Regan had thrown. Those were the good times, the times he couldn't make himself regret.

Myles smiled. "For three nights straight, the people of Fargelsi use their magic to launch glowing lanterns into the night sky."

"Why would they do such a thing?" Riona couldn't keep the scorn from her lips.

Red crept up Myles' neck. "Well, they're supposed to carry our worries to the skies above. Once a lantern stops glowing, it means the worry has faded from the fae who launched it."

"But that's ridiculous." Riona lifted a brow. "You can't get rid of what ails you by sending it to the sky."

Myles opened his mouth to respond, but the doors slamming open stopped the words. A messenger crossed the room to reach Myles.

Myles pushed his chair back and stood. "What has happened?"

The messenger leaned down to whisper something in Myles' ear and pressed a message into his hand. Myles nodded. "Please find the queen and bring her to our chambers. Brandon, can you get the kids fed and back to their nanny? Then, we will need you to join us as well."

"Of course." Brandon stood. "What's going on?"

"I'll explain later. Griff, you're with me. Now."

Griffin followed him out into the hall with Riona and Gulliver on his heels. "I didn't have to wear this ridiculous dress," Riona whispered. "Did I?"

"Probably not." It was most likely a test. Neeve wanted

to know how pliable Riona was, how far she was willing to go to please the queen.

Griffin sped up to walk at Myles' side. "Where are we going?"

"My rooms. We need to talk." Myles' jaw clenched, and he uncurled his fists. "You have not told us everything it seems."

Griffin didn't know what to say to that, but Myles was right. There was plenty they kept from the people of Fargelsi.

Myles slammed open the door and ushered them inside. He waved toward the white settee in the sitting room. "Have a seat." He turned his back on them and unfolded the parchment.

No one broke the long silence until the door opened once more and Neeve entered. She peeled gloves down her arms, releasing her hands as she set the gloves on the mantle. Myles handed her the message, and her expression didn't change as she read it. She lifted her eyes to her husband, and he gave her a short nod.

Neeve untied the front of her cloak. "We are at peace now in the three kingdoms." She draped her cloak over the end of a chair and lifted the hem of her gown so she could sit. "We've had this peace for the last ten years. My husband tells me this coincides with you, Griffin, entering the prison realm." She tapped a finger against her chin before lifting her other hand that held the message. "We received a note tonight telling us of a breach in the prison magic."

"A breach? How would anyone know?" Surely there weren't powerful enough fae to be able to spy on the people the world had forgotten.

Myles slumped into a wing-backed chair, crossing one leg over the other. "Darling queen wife, I think we need to tell them."

Worry flashed across the queen's face. "We do not know them."

"Yet, you've already given your support to Griff. Maybe it's time he had our secrets too." Myles turned tired eyes on Griff. "Regan is gone. You are a man without a master. Some probably call that freedom, but you... maybe not."

Griffin didn't take his eyes from Myles. "Whatever happened in the past is done. I am not that man anymore."

"No. I don't suppose any of us are the same." He rubbed his eyes. "It started when she was six."

"What started? Who was six?"

Myles sighed. "My niece, Tia."

His... "Brea and Lochlan's daughter?"

"Yes. She's powerful, Griff. Maybe even as powerful as her mom. She's ten now, but for the last four years, she's been plagued by dreams. They change, but the themes are always the same. Darkness. Fae with all sorts of features. Wings. Tails. Horns. She even dreamed of a giant green beast."

"An ogre," Gulliver piped in. "That's what they're called."

Gulliver was right. These images could mean only one thing. Tia saw the prison realm in her sleep. "But how? No one who enters the realm returns."

Neeve's shoulders dropped. "None of us know. At first, we thought they were simple nightmares, but then there was one constant."

"You." Myles met his gaze. "Tia described seeing you over and over. But I'm the only one who remembers you, the only one who could prove that Tia's dreams weren't just dreams."

Griffin rubbed his face. "This isn't possible."

"You haven't met this little girl. With her, everything is possible."

Griffin looked to Neeve. "And the message? Why did we have to leave dinner so suddenly?"

"It's from Iskalt, from Brea." She held it out.

Griffin's hands trembled as he unfolded Brea's words.

The dreams are growing worse. Tia spent all week in bed, mumbling about a man who has to come. One who has to save her. I don't know from what, but she's scaring me with tales of a breach in the prison magic, allowing this man she sees to escape.

Why does my girl need to be saved? And by this stranger? I can't help feeling something is coming for us, sister. Something more evil than we've faced before. Tia has taken to sitting in the north tower watching for this mystery fae to come. She claims she'll feel him moving toward her, and that will allow her to return to us, to her twin brother.

Please be on the lookout for this new evil, Neeve. Protect Myles because we all know he's the most likely one to do something stupid.

I love you both.

Brea

Griffin read the note three times. This child, his... niece... she saw him in her dreams?

He passed the note to Riona who read it to Gulliver.

Griffin wasn't a hero, he wasn't the man to save a child, yet this child believed in him. She knew he'd come, and he'd save her from some unknown evil.

Neeve rubbed her eyes. "Griff, I know there's a lot to think about, and you need to be smart about this."

Emotions warred within Griffin. A desire to follow the path that led to taking down the wall with the most powerful magic wielders in the realm. And an invisible pull toward this little girl.

"We were going to Iskalt, anyway." He stood. "We leave in an hour."

"You can't possibly consider going through the marshes in the dark." Neeve chimed in. "The Vatlands–"

Griffin cut her off. "–are not our way to Iskalt."

"Griffin." Myles crossed his arms. "You cannot be thinking what I know you are."

"We must cross Loch Villandi. I won't waste any more time. If we leave tonight, we can reach the shores by morning and hopefully get a fisherman to take us to Iskalt."

"No fisherman will risk their ship in the dangers of the Iskalt sea."

Griffin met Myles' gaze. "Everyone has a price."

CHAPTER SEVENTEEN

"Do you know who Queen Sorcha was?" Neeve leaned against the doorframe, watching Griffin prepare to leave. She'd brought him provisions and then stayed. Griffin had known Neeve before when they both resided in the Fargelsian palace. He didn't know if he'd ever get used to her being a queen, but somehow, it fit.

"I've known a little of her. She was Regan's grandmother, but Regan didn't speak much about her family."

Neeve met his eyes. "Sorcha was the most powerful Fargelsian to have ever lived. She could do spells none of us can even dream of. You obviously know how Fargelsian magic works. We have to speak the words of a spell to let it free. Well, Sorcha is said to have performed dangerous magic, the kind that would kill the average Fargelsian. But her spells were hidden away inside a book. Though, most Fargelsians think the book is a legend."

Griffin stopped packing the food and turned to her. "But you don't?"

Her brow furrowed. "I… I don't know. My father seems to think it is real, but I have a hard time believing the story."

Griffin crossed his arms. "What does the legend say?"

"Sorcha had a twin sister who knew she had to do something to stop the path Sorcha had set them on, spreading darkness across the kingdoms. So, she stole the book and hid it in the human realm with a network of guardians." She studied him for a long moment. "Rumor has it Regan searched for the book for decades."

He tried to remember a time when Regan revealed this to him, but she'd kept him in the dark. Griffin hated how much that hurt. "But she didn't find it?"

Neeve shrugged her shoulders. "We don't really know. The spells she used for the border wall were certainly more powerful than most. We assume they came from the book, but I don't know how she got them. Her arrogance may have prevented her from thinking the book was with mere humans."

"She wasn't—" He bit back the words, wishing he didn't still feel this urge to defend her.

"There's more." Neeve stepped into the room. "Sorcha created the prison realm."

He already knew that, but he started putting the pieces together. "She—" He stumbled back. "Are you telling me this book could bring down the prison magic?" It was exactly the kind of lead he'd been looking for.

She pursed her lips, thinking before speaking. "I believe it's the most logical conclusion."

"I need to find that book." He shoved the last item in his pack and slipped it over one shoulder. "Thank you, Neeve, for your hospitality."

"Griffin?"

He stopped in the doorway and looked back. "Myles' stories about the great Griffin O'Shea... I wouldn't trust that man with this information."

"Then, why do you trust me?"

She gave him a soft smile. "Because I know what it's like to spend years in captivity. Our prisons were different. But I fought against mine, and I managed to do good even with the oppression I endured. I very much hope you're planning to fight against yours."

Riona and Gulliver walked down the hall to join him as he gave the servant queen one final look. "For any wrongs I may have done you, your Majesty, I am more sorry than you could ever know."

She didn't remember his status in the palace or the fact he played a hand in keeping the Fargelsian people trapped in their kingdom, but the words weren't for her. He'd needed to say them.

"Wait for me!" Myles sprinted down the hall with a too large pack dangling from one hand. He panted as he joined them.

Neeve smiled at her husband. "Myles will be accompanying you to Iskalt."

Griffin's brows drew together. "That's—"

"A great idea." Myles grinned. "Yes, Griffy-Griff, I agree. No need to thank me for leaving my wife and kids to help you. They understand we have a special bond."

Griffin grunted. "We do not."

Myles slid an arm around his shoulders. "Now, is that any way to talk to the only person in the three kingdoms who even knows who you are?"

Neeve gave her husband an indulgent laugh before pulling him away from Griffin. He wrapped his arms around her, and Griffin shifted between his feet, uncomfortable with the moment between them.

"I'll be back as soon as I can," Myles whispered, resting his forehead against Neeve's.

"I don't like this, but it feels important. I can't shake that feeling. Whatever they find, it's going to change everything."

"Not everything." He kissed her long and slow.

Griffin cleared his throat. Myles pulled back with a sheepish grin.

Neeve stayed where she was as the four of them walked down the hall. Myles walked backward, not taking his eyes from his wife. "I love you, Neever Beaver!"

Griffin choked on a laugh. "That's your nickname for her?"

Myles gave one last wave and turned to join the group. "I mean... it's better than douchy Loch. And there aren't even any beavers here in the fae realm, so she just thinks I'm rhyming her name."

"What's a beaver?" Gulliver asked.

Myles ruffled his hair. "We're going to have a lot of time to talk on this adventure, little man. I'll tell you all about the humans."

"Oh joy, time to talk to Myles." Griffin shared an exasperated look with Riona. They walked across the bridge and took the horses Neeve promised them. Once they headed for the Dragur Forest, the tension winding through Griffin eased. The palace wasn't the same as Regan's, but he couldn't help seeing her around every corner.

Ahead, Myles and Gulliver chatted, but Griffin hung

back, thoughts of the spell book Neeve told him about rolling through his mind. Maybe it wasn't people he needed to gather to help bring down the prison magic.

Maybe it was words.

* * *

They rode across open ground, away from the swampy Vatlands Myles suggested they travel. Griffin knew that way was safer, but it was also much slower across Eastern Eldur to the Sea of Iskalt before they would reach the Ice Palace. It would take weeks. And weeks were something they didn't have.

There was only one other way into Iskalt. And none of them would like it. They stopped occasionally and rested only when they had to.

As soon as Griffin laid out his plans, he'd seen Myles' face grow steadily paler. Griffin didn't blame him. Their journey would be risky. It was not an undertaking many supported.

Riona and Gulliver didn't quite understand Myles' fear. Riona was born for the water. And Gulliver... he tried putting a brave face on for everything.

They reached the ramshackle dock at the southwestern edge of Lake Villandi which spanned the distance between Fargelsi and Iskalt. Crossing here would allow them to bypass Eldur—except for the mountain pass through the tip of the northern Vatlands that stood between Iskalt and the shores of Villandi.

Griffin slid down from his horse and peered into the crystal clear water. He couldn't see any of the mysterious creatures that lived in the depths, but he knew they were there.

A dark-skinned woman with pink magic flashing in her eyes walked toward them, her hands on her hips. "And who might you be?" Her expression wasn't unfriendly, just... wary.

Griffin walked toward her. "Griffin O'Shea." He stuck out a hand.

She clasped it, one eyebrow raised. "I didn't know there was another O'Shea in the world other than that blasted ice king."

"So, you're not a friend of Iskalt's?"

She smiled. "Oh, I'm a friend of Iskalt's, just not the royal couple."

Griffin could make that work, but before he spoke, Gulliver jumped down. "Well, my friend here is about to blow up their world, so he could use your help."

Now, she looked interested. "And how can I be of service?" She scanned each of their faces. Myles tried to obscure his with the hood as he dismounted.

"We need passage to Iskalt."

That surprised her. "What's a pretty boy like you going to do in Iskalt? Do you realize how cold it is there?"

Griffin had nothing to say to that. He was Iskaltian, he was born there, but he hadn't set foot in his kingdom since he was barely old enough to remember. Could he even claim to be a Prince of Iskalt anymore?

The woman laughed, a full laugh. "That question wasn't supposed to initiate a deep period of thought. Of course, I can give passage to anyone who pays."

"Get us to Iskalt without being captured by a royal

vessel, and you can keep our horses. They're good stock and will fetch a good price."

She rubbed her chin, letting the sun glint off a ruby ring. "So we're clear, my cargo is illegal. If you are caught on this ship, you may be sent to the prison realm."

Griffin and Riona shared a look.

Only Myles took issue with that. "How illegal?"

The captain ignored his question. "Welcome aboard. We leave tomorrow at first light. I'll take those horses now. My men can sell them when we're gone. With beasts like that, they may even fetch a price at the palace."

The captain's people led the horses away while Griffin made camp near the edge of the lake. He wished they had another means of getting into Iskalt, but even most fishing vessels avoided Lake Villandi, leaving them with few options but to trust a smuggler—the only fools brave enough to face the difficult crossing.

"What do you think she's bringing into Iskalt?" Gulliver asked.

"It's probably better if we do not know." He turned to Gulliver. "How's the tail?"

"The queen's healer sent me with some salve. It's helping."

"Good. Let me know if anything goes wrong, all right?"

Gulliver nodded, and Griffin clapped him on the shoulder.

The night in the palace of Fargelsi came back to him, the moment Riona decided she was in this with them. Griff didn't yet know what was at stake for her, but they all had things to lose if they didn't find what Egan wanted.

That night, as he looked to the stars above, he thought of

Shauna and the strong will Egan would try to break. Of Nessa, the little girl who'd never deserved any of this. It was for people like them that propelled him on this journey. He'd give them a real life, even if it meant unleashing Egan to do it.

His last battles were about kingdoms and who sat on the three thrones of the fae realm.

This time, he fought for people, for freedom.

For ideals that were larger than himself.

He shifted to watch Riona in her sleep. Was there a part of her that wanted to fight for the same things?

Maybe they were always meant to be on the same side.

CHAPTER EIGHTEEN

Griffin watched Myles lean over the side of the ship, heaving as the contents of his stomach streamed into the lake below. "I hate you, Griffin O'Shea," he grumbled in between bouts of nausea as the ship rocked. "I hate you so freaking much."

Riona chuckled from her spot sitting beside Griffin on the deck. "I don't think the king likes you very much."

"King Consort." Griffin didn't know why he corrected her. Maybe it was because Myles had risen to the position Regan once meant for him. He wasn't sure how he felt about that. "Where's Gulliver?"

Riona shrugged. "It's not my job to watch the boy."

The rocking intensified as water sloshed over the ship's side. Griffin lunged forward, tackling Myles' to the deck as water crashed over where he'd just been standing. Griffin had seen what happened when the average fae touched the Lake Villandi water. He'd once lived near the Villandi shores, and he'd seen many fishermen who thought they could master the lake throw themselves in to the waters after only touching a few drops.

Myles kicked him off. "I don't need you saving me, O'Shea."

The words stung, but Griffin only grunted and sat back on his heels. "You're welcome, human." He settled back next to Riona. Sanity said they should head below deck, but that only made Myles' sickness worse.

"Are all humans so rude?" Riona crossed her arms.

"No. And yes. Myles is just seasick. I don't pretend to know all humans, but the ones I've known can be pretty rude. My wife..." He let the words trail off, better left forgotten when they were only a day from setting foot in Iskalt.

"I thought the passing was supposed to be easy."

Griffin sighed. He hadn't properly prepared any of his companions. Only Myles had known what was in store for them. On the Fargelsian side of the expansive lake, the water appeared calm, beautiful—deceptively so. The closer one sailed to Iskalt, the more the waters churned, trying to keep ships from their shores. Some thought it was a kind of magic, but Griffin wondered if it was an omen for what lay ahead.

Iskalt held no hope, no warmth. At least, it hadn't before. If Lochlan was king now, why did the waters still churn?

The cracked wooden door slammed open, and the Captain screamed at them. "Below deck. Everyone. I won't have idiots accidentally touching the water and not-so-accidentally throwing themselves overboard."

"Not arguing with that." Myles, looking pale and tired, followed her.

Griffin tried to steady himself and get to his feet. He

reached a hand down to Riona. She shook her head, her braids clinging to her face. The colorful tattoos danced along her skin. Riona followed his gaze and pulled her sopping cloak to cover her arms.

"I'm not going inside," Riona yelled above the wind. "I belong out here." She closed her eyes as another blast of lake water smacked her in the face. Griffin tried to get to her, to push her out of the path of the water, but he wasn't fast enough. Yet, nothing happened. She didn't jump to the depths or hang over the side of the ship.

Griffin studied her for a moment longer, stumbling as the boat reared up. He lowered himself beside her, his hands searching for something, anything to hold on to. "You told us you were Asrai but it was hard to believe with our feet on solid ground." A fae of both Slyph and Asrai descent seemed like the stuff of legends.

She didn't hear him over the howling of the wind. She seemed to be mesmerized by the water, but not controlled by it.

"Griff!" Gulliver's worried face appeared as he opened the door. "It's too dangerous out there."

"He's right." Riona shoved Griffin's shoulder. "Go, be safe. I'll be fine out here."

Griffin met Gulliver's gaze. "I'm not leaving her." He'd left people behind before. If she meant what she'd said—that they needed to fight for each other in a world that had forgotten them—then this was him fighting for her.

The storm raged around them, turning the sky black as a torrent of rain pounded down. Another wave sloshed over the side of the boat. "Riona, please!" Griffin reached for her as she stood at the side of the deck, looking down into the water.

A bolt of lightning seemed to crack the sky in two, and it snapped Riona from her trance. Her eyes widened as they landed on Griffin. "Yes, you're right. We need to get below deck."

He wouldn't tell her he'd been saying that all along.

Riona pushed him toward the door as the wood beneath their feet creaked. They both stumbled down the narrow staircase to where the crew sat leaning against the cargo.

Griffin shook his head, brushing the rain soaked locks from his face. Riona did the same with her wings.

Gulliver sat with a number of the sailors, his face not nearly as green as Myles'. He jumped up when he saw Griffin. "Hey, Griff. You want some ale?"

"No. And neither do you." He took the mug from Gulliver's hand and passed it off to Riona. "Is there tea?"

Gulliver's shoulders dropped. "Yes, there's tea."

A crash sounded above, making every fae present jump. Smugglers took their chances on the massive lake, but they knew the risk. If this ship went down, it wasn't the water that would kill them.

Only the creatures in it.

"Do you hear that?" Riona asked.

Griffin tried to listen above the boisterous sailors. "What is it?"

"A melody." She turned to the stairs. "I need to get back up there."

"No." Griffin grabbed her wrist. "Stay here."

She ripped her arm out of his grasp. "Where is the music?"

Griffin and Gulliver shared a look. "Riona." He tried to listen. "Is it something in the water calling to you?"

She shook her head and yanked open the door, running back up into the rain.

"What is she doing?" the captain yelled. "I don't care if she does have wings, she's going to get herself killed."

Griffin couldn't let that happen. He sprinted up the steps, yelling back down. "Don't let the boy follow me." Because he would. That was Gulliver. Griffin ignored the rain pounding into him as he searched the deck for Riona. A wave crashed over the side, and he jumped up onto a crate, never stopping his search.

He shielded his eyes against the rain, and that was when he saw it. A movement in the sky. Riona battled the storm, her wings working furiously to keep her in the air. It was the most incredible sight he'd ever seen.

And it terrified him.

"Riona!" He didn't move from atop his crate as lake water flooded the deck. What was she doing? His eyes followed the path it looked like she was trying to take. The rain let up just enough for him to see the crags of Talam.

That wasn't right.

Their path wasn't meant to take them anywhere near the island. Movement atop the cliffs overlooking the beach had Griffin trying to get a better look. A man stood on the uninhabited island.

The water receded from the deck, and Griffin jumped down, yanked the door open, and thundered into the safety below deck.

"Captain," he called. "There's an island out there."

"Not possible," the captain yelled. "We aren't anywhere

near Talam." Her eyes pinned on Griffin. "Unless... the storm sent us off course. We need to get out there, but I refuse to risk my men. Where is your little winged friend?"

"By now, my guess is she's *on* the island."

The sound of splitting wood surrounded them, and horror flashed across the captain's face. "I have to go above deck. I need to save my ship." She climbed the stairs before disappearing out on the deck.

Wood cracked. Griffin didn't know much about boats, but he knew that wasn't a good thing.

She was going to need help. Griffin ascended the stairs to help the captain, but what he found...

"A wave crashing over the rail hit me." Fear shone in the captain's eyes as she climbed up onto the wooden rail.

Griffin ran toward her, trying to catch her by the legs, but he was too slow. Lifting one foot, the captain let it dangle over the dark waters.

Griffin's scream died in his throat as the captain stepped off the rail. As soon as she hit the water, something dragged her under.

Horror sliced through Griffin as he backed away. He looked to the island just in time to see the ship crash onto Talam's black sandy beach.

CHAPTER NINETEEN

Riona

As soon as the ship crashed, the storm faded away, letting the waters return to the glassy calm depths as they'd seen in Fargelsi.

The music went the way of the storm, no longer calling Riona. She flew down to the shipwreck, knowing how lucky they all were to have more likely beached the ship instead of crashing into the rocky shores at the north of the island.

The storm had caused damage, but Riona had other priorities. She lifted higher in the clearing skies, wondering if what she'd seen was an apparition or a product of magic.

Yet, as she neared where the man watched the ship down below, she knew it was real. She gave one flap of her wings, hovering over the ground before touching down.

The man didn't move.

Riona took his silence as a chance to marvel at how closely he resembled her. No, he didn't have dark skin. The opposite actually. But his pale, almost chalk-white skin was covered in tattoos just like hers. And the wings may have been black, but they could only belong to someone of their species.

"I thought I was the only one." Riona studied him from blond hair to odd clothing. "The song... was it you?"

He nodded, pulling out an odd instrument she'd never seen before.

"You caused the storm." She didn't know why she was so sure of it.

He didn't respond to her except to dip his head. "Your friends." His voice was lower than she'd expected. "They have all survived. Except the captain, unfortunately."

She had many questions for this man who was so like her. Where had he been all these years she thought she was the only one of their kind? But she had a more pressing matter. Giving him one last look, she kicked off the ground and flew toward the shipwreck.

"Griffin?" She landed on the deck. "Gulliver?"

Someone stumbled from the stairwell. The human. "That was quite the ride." Myles held the side of his head where blood seeped through his hair.

"Where are the others?"

"Coming." Myles fumbled his way off the boat and collapsed onto the black sand. Gulliver emerged next. "Where's Griffin?"

"Wasn't he with you?" Riona looked behind him.

Gulliver shook his head. "He went after you."

No. He wouldn't have been that stupid. A cough alerted her to someone else's presence. Running the length of the deck, she found Griffin leaning against a crate with blood trickling down his cheek.

"Riona!" Gulliver yelled. "Griff! There's someone coming."

The fae with the music. Riona extended a hand down to Griffin, pulling him up. He gave her a grateful smile, but she'd already looked past him to the waiting fae.

"Griffin O'Shea." The man rushed toward him, one hand out in greeting.

Griffin took it, confusion flashing across his face.

"Welcome to Talam. I was hoping to have visitors while I was here, but some of you were not expected." He sent Riona a look she couldn't decipher. "Come, come. I have a camp in the forest."

Griffin's jaw clenched. "We aren't leaving our ship."

"What if I promise to repair it if you come with me now?"

"Dark Fae don't have magic."

The man smiled. "True. But then, I never said the magic was in me." He tapped the instrument against his leg. "I'm Nihal, by the way."

"Well, Nihal," Myles started. "What is a Dark Fae doing in human clothes?"

"Ah, very good question. You're intelligent for a human. The truth is, I live in the human realm. No, I won't tell you why or how I traveled here. We will meet again one day and those answers will come."

Riona looked to the sailors who seemed lost without their captain.

"Stay with the boat," Griffin ordered, giving Riona a shrug. "Someone had to take charge." He lifted his voice again. "There should be some wares that are okay to eat in the galley. Just... be careful of the water."

Nihal had a skip in his step as he led them through the garden of boulders to the trees where he'd set up one meager tent.

Riona raised a brow. "This is where you live?"

Nihal smiled. "Only for one night. Then, I'll be back in my village in the human realm."

Emotions rolled through Riona, warring for supremacy. There were differences, but none so profound as their similarities.

"Why don't your tattoos move?"

"Ah." He grinned. "That is an answer for another time. We don't have long."

"Why?" Riona crossed her arms.

"Because there are things happening in Iskalt."

Griffin huffed out a breath. "We were on our way there. You delayed us."

He shook his head. "Your ship was headed for the smuggler's coast, and those men you're with would not have just let you go."

"What do you mean?" Myles asked.

Nihal gestured to the ground around a fledgling fire. "I received word of your departure from an ally in the Fargelsian court. As I started asking around the docks if anyone had seen your party, a common name surfaced. Captain Murphy."

Griffin averted his eyes at the name. Had he seen her perish?

"A king consort of Fargelsi." Nihal pointed to Myles then Griffin. "A forgotten prince of Iskalt. A woman who is one of the last of her kind. In joining together, you made yourself easy pickings."

Riona scowled. "Says the man who wrecked our ship."

Nihal sighed and pulled his instrument onto his lap. "Trust that I wouldn't have done so if there were another choice."

"Ever thought of not playing?" Riona wouldn't let this go.

"I have thought of it many times, yes. But I do not play for my pleasure. The piccolo allows me to perform magic I could not otherwise do. I do not use it lightly."

Riona rubbed her eyes. Between the rough seas, the flight through the storm, and now a cryptic fae who looked like her, she was ready to go to sleep and forget it all.

Nihal's eyes rolled back into his head, and his body slumped forward. Griffin scooted near him. "He's breathing."

Nihal's arm bent up with the piccolo in his grasp. He put it to his lips, and a sweet melody replaced the awkward air around them. A gust of wind blew through the trees. Riona ran to the edge of the cliffs, but the sea below still held its calmness.

Shouts came from the beach, but she couldn't make out the words. Jumping into the air, she flew toward the noise and touched down. "What happened?"

One of the sailors stared at her in disgust. "Ship's healing itself. Not even my magic could do that."

The piccolo's song reached the beach, and Riona could get lost in it. She flew back to where she'd left the others.

"The ship is repairing itself. We'll be able to leave at dawn."

Griffin opened his mouth to speak, but Nihal set his

instrument down and spoke as if nothing had just happened. "Dawn it is. Good luck on your journey."

That was it? That was all he had to say for himself. A Dark Fae who could make magic with his piccolo?

"I suggest you stay up here for the night rather than with those men." Those were Nihal's final words to them.

Riona looked to Griffin and nodded. Something inside begged her to trust Nihal.

And they were all too tired to do otherwise.

CHAPTER TWENTY

Griffin

Griffin woke the next morning to find Nihal standing atop the cliffs, looking into the rising sun. His dark wings stretched wide, making him a sight to behold.

Wiping the sleep from his eyes, Griffin joined him, his gaze going down to the beach and widening. "The smugglers. They're gone."

A pit opened inside him. Was this where they lost, where they failed? Was it because of a winged fae with magical music?

A smaller boat anchored not too far from the beach. "Is that a... fisherman?"

Nihal nodded. "That's Liam. He comes around here every few weeks to see if I have need of him to run messages for me."

"Messages for who?" When he didn't respond, Griffin nodded. "Right, another answer we'll get in time."

Nihal shrugged. "Did your clothes dry adequately over night? I don't exactly have a tune for that."

"They did, thank you." Griffin and the others had been soaked to the bone when they'd arrived, but Nihal had dry clothing waiting for them. "I don't suppose you'll ever tell us why you forced us into coming to Talam?"

Nihal shook his head with a hint of a smile on his lips. "Come. We must speak with Liam."

At the beach, a tiny wooden boat had been hauled from the water, and a man with gills running up his arms and neck smiled wide. "Nihal." He pulled him into a back-thumping hug.

"It's good to see you, Liam. Have you met my new friends? Griffin, Riona, Gulliver, and Myles." He cupped his hands around his mouth to whisper, "He's human."

"The human has ears." Myles didn't look offended.

Liam released a booming laugh.

Griffin couldn't take his eyes off the strange features. He'd thought all Dark Fae were in the prison realm, and here were two free ones standing right in front of him. How many more were there?

Nihal and Liam waded into the water, an act that seemed unnatural to Griffin who'd spent his life avoiding it. They spoke in hushed tones before returning. Nihal grinned wide. "Liam will take you to the shores of Iskalt. No need to land on the smuggler's coast because his boat carries the royal seal of Iskalt."

Liam nodded. "The king tasks me with many things."

"And I'm sure the king will thank you for this. You are bringing his brother home, after all."

Just hearing the words struck something in Griffin's gut. His brother. Home.

But Iskalt had never been his home.

"Nihal." Griffin stuck out a hand. "I don't think I'll ever understand you."

Nihal shook his hand. "Griffin O'Shea, you and I will cross paths again to find the secrets you seek." His eyes found Riona. "If things were different, my dear, you and I would be able to spend time comparing our upbringings as the last of our kind." He bowed. "Be safe. You think the storm yesterday was rough... well, the waters of Iskalt have drowned many men. Good luck." He lifted into the air with a giant flap of his wings and flew to the top of the cliffs, watching them for a moment longer before disappearing through a portal he shouldn't be able to make.

"That man..." Riona shook her head. "He caused the storm that almost killed us, yet... I want to trust him."

Griffin knew the feeling. But like Nihal said, he fully expected to see him again.

Griffin wondered if Nihal's final words had been a lie. Since leaving Talam, they'd had nothing but smooth sailing. Liam operated his boat alone, always running to different areas to keep them on track.

Griffin leaned against the rail, letting the sun warm his skin.

"You were with Captain Murphy before?" Liam asked.

Griffin nodded. "Well, until she died."

"How'd she die?"

"Jumped from her own ship."

Liam let out a low whistle. "The woman has a reputation even outside the smuggler's coast. She abducts those with well-connected families, the nobility, sometimes even humans. If no one will pay for them, she pushes them from the boat to die in the dangerous waters."

Griffin could hardly process the information. "She..." Was that what she had planned for their group? Myles was the only one anyone would pay for. A chill raced down his spine.

"Nihal..." Was that the reason he created the storm? "He saved us."

A grin slid across Liam's face. "He tends to do that. Calls himself a conduit, not like I know what that is. He was the first fae like me I've met. You know, dark." His eyes slid to where Riona and Gulliver soaked in the sun. It seemed even the hard Dark Fae enjoyed the warmth after the gray skies the day before.

"You'd be surprised what kind of fae exist."

Liam grunted. "Not sure anything can surprise me anymore."

Griffin pushed off the rail. "Can I ask you something?"

He nodded.

"Nihal said the second half of our journey would be more difficult. But this... the breeze and the glassy waters."

Liam grimaced. "We are still in Fargelsian waters. Wait until we reach Iskalt. That's where many ships sink."

Griffin began thinking they should have taken the weeks to cross the Vatlands and Eldur on horseback.

The first iceberg marking the entrance to Iskalt waters stood in their path. Liam tried his best to steer around it, enlisting the help of Myles who claimed he'd taken two sailing lessons as a kid, but they were too late. The wooden boat scraped along the iceberg, sending shards of ice raining down on the deck followed by freezing cold water. Griffin tried to steer clear of the water, but it got him anyway. He waited for the compulsion to jump but it never came.

"Iskalt spells their waters to keep the Fargelsian dangers out." Liam ran from one side of the ship to the other.

"They should spell their icebergs," Gulliver yelled.

"We're going to lose the ship!" Myles yelled.

Riona's eyes widened as the ship rocked sideways, trying to break free of the ice. She jumped to her feet, walking with deliberate steps to the side of the ship.

What was she doing? Griffin tried to rise, but the ship dug farther into the ice, knocking him back on his butt. The cry was stuck in his throat as Riona climbed onto the railing and dove into the icy waters with a mesmerizing grace.

He scrambled to his feet and stumbled to the railing to peer down into the dark, frothing water battering the iceberg on all sides.

"What was that?" Liam yelled.

Griffin searched for Riona, his heart beating rapidly. A loud crack filled the air as boards broke apart.

Liam took in a deep breath. "We can't take much more damage before we sink. Bring me the oars." Griffin didn't know what he planned to do with them, but he wasn't focused on him, not with Riona down in the freezing water.

Only months ago he'd faced Riona in a fight to the death. Now, he needed her to be okay. "I can't do this on my own, Riona." She was loyal to King Egan in a way only Griffin understood. He'd been there. She just needed to see she was worth so much more than what he deigned to give her.

But first, she needed to live.

Time stopped—or at least it felt like it.

Gulliver joined him at the rail despite Griffin's insistence he stay away. But if the ship was doing down, at least they'd be together.

Gulliver put a hand on Griffin's arm as time ticked on. Liam passed Griffin a long oar to use as leverage to try to break the ship free of the ice.

It wasn't working.

Until it was.

The ship groaned and cracked as it was freed of the ice.

And still, she didn't resurface.

No one other than Egan would miss Riona. Her kind had been forgotten by the realm, and the only one like her lived in the human realm.

"She's going to be okay," Gulliver said. "She's Riona."

Griffin couldn't take his eyes from the dark waters, he couldn't stop looking for the woman who'd saved them.

"Griffin," Liam shouted. "Is that... there's a body in the water."

Griffin ran the length of the ship, stopping next to the captain. "Get her out."

"Nets!" The captain ran toward where the net hung at the bow of the ship and got them into the water.

Griffin and Myles pulled the nets up and Riona with it. Her entire body shook, proof she still lived. "Get me something dry to wrap her in," Griffin pleaded as he gathered

Riona in his arms and headed for the stairs. He laid her on the table, not knowing what to do next. "Liam?"

The captain appeared in the doorway. "What is it?"

"I think we need to undress her, get her warm. Will you fetch Myles for me?" The human knew more about how to take care of someone when you didn't have magic.

Griffin blew out a breath. Myles groaned when he walked in. "I kind of hate you, Griff. I mean, who takes a ship across this cursed lake? You got us shipwrecked, almost killed by smugglers, and stuck on an iceberg." He sighed. "But what do you need from me?"

Griffin looked down at Riona and the tattoos fading from her skin as if draining her very life. "You packed clothes for the journey, right?" Griffin only had what was on his back.

Myles rummaged through his bag and handed Griffin a pair of linen pants and a cotton shirt.

Together, they managed to remove Riona's clothing—keeping their eyes averted out of respect.

"She really saved us?" Myles tugged the shirt over her head.

Griffin focused on drying the icy water from her hair and wings. He wished Egan had returned all of his magic. Then he'd have her dry in no time. "Riona is half Asrai and half Slyph."

"I have no idea what that means."

"Humans," Griffin grumbled. "They may resemble what you humans call mermaids."

"No way." Excitement laced his tone. "Riona is a mermaid?"

"Half-mermaid. She doesn't have a tail like the creatures of your stories, but she is drawn to the water."

"How did I not know such a fae existed?"

"They've been forgotten, just like many other kinds of fae trapped behind the prison barriers. Prisoners aren't the only fae being forgotten. It's why we're on this mission. We're going to change the world."

Griffin didn't sleep that night. The rocking of the boat subsided the closer they got to Iskalt as the waters calmed.

And still, he couldn't let himself rest. Riona woke up twice, but each time she could barely open her eyes. There were no fires on this vessel for obvious reasons, but Griffin wrapped her in whatever he could find.

He'd watched her most of the night as the blue faded from her lips, and her beautiful dark skin regained some of its undertones.

Gulliver tried to stay up, but he ended up passing out on a wooden bench next to Griffin. Liam was up on deck watching for any other dangers.

The air chilled as they neared the Iskalt shores, the biting cold burrowing deep into Griffin's bones.

For now, everything was calm. The fear that had lived with him about facing Brea and Lochlan was replaced with a new fear. He hadn't wanted to lose Riona. They were in this together. Did that make them... friends?

Her eyes fluttered open as if she could read his thoughts.

"Hi." Griffin smiled down at her. "Can I get you some water?"

She shook her head.

"You saved us." He knew without a doubt she'd pushed

the ship away from the iceberg. "I didn't know you were that strong."

She coughed, and when she spoke, her voice held a weakness that was so unlike her. "Only when I give in to my Asrai nature."

"In the palace, many were afraid of me. And then there's you," she whispered. "You've never been afraid of me. Not even as we fought in the pits. Why?"

He had so many answers for her. Because he thought he deserved every punishment. Because he was fighting for Nessa, for all his people.

But neither of those answers seemed sufficient, honest.

He looked into the flickering light of a single candle. "Because I know what it is like to be feared." He dropped his voice. "Fear is worse than hatred."

"It is." Her eyes fluttered shut again.

He looked from a sleeping Gulliver to a dozing Myles. Here, for once, neither of them had to be feared.

"Is Riona going to be okay?" Maybe Gulliver wasn't asleep.

Griffin softened his voice. "I think so."

They sat in silence for a long moment. "Griff?"

"Speak, Gullie."

"Do you ever regret the things you've done?"

Griffin's brow scrunched. "Is this what's keeping you up?"

"I think I know you. You raised me. But I've started wondering if I only know one side. Maybe there's a part of you—the part that followed the evil queen—you hide from us."

Griffin turned to face him, the flickering of the candle

highlighting the shadows on his face. "I will regret the things I did for the rest of my life." He sighed. He owed Gulliver the truth. "I like to tell people I'm not the same man I was, but I've never tested myself to see if what drove me all those years ago could get ahold of me now." He would soon once he saw Callum. Would the real Griffin finally show up? "I think... I think the two sides of me have merged. The one who cares about our people in Myrkur, who doesn't go a day without fearing for Shauna and Nessa... he's real. You've always had the real me."

He sucked in a breath. "But... I think Regan had the real me too."

Two halves, both wanting different things. Gulliver's expression fell like he didn't appreciate the complexities of that answer. Griffin had to constantly fight the side of him that sought power and adoration.

But he did, he fought it. And most of the time, he won.

"I need some air." Gulliver slid off the bench and headed up the stairs. Now that they were past the rough waters, the lake surface was calm.

Griffin relaxed back in his chair. "He's never going to think of me the same way."

He hadn't thought Riona was awake, so her voice surprised him. "You cannot change your nature, Griff. But you can fight it. He'll figure that out one day. You and I have darkness in us. We make little sense to someone with such obvious light."

The difference between him and Riona was that Griffin had people to yank him out of Regan's orbit, to make him question her when she still lived.

Who did Riona have to pull her from the darkness?

To make her see King Egan as he was.

Someone who could show her she deserved more than the bloodshed he foisted upon her.

She'd fallen asleep again, and he looked down into her face. "Me, Riona. You have me."

Chapter Twenty-One

The biting cold wasn't something Griffin would ever forget. He was a child when he last set foot in his home kingdom of Iskalt, before his uncle took his father's throne. Before Lochlan reclaimed it with an Eldurian army fortified by the Iskaltians still loyal to the royal line.

And Griffin hadn't been there. He should have stood at his brother's side, should have fought for their family.

Instead, he chose to forsake the only other person who mourned his parents the way he did. He barely remembered them, but he knew they'd have wanted their boys to fight for each other, not against each other.

They'd have been ashamed of him.

Riona stood at his side, wearing an outfit of Myles' that fit her awkwardly. Her wings were hidden underneath her shirt, folded in on themselves. Griffin never wanted her to hide such an integral part of herself, but it was her decision.

Just like it was her decision to let the tattoos fade into her skin.

Riona would do anything to secure the secrets of the prison realm, and Griff would do anything to bring those secrets down.

It seemed they were meant to be at odds, but just like everything else, their animosity faded into the sea. For now, they had similar goals.

"Griff." Gulliver's teeth chattered. "Is it always this cold in Iskalt?"

He looked sideways at Gulliver. "Most of the time, it's worse."

"And here I thought the icebergs were just friendly greetings from the ice king."

A laugh burst out of Myles. "More like a warning to keep smugglers from nearing the Iskalt shores. That's why they sail to the smuggler's coast north of here and then travel over the mountains to the villages from there. But I'm definitely telling Lochlan fae are calling him the ice king. It fits."

Their ship had made it through the rough waters to the calmer inlet and run aground on a sandy beach. It wouldn't be setting sail again anytime soon.

Their group trudged up the narrow path from the cove and stared across the expansive field of snow that spanned the distance between the palace and the nearest village.

Liam had grown quiet behind them, maybe mourning his boat.

"What will you do?" Griffin asked him.

He shrugged. "It was just a boat. We all survived, and that's what matters. Nihal will make sure I'm compensated."

Griffin nodded, amazed at the faith he had in the Dark Fae they'd met back on the island.

"What is this stuff?" Gulliver's eyes widened as he

leaned down, his hand hovering over the snow. "It's not going to kill me, is it?"

Griffin laughed. In Fargelsi, many things were deadly. Here in Iskalt, life was difficult, but the fae weren't surrounded by potential dangers. "It's snow, Gullie. Go ahead. Touch it."

A look of glee flashed across Gulliver's face. It reminded Griffin how young this boy still was, how ill prepared he was for what lay beyond the prison world he'd known all his life.

He stuck one finger in the snow. "It's cold!" He laughed as he scooped up a handful and then another. He took off running through the field, his steps leaving grooves on the smooth surface.

A snowflake hit Griffin's face, and he looked up to see the tiny flurries blanketing the sky.

Gulliver tilted his head back and caught snowflakes on his tongue, laughing each time.

Griffin could have watched him for hours. There was no snow in Myrkur, just like there'd been none in Eldur or Fargelsi. It was one of the wonders of Iskalt. Griffin shook the snowflakes from his hair, leaning down to scoop up a handful of snow. With a grin he took careful aim and landed the snowball against Gulliver's back.

Gulliver whirled around, trying to look at his back. "What did you *just* do?"

Griffin laughed when another snowball hit Gulliver's front, and he turned to see Riona's eyes dancing with humor.

"No way, you're both dead." Gulliver scooped up a snowball, and chaos ensued as all three adults ganged up on the kid.

Liam only watched them with a look of amusement.

Gulliver's shrieks of laughter did wonders to lift Griffin's mood. If nothing else, at least the kid got to experience his very first snowball fight.

Myles stepped up beside Griffin, his face flushed red from the cold. "We should keep moving and get to the palace. We aren't exactly dressed for this weather."

Griffin shook his head as he caught sight of Riona hopping through the snow drifts with tentative steps, a look of awe on her face. "Just give them a little longer Myles. In the prison realm, in Myrkur, these kinds of moments don't exist."

"What kind?"

"Wonder." In Myrkur, there was only survival. Here, in the safety of Iskalt, there was room for them to breathe.

A few travelers on the road winding through the field gave them odd looks, but Griffin didn't have the heart to interrupt Gulliver or Riona.

Liam clapped him on the shoulder. "This is where I take my leave of you."

"Will you be okay?"

The fisherman nodded. "A friend has an inn in the nearest village. I'll go there and try to find an Iskaltian ship heading back to Fargelsi."

"Go to the Fargelsian queen." Myles stepped in. "Tell her Myles sent you. She will see you are compensated for your ship."

"I don't know who you folks are, but from the moment Nihal introduced us, I knew you were working for good. Or else, he wouldn't have orchestrated your survival."

Griffin shook his hand, and Liam turned down the road, trudging through the snow.

Griffin let his gaze wander across the fields to the imposing palace at the other end. No one would ever call the Iskalt palace comfortable. It wasn't soothing and airy like Fargelsi. It didn't hold the beauty of the exotic Eldurian palace. Instead, it stood like a fortress meant to intimidate, to threaten.

At least, it had while his uncle Callum claimed it.

Now, it held a new kind of intimidation for Griffin. Behind those walls, Brea and Lochlan lived their life in ignorance, never knowing he'd once stood between them.

Griffin gestured for Myles to follow him, and they joined Gulliver and Riona. Gulliver's cheeks and nose were bright red, but he seemed impervious to the cold.

Riona's breath curled in front of her face, and she couldn't stop staring at it. "I've never seen magic other than your portals, Griffin." No one in Fargelsi had used it around them. "Is it always like this?"

Myles snorted. "That's not magic, it's science."

She turned to him, confusion tugging the corners of her lips down. "Science? I do not know this term."

"The cold air meets the warm moisture in your breath."

"Moisture? I did not spit."

"No..." Myles shook his head. "You know what, screw it. Yes, it's magic. Isn't it wonderful?"

Griffin held in a laugh. "We should head toward the palace."

"Do you think they'll give us an audience with the king?" Riona's fierce gaze met his. "Or do we have to fight our way in?"

"Whoa." Myles held up both hands. "No one is fighting their way into my best friend's castle. Dude, if you told me

I'd be saying a line like that ten years ago..." He laughed. "We'll get in to see the king *and* the queen."

"How do you know that?" Riona crossed her arms.

"It's called bestie privilege."

Riona opened her mouth to speak again, but Griffin cut her off. "Don't try to understand human speak, Riona. It usually makes little sense."

Myles only shrugged and walked toward the snowy path that would take them to the palace. "We're not going through the front entrance."

"Probably a good idea." Griffin brushed snow from his hair. "We don't need our presence here discussed throughout the villages. Gulliver, keep your sunglasses on once we're inside. Don't take them off until I tell you it's okay."

Gulliver nodded, checking to make sure his tail was still tucked away.

The closer they walked to the palace, the more Griffin wanted to turn around and brave the rough waters of Lake Villandi again. But he couldn't. Not this time.

"It's so big." Gulliver stared up at high stone towers and the fortified walls that wrapped around the palace. It was a fortress, but it was also beautiful in its own way.

The guards at the front gates watched them pass, but didn't speak as Myles led the group around to the south side of the palace grounds. They rounded the corner to find a frozen pond. Memories rushed in to swirl in Griffin's mind. He'd been so young when he left Iskalt as a child, the memories were normally only fragments. But he could see his brother so clearly running across the frozen pond with his friends.

Now, there were two children playing a game Griffin

didn't recognize. They had blades strapped to their feet and sticks in their hands.

A smile stretched across Myles' face. "That would be the prince and princess."

Suddenly, Griffin couldn't breathe. He'd known Brea and Lochlan probably had kids, but it still felt like a lance shot through him at the sight of them. His eyes followed the princess across the ice. She used an odd stick as she chased a black toy. "What are they doing?"

"Playing hockey." Myles laughed. "I made Lochlan take me to the human realm to get skates and sticks. If the kids had to live in a freezing kingdom, they'd at least get the benefits of it." He cupped his hands around his mouth. "Nice shot, Tia!"

Two guards obviously sent to watch the kids looked their way but didn't move. They kept a distance, probably at Brea's insistence. She wouldn't want her kids feeling smothered by security.

Tia jerked her head up. She was older than Griffin thought at first. Maybe eight or nine?

"Uncle Myles!" She dropped her stick and wobbled as she tried to run with the blades on her feet. Griffin saw it then, the complete adoration. The kid loved Myles... her uncle.

A relationship Griffin would never have with his brother's children.

Tia reached them and flung herself into Myles' arms. "What are you doing here? Mom said you were busy with your own brood—her word, not mine."

"It's a long story, but your cousins had to stay back in Fargelsi."

Her expression dropped. "Oh."

Myles put her down and wrapped an arm around her shoulders. "I'd like you to meet some friends of mine. This is Griffin."

She lifted her chin, regarding each of them with keen eyes. "Hello. I'm Tierney."

Griffin's gut clenched at the name. Queen Tierney. She'd been married to Brea's mother in Eldur. Until... Griffin met Myles' gaze in understanding. They both knew what Tierney's death in battle had done to Brea. It gave her the anger, the hatred she'd needed to defeat Regan.

Griffin bent down to meet the little girl's gaze. "Hi Tierney." She stared at him, recognition on her face.

"I wondered what your name was," she whispered. "I knew you'd come today. It's why I came down from the tower. Griffin." Power swirled in her intense gaze.

Griffin couldn't look away as the message Brea sent Neeve came back to him. Tierney saw the prison realm in her dreams, saw him.

One side of her mouth curved up. "You're going to save me. Not here. Not now. When the time is right. But I wish you'd save my brother instead."

The intensity left her eyes in an instant and she became just a little girl again with snow clinging to her strawberry blond hair and melting on her rosy cheeks. She gave them a full smile and turned to Gulliver. "Who are you?"

Griffin couldn't take his eyes off her as she chatted with the others. What did she mean he'd save her but not her brother?

Snapping out of his daze, Griffin dropped a hand on Gullie's shoulder. "This is Gulliver."

She scanned Gulliver from head to toe. "Gulliver is an odd name."

He raised a brow. "So is Tierney."

Tierney pursed her lips. "Okay. You can play hockey with us."

Before Gulliver could accept the invitation, a cry reached them followed by a splash.

Griffin didn't stop to consider what had happened. He ran as shouts filled the air. The ice cracked, dragging the prince below the surface.

"I'm coming, Toby!" Tierney's little voice rang out behind Griffin. She muttered a string of words he couldn't make out.

The ice undulated, sending fissures through every part of it. Magic. It had to be. But the only people who could have magic here were the guards. Unless... He cast one more glance toward the frantic kid whose lips hadn't stopped moving. The hair on Griffin's arms stood on end as another wave of erratic magic filled the air.

The prince pulled his head above the ice before a wave of magic sent him back under.

Griffin reached the edge of the pond and tested the ice with his foot. Cracks spidered out from his weight. He'd never wished for his magic to return more than in this moment.

Tierney skidded to a halt beside him, her hair sticking to her face.

Griffin could feel it. Her magic. The power she possessed. He turned to her. "Pull your magic back in."

"I need to save him."

"Kid, you're going to get him killed." *Think, Griffin.* He

couldn't remember how to reverse Fargelsian magic. "Just don't utter another word."

The guards reached them, and Griffin gestured to Tierney. "Get the princess away from here."

Fat tears slid down her cheeks, but the guards pulled her away, taking orders from a man they didn't know.

A man who had to save Brea's son.

What had Tierney called him? Toby.

"I'm coming, Toby." He couldn't stand in any one place too long, or the ice wouldn't hold him. Sucking in a breath, he stepped out onto the ice, now broken by a little girl's uncontrollable magic.

With light feet, he hopped across the surface. The prince hadn't come up in too long. Adrenaline spiked through Griffin as he reached the hole in the ice Toby had fallen through. There was no sign of the prince, no sign of life at all.

Griffin stuck a hand down into the icy water, trying to find him. Myles, Riona, and Gulliver waited at the edge of the pond, yelling for Toby.

"Stay off the ice!" Griffin ordered. He unclasped his cloak around his neck and threw it onto the ice behind him.

He was Iskaltian. The cold shouldn't bother him.

And yet, he hesitated.

Sucking in a deep breath, he plunged into the water, letting it sting his eyes as he kept them open. The pond wasn't deep, but it was dark, only letting light through where the ice cracked above.

Griffin's entire body went numb from the cold. He kicked his legs as he searched everywhere for the young prince. Even after ten years, he couldn't let anything break Brea's heart the way the death of her son would.

His lungs squeezed, desperate for more air as his heart beat uncontrollably.

And then he saw him. The young prince with his dark hair, so unlike his sister's. Griffin reached for the boy, relief flooding him. He wrapped an arm around Toby's waist and dragged him back to the opening in the ice.

A hand reached down to help lift the prince. Griffin took the help without thinking where it could come from with the ice so splintered.

Whoever it was dragged Toby from the water. Griffin gripped the jagged edges of the ice and hauled himself out of the icy pond. His entire body shook as he tried to crawl toward the shore. The cracks surrounding him widened, and that was when he saw her.

Riona, wings unfurled behind her set Toby on solid ground before returning for Griffin. From the air. She was flying, showing her otherness to Iskalt with no thought to what could happen.

Griffin had only seen her fly to get to Nihal. The Slyph rarely used their wings to fly. Only when faced with battle would they take to the skies.

Yet here, to save his life, to save a prince she didn't know... she was Griffin's guardian, come to his rescue. As his eyes slid shut, her hands lifted him from the ice. The last thing he remembered was soaring through the sky.

Warmth enveloped Griffin, and a smile curved his lips. Warmth could only mean one thing. He was safe in Fargelsi with Queen Regan, the only woman who'd ever taken care of him.

And Brea. His wife.

A sigh rattled through his chest as he pulled Brea against him. She fit him like nothing ever had before. The marriage magic was only a few days old, but they'd have a lifetime to explore what it meant, to come to terms with the binding force that could never be torn away.

And Griffin didn't plan to do either anytime soon. In the coming years, Brea would grow into her role as a Fargelsi royal. And their children... he smiled at the thought. They'd be remarkable children, holding the magic of all three realms within them. Brea was of Eldur and Fargelsi. Griffin could command Iskalt power. As long as they remained together, no one would defeat them.

"Brea," he whispered on a sigh. His Brea.

Regan had forced her into the marriage, taking advantage of her naiveté, but the magic made her feel things for Griffin. He knew it did.

"Griffin." Her voice sounded far off, like she wasn't lying right beside him.

"I love you, Brea."

Pressure pulsed in his chest as if someone slammed their fist into it. Warmth hit his lips, and he sighed into the kiss.

"Griffin, if you don't wake up right this freaking second..." That was Myles. Wait, he shouldn't be there. Brea had traded herself, her freedom to make sure Myles and Neeve were released from Fargelsi.

His eyes slid open slowly, painfully. He sucked in a breath, but his lungs were raw, and pain rippled through him. And there she was, Brea Robinson. The girl he'd abducted from the human realm, the one who was now his wife.

He reached up, sliding his hand to the back of her neck. Brea froze. "Sir, I—"

Griffin cut her off by pulling her closer and rising up to meet her kiss. She didn't stop him at first, giving in to the irrational pull between them.

And then she punched him and shot to her feet, one finger on her lips. "Saving my son does not give you the right to kiss your queen."

The fog in Griffin's mind cleared. He wasn't in Fargelsi with Regan and Brea. Regan had been dead for ten years, and Brea was no longer his wife.

No one spoke for a long moment as Griffin realized what he'd just done.

"Myles," Brea growled. "I will not banish your friends

from the palace." Her suspicious gaze slid over Riona who'd left her wings bared. "They saved my son. But they are your responsibility."

Myles smirked. "I am a king too. You can't just order me around."

She stepped toward him. "Care to bet on that?"

They stood in a silent stand off for a long moment before Myles pulled Brea into a hug. "I missed you."

She rested her chin on his shoulder. "I missed you so much I don't even care that you brought a pack of bizarre strangers with you."

Strangers. That was what they were to her.

The door to the sitting room burst open, revealing the king—Griffin's brother. Lochlan's gaze darted between the fae huddled near the fire. "Where's my son? Tobias... he... I heard. Is he okay?"

Brea nodded. "He's in his rooms sleeping. One of the healers is keeping a watch by his bed, as is *your* daughter."

Lochlan's brow shot up. "What did she do? You only call her mine when she's causing trouble."

Griffin wanted to laugh at that because it should have been the other way around. Brea was the troublemaker. But right then, he felt like an intruder on their family moment.

Brea sighed. "Someone has to teach Tia to control her magic—better yet, not to use it—or we're in for many years of this sporadic destruction before she takes any of her Fargelsian classes seriously. And heaven help us when she gains both her Eldurian and Iskalt powers. That child... She could have killed her brother today."

Lochlan rubbed tired eyes. "That girl is going to be the death of me."

Brea's expression softened as she stepped toward her husband and wrapped her arms around his waist. "We will get through it. We always do."

Myles groaned. "We should probably go before you guys start with all the kissing and the self-sacrificing vows." He put a hand to his chest. "I would die for you, my douchey Loch." He deepened his voice. "Brea, you are the stars in the sky. Yada, yada, puke."

Lochlan leaned into Brea. "Why do we let him visit again?"

She only smiled and shook her head, exhaustion weighing her down. "It's not like he and Neeve aren't the same way."

Myles laughed at that. "No, our relationship goes something like this. Myles, I need you to do a thing. It's a hard thing, but you're the manliest man I know, so it has to be you." He shrugged. "Then, I do the thing."

Ten years, and these people hadn't changed a bit. Griffin watched them interact, knowing he could have been part of their lives if he'd made different choices. This could have been his family.

"These people are strange," Riona whispered.

"That's always been the best thing about them." A shiver raced down his spine, and a thought struck him. "How did I end up in dry clothes?" He looked to Myles.

Myles pointed to Riona who gave him an unapologetic look. "It was either strip you or let you die. You did the same to me. Now we're even."

The ensuing silence told him Brea and Lochlan no longer chatted with Myles. Instead, both sets of eyes settled on Griffin. "Do I want to know?" he asked his wife.

"I'm not sure yet." She pursed her lips. "Go to Tobias. He and Tia need you. I'll figure out what's happening here, and then I must go nurse Ciara."

Lochlan swept his eyes through the room once more before turning and shutting the door behind him.

Brea took a seat in a high backed wooden chair that looked almost like a throne. It suited her.

Griffin scooted closer to the fire.

"If I told my husband you kissed me, you'd have more than just the one black eye." She crossed her arms. "And yet, I do not wish you harm. Who are you, sir, and why did it feel wrong to hit you?"

When no one answered, her eyes settled on Myles. "What don't I know?"

Myles sighed. "Well, this is the second time I've been abducted by Griffin O'Shea."

"We did not abduct you," Griffin protested. "I'd have been happy to leave you at home."

Brea's eyes widened as they bounced from Myles to Griffin and back again, ignoring Griffin's words to focus on Myles'. "You mean the man from your stories?"

"No, the man from our histories. Brea, I've been telling you about Griffin since he crossed into the prison realm."

"My husband told me there is no way out of the prison realm. So, I ask again, who are you?"

Griffin pushed himself up despite the ache in his bones. He held back the bit about being the man her daughter saw in her dreams. Brea probably didn't even know they were more than dreams. "Many years ago, I was your husband."

Why was Griffin such an idiot? He had to lead with the husband bit. But looking into her eyes, he couldn't hold it back. Brea Robinson was every bit as beautiful as he remembered. Dark hair framed her pale skin. Her eyes... he sucked in a breath. They would forever haunt him.

And her kiss... he couldn't bring himself to regret that. The marriage magic might be broken, but he still felt the small tug of it, pulling him to her.

He had to remind himself he wasn't here to catch up with old friends—or enemies. They needed information and quickly if he was to save Shauna and Nessa. They were his family now.

Brea left them hours ago, not letting him finish explaining who he was. She hadn't wanted to hear much beyond, *I was once your husband.*

Myles led them to the suite of rooms he and his family normally used when visiting. Servants bustled around—many more than in Fargelsi. They opened drapes, pounding the dust from them, and started a fire.

Griffin barely had the energy to stand, so he lowered himself to the woven carpet before the hearth, letting the flames thaw the ice inside him. He'd thought a lot about what it would be like seeing Brea and Lochlan again.

He'd never counted on it hurting this much.

Riona busied herself cleaning up in the washroom while Gulliver lounged on the bed, his eyes sliding shut. Myles left them to their own devices so he could check on the kids.

Griffin stared into the flames, letting them clear his mind. He was like Myles once, all charm and hilarity. He'd been an easy person, one who liked jokes and smiled every chance he got. The prison realm tore that out of him, leaving behind a man who worried too much, cared too much, lost too much.

Riona stepped from the washroom, her face impassive—a mask she seemed to have perfected. She sank onto the carpet beside him and stretched her wings to the flames to dry them.

"Did you grow up in this palace?" she asked.

He shook his head. "I was young when I left. My mother and father were killed."

She flicked water from a wing tip. "My mother and father died when I was young too." She stretched her arms out, sighing as the tattoos darkened, the vibrant colors returning to the surface.

"Does it pain you to hide them?"

"Yes. But I do it because out here, outside Myrkur, they don't understand what it is to be different. Eldur, Fargelsi, Iskalt… sure, there's a difference in how they use their power, but if one fae from each kingdom walked toward you, would you be able to tell the difference?"

"Probably not." Eldurians often had darker skin, but then, so did some Fargelsian fae. Even in Iskalt, skin color varied, but at the end of the day, it didn't separate them from the fae of other kingdoms. Not like Riona's tattoos and wings.

"That is why this Queen Sorcha didn't only wish to send prisoners away. Anyone who is different has been forgotten by your world."

"Is that why you accepted this quest for Egan? To bring all fae together into the light?"

She took a long moment before responding. "No. I came because I had no other choice."

A knock on the door interrupted them. Griffin pushed to his feet and crossed the room. He pulled open the door, surprised to find Lochlan on the other side. His brother had changed more than Brea had over the years. Fine lines creased his brow.

And a kid dangled from one of his arms, squirming to get free. "Papa, down."

Lochlan looked to Griffin like he was just another father who knew the way of children. "As soon as I put her down, she's going to run."

"Do you... want to come in?" He didn't know what answer he hoped for.

"I have to get back to my son's side, but you and I need to talk. Please, come with me." He hoisted the little girl into his arms. "This is Kayleigh, the kitchen's worst pastry thief. Which is why she's with us." He chuckled to himself. "She stole an entire pie yesterday and shared it with the stray cats in the stables."

Seeing the serious Lochlan smile and wrestle with his daughter wasn't something Griffin ever thought he'd witness.

Lochlan gave him a brief smile, another thing Griffin rarely earned in their lives before.

Griffin followed him down the long hall where colorful portraits adorned the walls. This castle was once his home, yet he knew little of it. They reached a series of doors and stopped at the one in the middle before Lochlan pushed it open.

Tobias slept in an ornate four-poster bed. His sister had fallen asleep in a chair beside it.

"Can you hold Kayleigh for a moment?" Lochlan passed the kid over before Griffin could tell him how not a kid fae he was. The only one he'd ever been drawn to was Gulliver. Kayleigh got an impish look on her face before trying to break free. Griffin tightened his grip.

Lochlan bent to lift Tierney and put her in bed beside her brother. He placed a kiss on her head and straightened.

Brea appeared in the doorway and froze. She was in the middle of nursing a baby. "Sorry, I didn't mean to interrupt you two." She looked to Griffin. "You can put Kay down."

Griffin did as he was told, but Kayleigh didn't try to run off again. Instead, she took her mother's hand. When they were gone, Lochlan shut the door with a laugh. "Those kids obey my wife much more than me." He gestured to the two chairs next to the bed. "Sit. Please."

Where was the commanding Lochlan Griffin had known, the *douchey* Loch—as Myles called him.

"So." Lochlan rested his elbows on his knees and leaned forward. "Myles told me about your perilous journey to reach our shores. Not many ships brave the Iskalt bays anymore." He paused, rubbing his chin. "In fact, we found a smuggler vessel capsized about a mile out to sea from what they call the smuggler's coast."

Griffin's face paled. The other ship... He thought back to Nihal and the music with a mind of its own. Was that the true reason the music wanted them on a different vessel?

"You look pensive."

Griffin snapped himself out of the dark thoughts. "I am, sorry. It's been a long journey to reach Iskalt."

Lochlan offered him a tentative smile. "Myles has been entertaining us with stories of Griffin O'Shea for the last ten years. He claims I had a brother who was sent to the prison realm. I didn't believe him."

"And now?"

"Now, I am sitting face to face with someone who strongly resembles my father and escaped the prison realm—which is supposed to be impossible. We don't know much about the magical barrier, but crossing it is supposed to be a one way trip. It doesn't let anyone leave. You portaled out, didn't you?"

Lochlan had always been the smartest among them. "We did."

"I knew it. Only an O'Shea can open a portal to the human realm." He paused. "Myles says I should thank you for saving my son's life."

Griffin shrugged. "I did not do it for your thanks."

"You did it because he's your nephew."

"No. He was a kid in danger. I had no thought to his blood relations."

Lochlan rubbed the back of his neck. "Are you sure you're the Griffin from Myles' stories? Because that man wouldn't have jumped into a freezing pond to save a random stranger."

"I'm not sure who I am anymore." The truth slipped out. Maybe it was the kind of thing he wanted to be able to say to his brother and have him understand. He wanted to tell him of his life over the last ten years. "But I do understand loss. I wouldn't wish it on anyone."

"Are you a father? I'm sorry, I don't know what's possible in the prison realm."

"I have not sired children if that's what you're asking. But one thing I've learned is that it doesn't matter who gave birth to the child or sired them, only who loves them with their entire heart. I have people who are counting on me."

Lochlan nodded, but his eyes glazed over like he was deep in thought. "Were we good brothers? I know the stories about Regan and your loyalty, but was there any point where we were truly a family?"

The question surprised Griffin. He wasn't ready for it. "Those moments were fleeting. I wish I had a different answer for you."

"Over the last ten years, I've tried to remember you. I even traveled to a few of the places Myles said we were together. I don't understand how every memory could have just vanished without a trace left behind."

Griffin stared at the serene faces of the sleeping children. They didn't yet know how dangerous this world was. "I think, no, I know that it's probably a good thing you don't remember. If you did, you'd never trust me, and this conversation wouldn't happen."

Lochlan's brow creased like he was thinking too hard. "The only blood relation I have—other than my children—is sitting in my dungeons."

Griffin studied his brother, trying to see if the years of separation had been good for him. They weren't the kind of family who was there for each other or the kind to offer encouraging words. But Lochlan didn't know that. He didn't know that when Griffin put a hand on his arm, it was the first time he could ever remember wanting to take his brother's worries.

Pain lanced through him, but it wasn't a physical type of pain. The world continued to churn. As Griffin was erased from the collective memory of the three kingdoms, life went on without him—as if he'd never been there at all.

"Brea won't let Myles discuss you in front of her."

Lochlan sighed. "But I've seen it every day. There is something missing from her. And she chooses to ignore it. To some people, she's a queen. To me, she's a wife. To my kids, she's a mother. But to herself... I think that's where she gets lost. This pain, it's the only thing she holds back. Our marriage sealed her in a new magical bond, but Myles tells me she once married you. Sometimes, I fear pieces of the bond between you never went away."

"Why are you telling me this?" Griffin met his gaze. "You don't know me."

"But I do." A breath rushed out of him. "Myles comes to me when he needs to visit his parents in the human realm. For ten years, we've been making trades, each one the same. I take him to visit his parents, and he tells me more of this man he says is my brother. I know about your perverse loyalties and that you switched sides, fighting against Regan's soldiers with me. You saved Brea, Alona, and Brandon. And you loved my wife."

"With everything I had." Memories rushed in at him. He'd done what Lochlan said, breaking Brea and her father, Brandon, out of the palace along with Alona, who now sat on the Eldurian throne. These kingdoms owed him for their peace, but he'd never deserved thanks.

Lochlan's haunted eyes met his. "I'm thankful. If you did not love her, I wouldn't have Brea at my side. Is that odd? That I'm glad you loved my wife?"

He said loved in the past tense, but just seeing Brea had brought all his old feelings rushing to the surface.

Lochlan reached forward, pushing a lock of strawberry blond hair from his daughter's face. "Sometimes, I wonder..." He shook his head. "I used to wish for family. I had two moms growing up, despite our lack of a blood relationship. I had a girl who was like a sister and a best friend. I found Brea... but sometimes, I think of the brother Myles claims I can't remember. I never thought I'd meet you."

A long silence stretched between them before Griffin leaned forward. "I wonder too." He wondered what his life would be like if he hadn't chosen Regan, if he'd grown up in Eldur like Lochlan instead of Fargelsi.

Would he be free?

Would he be happy?

"You may not think you deserve thanks for saving my son, but you have it. Any request, anything you need from me during your stay here, you only have to ask. I may not know you well, Griffin." Lochlan stood and clapped a hand on Griffin's shoulder. "But I do believe you're my brother. Whatever that means for us... we'll figure it out. I'm not leaving Tia and Toby, but you should return to your people and get some rest."

Thoroughly dismissed, Griffin left Lochlan behind. A presence loomed near the doorway in the darkened hall. He expected to see Brea, the woman who didn't like to see people hurting.

Instead, when the figure turned, his eyes clashed with Riona's.

Griffin sucked in a deep breath, trying to calm his rapidly beating heart after the single best conversation he'd ever had with his brother. He stopped moving, his feet refusing to go forward as the emotions he'd held at bay for the last ten years toppled the carefully constructed walls around his heart.

He hadn't let himself miss them. Brea and Lochlan.

Because if he missed them, he'd have to admit to himself he loved them, that he'd made so many mistakes that had hurt the two people he cared about most.

Tears gathered in his eyes, but he didn't let them fall.

Riona said nothing as she approached, and Griffin was thankful for her silence. He didn't know what she'd heard, but it didn't matter.

He was used to loss. He'd come to terms with leaving his family behind, but he was never supposed to get them back.

CHAPTER TWENTY-THREE

Griffin straightened his tunic—borrowed from his brother, the king. The ice blue cloth was fine with simple navy embroidery along the shoulders that were a little loose on his narrow frame. A decade in the prison realm had robbed him of the strong physique he'd once had. The trousers were comfortable and simple. Not the clothes of a king.

Making his way down the wide, stark hallway from his rooms, Griffin studied the tapestries along the way to the dining hall. Depicting the history of Iskalt, he wished he'd had memories of walking this hallway, of living in this palace, but he was so young when he'd been forced to leave.

Sounds of laughter drifted from the dining hall.

Griffin had dined in the halls of many palaces where kings and queens were attended by their court. Iskalt was different, and he suspected that was Brea's doing. He peered into the dining hall, watching Brea and Loch with their young family at the lone table at the opposite end of the room. Toby and Tia sat on either side of their father, vying for his attention—which, like a good father, Lochlan divided equally among them.

Kayleigh sat beside her mother, who balanced baby Ciara on one arm and poured a tumbler of juice for Kayleigh with the other. They were a beautiful family, happy to entertain their strange guests.

"You have a tail," Tierney said, eyeing Gulliver's bandaged tail flicking nervously behind him. Griffin didn't realize he'd stopped hiding it.

"I do," Gulliver said. "I'm Tuatha De Dannan, land fae from Myrkur."

"You just said a lot of things that don't make sense," Tia said, picking at her dinner. "And you have cat eyes."

"Is that okay?" Gulliver asked, frowning as if not quite sure what to make of the assertive princess.

"It's cool." Tia popped a green bean into her mouth. "You just don't see that every day."

"What happened to your tail?" Toby asked, leaning around his father to stare at Gulliver's bandages.

"Tobias, that is a rude question," Lochlan said.

"It's okay, your Majesty. It got cut off." Gulliver examined the strange contents of his plate. It looked suspiciously like human food. "Some bad people did it, but Griff saved me."

"Will it grow back?" Tia asked.

"I sure hope so." Gulliver's truncated tail thumped against the back of his chair. "It used to have a mighty fine tip, flat and shaped like a leaf. That's where all the feeling was. I feel a bit clumsy without it."

"That's so cool," Toby said. "I wish I had a tail."

Griffin smiled as Gulliver puffed out his chest. It was nice to see the royal twins had accepted Gulliver so easily.

"Oh, no, no, your Majesty. I couldn't." Riona's terrified voice caught Griffin's attention.

"Just hold her for a minute." Brea shoved Ciara into Riona's arms. "She won't break."

"Are you sure about that? She's so tiny." Riona held the princess like she was made of glass. "And such a sweet face." Riona scowled down at the little girl in her arms. "Just don't cry, okay?"

"Don't let that sweet innocent face fool you," Brea said. "That one is a little monster. And spoiled rotten. We can thank her father for that." Brea bent over Kayleigh's plate to cut her meat into small bites she could manage on her own.

"Don't linger in the doorway, Griff." Myles clapped him on the back. "I'm starving." Myles moved past him and stopped at the head of the table. "Really, Brea? Fish sticks and green beans? Did you send your husband grocery shopping at Target again?"

Ciara started to cry, and Riona groaned. "No, baby princess. We had a deal. No crying." Myles took pity on her and rescued the squirming child from her unfamiliar arms.

"I grew up on this stuff. I want my kids to like simple food and not the fancy stuff the kitchens insist on preparing for them." Brea shrugged.

"So, all those preservatives and fillers are okay? You know there's like hardly any real fish in those things."

"They taste like the scum at the bottom of a fishing vessel," Lochlan said. "But thanks to Brea, fish sticks are one of maybe three things they'll eat without a tantrum."

"Hers or theirs?" Myles asked with a smirk.

"Both." Lochlan refilled the twin's glasses with more juice, topping off Gulliver's too without a second thought. It was strange to see Lochlan being a father.

"You going to linger over there and watch this poor excuse of a dinner, or are you going to join us?" Lochlan cast a glance over his shoulder at Griffin.

"Not quite what I had in mind when the king of Iskalt invited me to dinner." Griffin took the empty seat beside Riona.

"We will eat after the children are done." Brea pushed Kayleigh's plate back in front of her child with a frown that said 'finish your vegetables.'

"Can we take Gullie sledding tomorrow?" Toby asked. "Can you believe he's never been?"

"It doesn't snow where Gulliver comes from," Lochlan said. "You'll have to show him all our favorite winter games. But not tomorrow, you and your sister are coming with me to visit the northern villages to investigate the border at Loch Villandi. You love seeing the icebergs."

"Aw, Papa, can't we stay and play with Gullie?" Tia begged. "Your king trips are boring."

"They aren't boring, they're educational."

"That means boring, Dad," Toby said.

Griffin snorted into his wineglass, trying to cover up his laughter.

"My children amuse you?" Lochlan turned to him with a smirk.

"You know what they say about kids speaking the truth." Griffin shrugged, enjoying the rare opportunity to give his brother a hard time. He had to remind himself over and over that this was not his family. Not anymore. They were kind and receptive, but they didn't know him. He was a stranger they were compelled to reach out to, but if they knew the sins of his past… Griffin would be left out in the cold before he could blink.

"Okay, kids, go with Nicola," Brea announced as a servant entered the room. "She's going to take you to the kitchens for dessert." Brea stood and lifted the sleeping Ciara from Myles' arms to hand her to Nicola.

"Come with me, children." Nicola held out her hand for Kayleigh. "Let's let your mother and father have a nice dinner with their guests."

"You're a lifesaver." Brea regarded her servant with a sense of gratitude few in her position would have for those in their employ.

A small hand tapped Griffin's shoulder. He turned to find a pair of violet eyes staring at him.

"Thank you for saving me, Uncle Griff." Tobias threw his arms around Griffin's shoulders and patted him on the back.

Startled, Griffin returned the hug.

"Goodnight, Uncle Griff!" Tia hugged his other side. "Can Gullie come with us for dessert?"

"Yes, he can, if he wants." Griffin eyed Gulliver, not willing to make him go if he didn't want to. But Gulliver followed the twins without a second glance at Griffin. When food was involved, that kid would go anywhere.

After the kids retired for the evening, Griffin actually enjoyed the meal with Brea and Lochlan. It was surreal, telling them stories of his childhood in Fargelsi and hearing similar ones of Lochlan's in Eldur. Riona seemed to enjoy the stories, but she had little to add to the conversation. Her childhood experiences were a million miles away from theirs.

"These two princes had it easy," Brea said, laughing at Lochlan's story about growing up with the Eldurian princess, Alona, and having to share a tutor. "We had to go to school with all the commoners, right Myles?"

"Who are you kidding? We were the commoners." Myles snorted, sipping on his wine after dinner. "Though, I was the popular one. Most everyone else just thought Brea was weird."

"I was fae in the human realm who spent too much time in mental hospitals because I saw fae everywhere I went, of course I was weird!" Brea threw a half-eaten roll at him.

"Oh, you grew up in the human realm?" Riona asked. "That explains a lot."

"I didn't know I was fae until I came here when I was almost eighteen." Brea's eyes went glassy as her memory glossed over the details of her arrival in the fae realm. Griffin had been the one to bring her here, but her memories wouldn't reflect that detail.

"And you are now Queen of Iskalt?"

"I am not a queen." Brea stood to refill their wineglasses. "My husband is the king. I just live here."

Griffin couldn't take his eyes away from her. She was still so... Brea. Still the same woman he fell in love with and married all those years ago. He found himself hanging on her every word, eager to hear more about her life.

Myles was the first to retire and then Riona. Soon, it was just Brea and Griffin after Lochlan left to go check on the kids.

Brea moved to clear the table herself rather than call a servant to do it at this late hour.

Griffin chuckled as he watched her.

"What's so funny?" She quirked a smile at him as she wiped the crumbs off the table.

"That was always one of the things I loved most about you, Brea. You never gave up your human roots just because you found out you were fae. I'm glad to see marrying a fae king hasn't changed that about you." Griffin took a sip of his wine, unable to keep the smile from his face.

Brea frowned at him for a moment before she gasped. "You're G. From the letter."

"What letter?" Griffin asked, unnerved by her startled expression.

"*Number seven. I love that none of this scares you. I miss you. -G.*" Her voice was barely a whisper.

"Ahh, number seven. The one you never received." Griffin nodded. "I once told you one of my top ten reasons for loving you, and you made me tell you the other nine, but I gave them to you slowly over time. I left that one for Lochlan to give you, but he never did."

Brea leaned back in her chair. "I like this time of night. The palace goes quiet, and I can just be."

Griffin chuckled. "You never wanted to be a royal, yet three kingdoms tried to make you theirs."

She looked to him with a smile. "First, it was Regan wanting to use me as a puppet. Then, Eldur. My mothers tried very hard, but that was never meant to be my throne. Iskalt though... It's..."

"Cold? Ugly?" Griffin laughed.

"Yes." She laughed. "But it feels right."

One corner of Griffin's mouth tipped up. "I missed your laugh. More than anything about you. Ten years without Brea Robinson's laugh is a tragedy."

Her smiled turned sad. "I get the feeling you and I have been through a lot together."

"More than you could imagine."

She reached over and put her hand over his.

He wanted to tell her their entire story, that they'd once shared a life together, but he couldn't get the words out. Something told him it wasn't the right time.

"I'm happy you're here. I'm happy to see you and Lochlan getting along. It feels like our family is complete with you here, but I can't recall why."

"Without the memories to go with those feelings, I can imagine it must be disturbing." Griffin withdrew his hand from under hers.

"I don't like it," Brea said. "So, maybe you can tell me our story, help me relearn the memories I've lost."

A pang of horror shot through Griffin at the suggestion. "No, you don't want me to do that, Brea." He scooted his chair back, preparing to stand. "You should keep your memories happy. You don't want to remember me as I was." His hand cupped her cheek and the familiar sensation of her skin against his came crashing back to him.

"You are my husband's brother. My children's uncle." Brea stood. "And to me... I don't know what you are. I mean, I know what you've told me, but I'm missing so much. That's the problem, Griff. It's me. Was I in love with you?"

The words sat on the tip of his tongue, but he swallowed them and stood, breaking eye contact with her. "I'm sorry I don't have the answers you seek." The words were like acid on his tongue.

Her shoulders fell, and she nodded. "I suppose you are just as confused as the rest of us. I must leave you now if I'm going to kiss my kids goodnight." Her strained expression didn't match her words.

With that, she turned and fled the dining hall.

Griffin stayed behind to finish his wine—and the pitcher, trying to forget the pull toward his brother's wife. By the time he shuffled back to his room, he was unsteady on his feet and convinced he was going to ruin his second chance.

"What are you doing?" Riona stuck her head into the hall. "You're making a racket out there."

"I am?" Griffin turned bleary eyes on her. She was a vision with her white wings fluttering behind her and her swirling tattoos pulsing across her dark skin. But she wasn't Brea. He swayed on his feet. "Did you come out here to annoy me, or have you decided you like me? I think you like me." A hiccup escaped his lips.

Riona pressed her lips into a thin line. "You're hardly likable, particularly in this state." She moved to catch him before he stumbled.

"I'm in love with Brea, did you notice?"

"You're drunk. I noticed *that*." She draped his arm over her shoulder.

"Yes, very drunk." He grinned down at her. "That's the only thing you can do when you realize you're still in love with your ex-wife who is now married to your estranged brother. Wine. Copious amounts of wine."

Without a word, Riona stepped into his arms, and rose up on her toes, giving him no warning before she kissed him.

Her lips were warm and inviting, and she fit perfectly against him. Griffin's heart pounded beneath his ribs as he reached for her, letting a hand trail down the length of her delicate wings. A shiver ran through her body at his touch, and he very much wanted to make her do that again, but she stepped away.

"Did you feel something when I kissed you?" She peered into his gaze.

"I did." He closed the distance between them, but she pressed a hand against his chest.

"Then, you aren't in love with Brea. Maybe you never were."

"How can you know that?" Griffin wanted it to be true. Needed it to be true.

"You were young and fancied yourself in love with the girl she was, but maybe you were just infatuated. Maybe you're recalling how you once felt about her, and you just want to feel like that again—but not necessarily with her."

Griffin frowned at that. For ten years, he'd struggled day to day just to survive. Being here with Brea brought back memories of being in love—memories of a short time when he was happy before everything fell apart. Who wouldn't want to recapture those feelings if given a chance?

"I hope you are right, Riona." He stumbled into his room with her assistance where he collapsed on the bed. "I don't want my brother to have to kill me for falling in love with his wife. Again."

CHAPTER TWENTY-FOUR

"Do you have many memories of Iskalt? Or were you too young?" Lochlan asked as they rode along the palace trails through the woods. Griffin was helping Lochlan "survey the land," but it was really just an excuse to spend some time together so Lochlan could figure out how he felt about Griffin's return. His brother had always been nothing if not predictable.

"Nothing concrete, but I do remember flashes of mother and father and you." Griffin rode quietly beside Lochlan along the winding trail that wrapped around the lake where the kids were ice-skating when Griffin first arrived only a few days ago.

"You remember me?" Lochlan glanced at him. "You couldn't have been more than two years old when they died."

"I have a vague memory of the day of their funeral. Callum wanted you by his side, but no one could find you. So, I wandered away, looking for you. I found you down here by the lake."

"You walked all the way down here on your own, and no one stopped you?"

"That's usually the way it goes with spare princes. No one notices the second born too much."

"I remember coming down here alone," Lochlan said. "I was only four." He shook his head. "If any of my children wandered off like that, I'd kill them."

"Callum probably didn't send anyone after me, hoping I'd disappear." Griffin suspected that was what Callum would have preferred of both boys that day.

"And then, he sent you to live in Fargelsi and me in Eldur. Were we ever friends after that?"

"Not really. We were so young, and I think we both had to think of ourselves at the time. New kingdoms. New families."

"And Regan was truly your family?" Lochlan gave him a skeptical look.

"I was a child, Loch. Hardly more than a baby when I lost my family. She's all I ever had, and she was good to me. She was my mother as much, if not more than Faolan was to you. I didn't learn of Regan's true motives until I was a grown man."

"And by then, it was too late, you already loved her."

"I did," Griffin managed in a whisper. Could it be possible that without the biases of their memories, the people he wanted to love might actually understand his past actions? "I owed her my life and my loyalty."

"As much as I owed the same to Faolan and Tierney. They raised me as one of their own. I would die for them."

"Had they proved to be evil as Regan, can you imagine

how torn you might be between doing the right thing and fighting for the women who raised you?"

"An impossible choice, brother." Lochlan led them down the trail to the north side of the lake.

"I need to speak with Callum." Griffin urged his horse to follow. He'd come to realize over the last few days that if Regan had been searching for Sorcha's book as Neeve claimed, if she'd found it—there might only be one man alive who knew where it was.

"I will go with you. We will find the information you need. We cannot release the whole of Myrkur, but we can and should free those who do not deserve to be there. I shudder to think of all the awful fae we've sent there over the generations thinking there was nothing but a prison waiting for them on the other side." Lochlan stopped at the center of the path, gazing across the lake. "What is that blasted child doing now?" He dug his heels into his horse's flanks and charged down the trail around to the east side of the lake where the kids were playing.

Only, two of them were on the ice, again.

"Gullie!" Griffin galloped behind his brother, his heart racing in his chest at the sight of Gulliver on skates with the petite Tia trying to teach him.

"Tierney Enis O'Shea, get off that ice this instant!" Lochlan flung himself off his horse and marched out onto the ice. It cracked under his weight, and he jumped back.

"I tried to talk her out of it, Papa," Toby said. "You know how she is."

"It's okay, Papa. I fixed it." Tia skated in circles around Gulliver, showing him how to balance his weight on the blades. "He's never skated before, we had to teach him so he can play hockey with us next time."

"Gulliver, come back here, now." Griffin tried to keep the panic out of his voice. He had images of Gulliver falling through the ice and never seeing him again.

"I'm not so good at the moving part, Griff." Gulliver tried to turn toward the adults.

"Don't fall!" Lochlan and Griffin yelled at the same time.

"Papa, it won't break this time," Tia insisted, a wave of magic hit Griffin in his chest, and for a moment, he couldn't breathe.

"Tia, rein in your magic, sweetheart," Lochlan's voice was calm and commanding. "Just like we've been practicing. Now, help Gullie skate toward me." He crouched down on the ground.

Tia rolled her eyes and took Gulliver's hand, guiding him toward the shore.

A loud crack echoed across the lake, making the frozen surface tremble beneath the children's feet. A huge shelf of ice broke just behind them, floating away to crumble and sink into the frigid waters below.

"Papa?" Tia's voice shook as she clutched Gulliver's hand.

"It's okay, Tia. Keep coming toward me." Lochlan's hands shook as badly as Griffin's. He wanted to run out on the ice and snatch Gulliver up in his arms and bring him to safety.

"Tia, wait!" Gulliver cried as he lost his balance and crashed to the ice. Cracks spidered out around him.

"Tia, run to me, baby," Lochlan said. "We'll take care of Gullie, but you have to get off the ice."

"I'm sorry, Gullie." A big tear ran down Tia's face as she ran to her father.

"Gullie, can you crawl toward us?" Lochlan asked. "Keep your weight distributed across the surface, and it won't crack anymore."

He wasn't far, but Griffin knew he was frozen in fear.

"You can do it, Gulliver. Just inch your way toward me." Griffin belly crawled out onto the ice. He was so close, but they were running out of time. "Just do what I do." He inched forward, prepared to take another dive into the lake if that was what it took.

Slowly, Gulliver crept toward him, bright tears shone in his eyes. "That's it, son. I've got you." Griffin swept him up in his arms and ran for the shore just as the ice shattered around them.

Gulliver clung to him like he did when he was just a little boy, and Griffin held on tight. "You're okay, you're okay," he murmured, refusing to let him go after they reached the safety of the shore.

"Tierney, what do you have to say for yourself?" Lochlan towered over her with his arms crossed over his chest.

"I'm sorry." She lowered her head, sniffing back tears. "I thought I could keep it from breaking again."

"The problem is you don't think." Lochlan knelt before her. "You have magic no one else has. We can't teach you how to control it if you don't listen to us."

"I'm sorry, Papa." She wiped her tears away. "I won't let that happen again."

"See that you don't." Lochlan stood and scooped her up in his arms, taking Toby by the hand. "You are not allowed to even look at the lake without adult supervision. Is that clear?"

"Yes, Papa," the twins said in unison.

"I'm sorry, Gullie." Tia sniffed again. "Sorry, Uncle Griff."

"Is he okay?" Lochlan asked as they made their way up to the palace, leading their horses behind them.

"Just shook him up a little. He's fine." Griffin carried Gulliver up to the palace kitchen for hot chocolate to warm him up. He was too old to carry, but he'd scared Griffin half to death.

"After your hot chocolate, you go find your mother and tell her what happened," Lochlan instructed.

"Do we have to?" Tia's bottom lip trembled. "She'll be so mad."

"Yes, you have to. And I better not find out you've given her an embellished version of the tale either."

"You okay, or do you want me to stay and have hot chocolate with you?" Griffin set Gulliver down and crouched to his level.

"I'm okay, Griff."

"Maybe try not letting Princess Tia talk you into anything dangerous again."

"She's kind of bossy," Gulliver whispered.

"She gets that from her mother." Lochlan gave him a wink.

"Truer words have never been spoken." Griffin stood to follow Lochlan from the kitchen.

"I had thought Gulliver was a kind of servant, but he's a son to you, isn't he?" Lochlan asked as they made their way down into the depths of the castle.

"I found him when he was just three years old living in a slum just outside the Myrkur Castle. We've been together ever since." Griffin wasn't sure when it had happened, but somewhere through the years, Gulliver had become his child. "Blood doesn't always matter when it comes to family." He thought of Shauna and Nessa back in Myr, and it renewed his urgency to speak with Callum.

"It's the people that matter," Lochlan agreed. "He's a good boy."

"Just mind your valuables when he's around. He likes to collect things that aren't his." Griffin slapped Lochlan on the back and handed him a jeweled knife. "Pretty sure that belongs to you. I found it in his room last night. I try to remember to shake him down every couple of days to make sure he hasn't stolen anything truly valuable. He's been on his best behavior since we arrived."

"Well, since mine tried to kill yours, I think we can call it even." Lochlan tucked the knife into his belt. They walked along the dank corridors lit with torchlight.

"Callum's been down here for the last decade?" Griffin shivered in the cold. He couldn't imagine living out a sentence like that. "Why not send him to the prison world with all the other prisoners?"

Lochlan frowned at the question. "I didn't want us to forget what he'd done. How much harm he and Regan brought to our people."

Griffin nodded. "It is wise not to allow yourselves to forget the past."

"But what I don't understand is why I sent my own brother to the prison realm."

"That's what you think?" Griffin turned to him in the dim light.

"Someone sent you." Lochlan shrugged as if the weight of the three realms rested on his shoulders. "You are a Prince of Iskalt, your punishment would have fallen to me."

"It was my choice, Loch. I knew I had to pay for my crimes, but I chose the path that would be better for everyone." Really, the path that would end the marriage magic between him and Brea. But he didn't say that.

"You sacrificed yourself for our happiness?" Lochlan stopped and turned toward his brother.

"I did so much bad. I didn't belong in your lives after that. It was better for you to forget the pain I caused."

Lochlan grew silent as they traveled deeper into the dungeons with only the torchlight to guide their way. Myrkur might not be the best place to live, but at least Griffin hadn't been confined to the freezing dungeons of Iskalt for the last decade. Sure, Myrkur was always dark, and that in itself could be stifling to a man used to the sun, but at least there was a sky. Fresh air and companionship.

"You've brought me a guest, nephew? How unlike you." Dirty hands with cracked nails gripped the cell bars, humming with the magic keeping Griffin's uncle from portaling to his freedom in the human world.

"Your nephew has come to speak with you," Lochlan said.

"Another one?" Callum peered out at Griffin in confusion.

"I've come from the prison world, so you do not

remember me," Griffin explained, taking a step forward in the torchlight. "But I am an O'Shea."

"Why don't you portal me out of this hell hole, and maybe I'll be inclined to believe you?"

"Nice try, old man." Lochlan moved to stand beside Griffin. "My brother has some questions for you. Should you answer them honestly, I'll see to some improvements to your accommodations."

"I want a fireplace, two new blankets, and some whiskey. Lots of it," Callum said.

Lochlan nodded for Griffin to continue.

"You once attempted to create a magical boundary around a village in Iskalt. Where did you learn such magic? I need you to tell me everything you know about boundary spells."

Callum's hands dropped from the cell bars, and he stepped back into the shadows. Lowering his gaunt frame onto a wooden stool, he leaned back against the wall with a sigh. "Boundary magic? That will cost you a lot more than a blanket and some whiskey." His seldom-used voice grated in his throat.

"If your information helps my brother, I will increase your comforts as I see fit. Now, talk."

"Regan knew of such magic. She created the spell around Fargelsi. Complicated magic, that was. She tried to teach me, but I failed to construct the spell properly."

"And you killed an entire village of Iskaltians in your experiment," Lochlan muttered.

"Where did she learn how to create the barrier around Gelsi?" Griffin pressed. "Did she have a page from the book of Sorcha?"

Callum's eyes widened. "You're looking for the book. Now, tell me why an O'Shea strives for such power?" When Griffin didn't answer, Callum leaned closer to the bars. "Are you looking to destroy a boundary spell, boy? Now, what is the most powerful boundary in the realm?"

He tapped his chin, a smile curving his lips. "The prison realm."

Griffin crossed his arms. "I do not know why my king wants the book."

"Your king?" His grin widened. "I smell lies, nephew. Why are you lying to me?" He muttered to himself as he drifted away from the bars. "A king. The prison realm has a king. What might he offer to bring down the magic?"

"Get to the point, old man." Lochlan growled. "Can you help Griffin or not?"

"Help him steal the most powerful book in existence?" He crossed his arms. "No. You don't want to play with that book, boys."

Griffin crouched down to meet his uncle's gaze in the dim light of his cell. "That book has led to the suffering of thousands. We need to find it so we can end that suffering."

Callum barked out a rough laugh.

"If you ever wanted to make amends for the wrongs you've done, this is your one chance," Lochlan added.

"Aye." Callum nodded. "I know where the book is kept, but you won't find it. Sorcha's twin hid it in the human realm. Her ancestors safeguard it now." His hands balled into fists as if aching to get his hands on the book once more. "Regan managed to find it long before she ever did anything with the spells. I took her to study it, to find what would give her the power she sought to overtake her brother. But the keepers of the book wouldn't let her copy any of the spells. It wasn't until years later when an odd fellow appeared in Fargelsi with scrolls containing powerful spells that Regan gained access to the power she sought. Those spells were going to make the strongest alliance in history. No one would have been able to defeat us."

Griffin met the cold eyes of his uncle. "But you were defeated, Uncle. And now, you'll be able to watch the book you wanted for your own personal gain create peace instead."

"So you know where it is kept?" Lochlan folded his arms across his chest.

"I do not. The location changes. I only know who is protecting it. But I'll let you boys find that out for yourselves."

"Papa!" Tierney's screech echoed along the dungeon walls.

"Papa?" Toby and Tia stumbled into the room, their breath billowing into a cloud of white around their pale faces.

"Twins?" Callum stood, grabbing the bars of his cell. "O'Rourke Twins?"

Griffin wanted to contradict him to tell him the twins were only of Iskalt, but that wouldn't be true. Not when their grandfather was an O'Rourke.

"What is it, Tia?" Lochlan crouched in front of her.

"It's Gullie!" she wailed, throwing her arms around her father's neck.

"What happened now?" Lochlan directed his question to his son.

"She tried to fix his tail." Toby stared at his feet, not meeting his father's eye.

"Who is that?" Tia sniffed her tears back, staring at Callum.

"I'm your great uncle Callum, sweet girl." He tried to smile, but between his grating voice and the layer of grime covering his face and hands, he was a gruesome sight.

Tia clung to her father even tighter, burying her face against his neck.

"Don't speak to my daughter, old man," Lochlan growled.

"Go to Ireland," Callum said suddenly. "An old fishing village called Bealadannan. Look for a Gelsi woman by the name of Ashlin Carrik. She will guide you."

Toby stared at Callum, eyes wide with horror, like he'd seen some awful omen in his great uncle's eyes.

"What's wrong with Gullie?" Griffin asked, breaking Toby away from Callum's ferocious gaze. It seemed Princess Tierney O'Shea was determined to 'help' Gulliver into an early grave.

"She grew his tail back," Toby said proudly. "But now, he won't wake up."

Griffin scooped Toby up in his arms and ran for the stairs, Lochlan and Tia right behind him.

"We aren't done with this conversation, boys!" Callum bellowed behind them. "You'll both be needing that book now." His maniacal laughter rang out behind them.

CHAPTER TWENTY-FIVE

"Gulliver?" Not sure what to expect, Griffin raced into the royal nursery where the kids played most afternoons.

"Griff, look at it! Isn't it beautiful?" Gulliver swished his new tail around.

"Are you okay?" Griffin went down on his knees to inspect Gulliver for any injuries. Magic gone wrong could lead to any number of issues. Some that might not be visible at first.

"Griffin, I am so sorry!" Brea wrung her hands. "That child of mine has a mind of her own."

"Kind of like her mother," Griffin said wryly, trying not to let his worry for Gulliver lead to anger with the strong-willed princess.

"Tia is so stubborn, and I just don't understand it." Brea paced the nursery with baby Ciara cradled in a human looking contraption she wore like a sling over her shoulder. The baby princess slept through her mother's anxiety. "It's like we don't speak the same language. Her Gelsi magic is so volatile. Even Neeve has never seen anything like it. She soaks up her lessons like a sponge, and she's constantly trying things she can't possibly handle at her age. I shudder to think what she'll be like when she comes of age and inherits the magic of Iskalt and Eldur as well. By then, she'll likely be easier to reason with. It's hard to reason with a ten year old who thinks she knows everything."

"I'm fine, Griff," Gulliver whispered. "Better than ever." His tail snaked up over his shoulder, and the freshly grown tip—shaped like a leaf—patted Griffin on the face. "I'm not so sure the queen is though." He watched Brea's furious pacing.

"Why don't you go find Riona and show her your new tail? And maybe stay away from Tia for a few days," he added under his breath.

Gulliver nodded. "She didn't mean to hurt me, Griff. Something weird happened when she used her magic. It was like it... bounced off me at first."

"Loch," Brea sighed when her husband joined them. Tia still clinging to his neck. "What are we going to do with her?"

Lochlan marched into the room, setting Tia on her feet before her mother. "Apologize to Uncle Griff." He stood, sighing with regret.

"I'm really sorry, Uncle Griff." Tia sniffed, her big dragon-sized tears tore at his heart.

Griffin crouched down to her level. "I'm not going to say it's all right, Tia. You have to listen to your parents about using your Gelsi magic. You know, I grew up in Fargelsi, and children there learn the words of power as they grow up. But you are very strong. You learn fast, but that doesn't mean you're ready to use your magic whenever you feel like it." Griffin glanced up at Brea and Loch, hoping he hadn't overstepped.

"Maybe it will help to hear it from someone new." Brea shrugged, urging him to continue.

"I'm afraid I can't let Gullie play with you anymore, Tia. Not without adult supervision." Griffin stood to his full height to tower over her.

"I would never hurt Gullie, Uncle Griff. Not on purpose." Tia's bottom lip trembled.

"Then, you should think about that, sweetheart." Brea took her hand. "You can't experiment on your friends. It's not safe."

"I wasn't experimenting." Tia jerked her hand out of her mother's grasp and ran from the room.

"I'm sorry," Griffin said. "I was too hard on her."

"No, she needed to hear it from you, brother. Gulliver is your child, you have to protect him. Even from pint-size princesses with too much magic and not enough sense."

"What about Toby?" Griffin asked. "He doesn't seem to give you any trouble with his magic."

Brea's eyes filled with tears, and he wondered if he'd said the wrong thing.

"Toby doesn't have magic," Lochlan said. "Not of his own. His only power seems to be in amplifying Tia's. Now that he's old enough to understand, he seldom helps her outside of their lessons."

"We won't be gone long, Brea," Lochlan insisted. "Just a couple of hours to glamour a few humans and ask some questions. We'll be back before you know it."

"You're always too cavalier about glamouring humans," Brea huffed. "I was one of those humans you glamoured for half my life."

"You. Have. Never. Been. Human," Lochlan growled, and Griffin stifled his laughter behind a pastry he stuffed in his mouth. Those two deserved each other.

"You know what I mean." Brea glowered back at him. "For almost eighteen years, I thought I was human."

"Don't blame me for doing your mothers' bidding. You know they just wanted to keep you safe."

"I know. I just like giving you a hard time for it. Bring me back something Irish—and Myles, don't let him forget the usual."

"I know, I know. Starbucks frapachinos and Godiva chocolate." Myles pulled on a human jacket over his stylish human clothes.

"You three are an odd sort of royal." Griffin shook his head.

"So not a royal," Brea called over her shoulder as she left them.

"We better hurry, Gullie wants cheeseburgers." Griffin stood to grab his coat he'd bought at the pawnshop.

"I thought we needed to make this a quick trip so your lady friend doesn't find out we were gone."

"She's not my *lady friend*." Griffin scowled at his brother.

"Seriously, Loch, who says lady friend?" Myles grinned and nudged Griffin playfully.

"Only old, out of touch, uptight kings, I guess." Griffin nudged Myles back. He enjoyed needling his older brother. For the first time, it felt like they truly were brothers. He planned to enjoy it for however long it lasted.

"Well, whoever she is, we better get going before she shows up." Lochlan shoved them both toward the inner courtyard where night was falling.

"And *we* are going where again?" Riona marched in with a guilty looking Gulliver behind her. Both were wearing their human clothes and had their bags tossed over their shoulders. Ever since Griffin had the nerve to speak with Callum without Riona, she had taken to following him everywhere and listening in on his conversations.

"We are just following a lead we got from Callum," Griffin admitted with a sigh. He still wasn't sure he could trust her. As far as Riona knew, they were seeking a way to bring the border around Myrkur down so they could take that information back to Egan. But Griffin had seen that done before. The moment Brea and her army broke through the Gelsi border magic, the entire barrier failed and thousands of Fargelsians, previously trapped, flooded into Eldur and Iskalt. He would not let that happen with Myrkur. Not until they found a way to separate the criminals from the innocent. If they were going to do this, they were going to do it right.

"You will tell me about this lead when we get to this Ireland place." Riona's wings bristled with annoyance.

Griffin quirked a smile at her. She was so easily annoyed, and her wings always gave her away. Just like Gulliver's tail. He found it oddly... alluring.

"Yeah, it'll be a miracle if we get any actual work done on this trip," Lochlan muttered as he followed them into the moonlit inner courtyard.

They portaled into the human world atop a grassy green hill on the rocky shores of Ireland. They were greeted with blue skies and bright sunshine. And Finn Donovan, the king consort of Eldur.

"Finn? What are you doing here?" Griffin looked between Lochlan's friend to the Kings of Iskalt and Fargelsi in confusion.

"Finn has been doing some... research for us in the human realm," Lochlan said. "I asked him to meet us here."

"Who's this the guy?" Finn lifted his chin at Griffin.

"My brother, Griffin. This is my... other brother, Finn," Lochlan said awkwardly.

"Can we dispense with the whole I don't know you because I forgot you explanations and just go with, it's nice to meet you, I know you're my brother's best friend?" Griffin gave Finn a nod. "We don't have much time here, and we need to make the most of it."

"I don't like this," Riona said.

"Of course she doesn't." Lochlan rolled his eyes.

"There are too many people involved." Riona glared back at him.

"Which is why I tried to tell everyone it should just be me and Griff on this trip, but no one listens to me," Lochlan grumbled, crossing his arms over his chest.

"Riona, Gulliver, don't move until Finn glamours you."

Finn stepped in front of them and lifted a hand. "What?" His eyes bounced from Riona to Gulliver before landing on Griffin. "You said they have no magic."

"They don't."

"My glamour won't work. Something is blocking it."

Myles shrugged. "Could be because they're already glamoured.

All eyes turned to him. "Speak, human," Lochlan bit out.

Griffin stepped closer, seeing Riona as the fae she always appeared to be. He rounded her to examine her wings.

"You wouldn't have noticed last time you portaled because you didn't have a human with you. Look at me, I'm a human glamour detector." Myles smiled proudly.

Lochlan met his gaze. "It's not a glamour. Finn's magic didn't work."

"Then it's something they're doing on their own. Maybe Dark Fae have like a... natural glamour? How cool is that?"

Griffin looked to Riona. "You... do Dark Fae glamour themselves without magic?"

She shrugged. "As long as no one can see, we're good. You all should do something about those ears though." She pushed past him.

She was right. They didn't have much time. Finn glamoured himself along with Griffin and Lochlan.

Lochlan met his friend's gaze. "Any luck, Finn?"

"I found her, but she's not exactly cooperative... or competent."

"Who?" Riona demanded.

Lochlan turned to Griffin with hands fisted at his sides. "Catch her up to speed, will you? Her infernal questions are getting us nowhere."

"Callum gave us the name of a woman who might lead us to the source of the boundary magic," Griffin whispered a hasty explanation she would like. "If all goes well, we might actually find something that will please Egan when we return."

He didn't miss the look of disappointment on her face.

"She's not going to like a troop of Fae descending on her all at once," Finn said. "She's really old and kind of cranky."

"Griff and I will go with Riona," Lochlan said. "Gulliver, you stay here with Myles and Finn."

"We'll be right back," Griffin said. "No stealing anything while I'm gone."

"Yes, sir." Gulliver rubbed a tail Griffin really hoped no one else could see.

Griffin and Lochlan walked down the hill toward the village, Riona following quickly behind.

"I will do the talking," all three of them said at the same time.

Lochlan sighed. "Let's agree to let Griffin speak."

"Was it necessary to bring him?" Riona asked. "You can portal here just as well as he can."

"Enough, you two." Griffin picked up the pace. The sooner they finished this, the sooner he could put some distance between Lochlan and Riona. They didn't trust each other and had taken an immediate disliking of one another.

The village of Bealadannan was old and crumbling, like some historical site come alive after a long dormant sleep to join the modern world. Cars and cellphones looked out of place in a village like this.

"Finn says she lives on the cliffside near the edge of town."

The town was little more than a few cobblestone streets and a marina where fishermen came and went with their day's catch.

Ashlin Carrik turned out to be an old crone of a fae woman. She stood waiting on her dilapidated front stoop, her cane tapping against the cracked concrete.

"If you're after Sorcha's book, you'll have to do better than a couple of O'Shea princes." She turned back into her house, leaving the door open for them to follow. "Or has one of you managed to become king of Iskalt?"

"I am Iskalt's king, madam." Lochlan gave the old woman a curt nod.

"Sit, sit." She gestured at the table in the corner of her one-room home. "I'll tell you what I know, and you can be gone with tonight's moon." She busied herself making tea and stoking the fire in the already too warm room.

"You're the one who married the O'Rourke girl, then?" She lowered herself into a seat beside Lochlan.

"My wife is the daughter of Faolan and Tierney Cahill."

"And Brandon O'Rourke is her father. She's the Eldur-Fargelsi weapon, and she's had a few children, hasn't she? That's why you're here seeking the O'Rourke book of spells. You want to understand twin magic, yes?"

"Twin magic?" Lochlan frowned, stunned into silence.

"How do you know so much about us?" Griffin asked, casting a wary glance at Riona, wondering again if he could trust her.

Ashlin just smiled—an act that took years from her weathered face—and shrugged.

"We are here to ask about ways to destroy—" Riona said, but Lochlan held up his hand to stop her.

"What do you mean by twin magic?"

"The O'Rourke line is riddled with twins, or didn't you know?" She poured them each a steaming cup of tea, the aromas of lavender, citrus, and lemongrass hung heavy in the air. "I suppose it has been a while. Regan never had children, so the last twins were Sorcha and her sister, Grainne, until your twins were born that is." She passed around a tin of biscuits, but no one was interested.

"What have my children to do with this book?" Lochlan managed to ask in a choked whisper.

"The O'Rourke book of spells holds many secrets to dangerous magic. High on that list is twin magic. When did you notice your girl had great power?"

"How do you know this?" Lochlan's voice shook with fear.

"I am old, dear. And I may choose to live in the human realm, but I am not useless. Not yet, anyway." She stirred honey into her tea and took a careful sip. "Your girl? She is strong, yes?"

"Very," Lochlan said.

"And your boy has no magic to speak of. Only enough to boost his sister's, yes?"

"Yes."

"In the right hands, the O'Rourke book of power can teach the best ways to raise such twins. To teach them how to control their magic *together*. That is key."

"And in the wrong hands?" Griffin asked.

"It can teach an O'Rourke woman how to break free of the twin who holds her back."

Riona kicked Griffin under the table.

"Where might we find this book?" Griffin asked, shooting Riona a glare. They didn't need to ask this woman about the barrier magic. They just needed the book.

"Grainne brought the book here to the human realm to keep it from any future O'Rourke twins. Her descendants still watch over the book."

"Where is it?" Riona asked. "It would help his majesty and his wife a great deal if they could learn how to help their twins now, before they are grown and it is too late."

"To my knowledge, it was buried with Grainne in the village cemetery. Hers is the largest headstone at the center of the churchyard."

"Thank you." Lochlan reached for the woman's hands. "If there is anything I can do for you..."

"Leave me be." She gave him a sad smile. "The happenings of kings and queens no longer concerns me. Just... watch your back, your Majesty. And take care of those twins."

After an hour of digging in the fading afternoon sun beside Finn, Griffin's arms ached. Grainne's grave was old, and the ground was hardened with time and erosion.

"It's clear." Griffin called up to his pacing brother. "Myles, help us lift the lid, it's heavy."

The three men lifted and groaned as they slid the stone sarcophagus lid aside.

"Is it there? What do you see?" Lochlan leaned over the grave.

"Nothing." Myles climbed out.

"No book?" Lochlan's shoulder's drooped.

"No body." Griffin climbed out and offered a hand to Finn.

"We should go back and ask the old crone to explain this," Riona said.

"She's right, Loch. This is the lead we've been looking for. We need that book."

"You've been looking for something to help the twins, haven't you?" Griffin put it together. "That's what Finn has been researching in the human realm."

"We couldn't find answers in any of the three kingdoms." Lochlan rubbed a tired hand over his face. "We've known for a long time that Tia needs more help than we can give her. We can't keep a magic tutor for longer than a few months."

"It was my idea, to research human folklore," Myles said. "Finn and I have taken turns researching for the last five years, but this is as close as we've ever come to an actual answer."

"Then, we need to go back and ask more questions." Griffin tossed his shovel down.

"We'll stay and fix this. You three go," Finn said. "We'll meet you there when we're done."

Riona and Griffin followed Lochlan back across the

village to the old woman's home, but when they arrived, she wasn't there.

"We'll wait until she comes back." Lochlan sat down on the front step.

Griffin walked around the old cottage. Something wasn't right. The back door stood ajar, and he peeked into the empty room, his heart hammering in his chest.

A teakettle hung over the fire with steam pouring from its mouth.

"Loch!" Griffin raced around to the front of the house. "Time to go."

"What? No, I'm not leaving until I have answers."

"We're not going to get them here." He rested a hand against Lochlan's shoulder. "She's hiding from us. Something isn't right."

"She's just an old woman. She can't have gone far."

"No, Loch, she doesn't want us here. I think this was some kind of set up. It could be a trap. We need to get back home."

"Brea!" Lochlan called the moment he stepped through the portal into the palace courtyard they'd left from only hours before. Moonlight was fading from the early morning sky.

"Loch!" Brea sobbed, stumbling across the grassy courtyard to reach him.

"What happened?" He gripped Brea by the shoulders, peering into her bloodshot eyes.

"Callum," her voice shook. "He's escaped."

"How?" Griffin wanted to go to her, to comfort her, but

that wasn't his place anymore. Never had been. "His cell was magically sealed."

"I didn't know it, Loch. I should have been paying more attention. What kind of mother am I? I didn't know they were going down to visit him. They never knew he was in the dungeons before the other day. Tia was curious. You know how she is." Brea's shoulders shook with the effort to speak.

"What happened, Brea? You're scaring me." Lochlan pulled her into his arms.

"He took them, Loch. Our babies. He... He must have talked Tia into letting him out. She would have taken it as a challenge to break through the magical barriers."

"He has Tia and Toby?" Lochlan's hands shook.

"Yes. What does he want with them, Loch? They're just children! You have to find him." Brea shoved her husband back into the fading moonlight. "Give him whatever he wants, just bring them home."

"He wants the book, Brea. He's going to use our little girl as a weapon."

EPILOGUE

Tierney: three months later

Tia focused on the warm pressure in her hand to remind herself she wasn't alone as she stared at the rocky crags of a place Callum called Ireland. She'd clung to each of his words, hoping he'd reveal a plan to bring Tia and Toby back to their parents, back to where it was safe.

But she'd started wondering if there was a safe place for her in either of the worlds.

Magic was her constant companion, thrumming through her body, looking for weaknesses to break through. It took all her willpower to keep from uttering spells that would set it free.

Energy traveled up her arm from Tobias' hand, and she tore hers away so violently she fell back onto her butt. The grassy shore softened her fall, but nothing could soften the confusion in her twin's eyes.

Tia gasped for breath as if a hand squeezed her lungs.

At ten years old, her magic should lay mostly dormant inside her, but it never had. Her earliest memories were of her accidentally using it on servants and friends. It was why she no longer invited friends to the palace. Once, she'd even tried distancing herself from her brother, but he didn't let her.

Below the cliffs, water twisted and frothed. She peered over the edge, wondering if there was a way to end the desperation of the last three months. Behind her, Tobias never took his eyes off her. She could feel his measured gaze. He was the calm twin, her safety. Yet, his touch made her magic grow and coil inside her.

Turning, her eyes met his. They had always been together in all things, but this time was different. "I can't..." She steeled her gaze. "You can't touch me, Toby. Because every time you do, it feels like I'm going to explode."

He pursed his lips. It had taken a long time for him to believe he amplified her magic because he couldn't feel it. When she spoke Fargelsian words of power, he didn't feel the flashes of invincibility that roared through her.

Toby was just Toby, a boy who might never fit into the world of magic, but one she'd protect with everything she had.

Tierney didn't know why Callum took them, why they'd hidden in the human realm for months.

She only knew it couldn't be good, that he had a use for her.

And whatever that use was, it would most likely hurt the people she loved.

Turning away from her brother, a brother she'd almost killed many times with her errant magic, she peered down at the waves. An icy breeze lifted the hair from her neck, sending a shiver down her spine.

Straightening her posture, she didn't let the cold get to her. She was an Iskalt princess. Brave. Loyal. Fierce. Everything her mother taught her. Her father tried to instill discipline and work ethic, but she would always be more like her mother. A rebel.

"I'm sorry, Toby," she whispered, wondering if the words would haunt him the rest of his life. "This is all my fault." She leaned in, careful not to touch him. "We need to run." She glanced back at the stone cottage where Callum poured over maps and old legends. "When the time comes, we need to get away. Will you be ready?"

He nodded, his face growing ashy. Tia hated the life Toby had to live because of her. She wanted more for him. Running away wouldn't get them back to the fae realm, but at least they'd have a chance. They only had to wait for their moment.

As if hearing their conversation, Callum walked outside and stood looking over the cliffs. "Want to see what happens when you run from me, young fae?"

Tia swallowed, inching closer. Fear kicked her heartbeat up a notch as she pushed Toby behind her, muttering under her breath. Her Fargelsian magic, the only kind she could draw on, pooled in her fingertips. But she didn't know the words to set it free. Callum reached out and yanked her toward the cliff. Her scream died in her throat as he held her leaning over the edge. His words were soft enough for her ears alone.

"If you defy me, it won't be the brave magical princess paying the price. I will take your brother, and you will never see him again."

Toby's scream sent relief flooding through her. He yelled

her name, and she met Callum's dark gaze. For now, her brother was here with her and she could protect him.

"Do you understand now?" Callum loosened his grip, and she tried not to stare at the rocks below. She nodded and he pulled her back, releasing her.

She dropped to her knees, her entire body collapsing in on itself. "Yes. I understand. Please, just don't hurt Toby."

Callum lifted his eyes to the dusk. Tia didn't have access to her Iskalt night magic yet, but she saw the moment her uncle's came alive in his eyes.

He turned, swiping his hand through the air and shoving Toby through a portal before closing it, swallowing Toby's scream.

"Please," Tia yelled. "Bring him back. I'll do whatever you want."

A smile curled his lips, and a portal opened nearby. Toby fell through, his entire body shaking. Tia crawled toward him. "Tell me you're okay." She wanted to take his hand, to drag him in to a bone-crushing hug. But she couldn't control her magic while touching him.

Toby rolled onto his side as his body heaved, and vomit splashed the grass.

Tia pulled her knees up to her chest, tears stinging her eyes. "Toby, I'm sorry."

No more dangerous escape plans. Tia would never again risk her brother's life.

Callum's boots bent the grass as he walked toward them. A look of disgust twisted on his face.

Tia met his gaze, not daring to look away.

"If you try to run from me, I won't be so generous in your punishments." Callum's scowl never left his face. It had been three months since he pulled them into the human realm, three months of him refusing to tell them why.

Tierney backed away from Tobias, letting the power settle inside her.

Toby rolled onto his back. "What do you want from us?"

Callum rubbed the back of his neck and glanced over his shoulder to the tiny cottage they'd been staying in. "Supper is ready. Eat or don't. I don't care. In the morning, I'm leaving for a few days."

Callum left them periodically to chase down leads on whatever he was searching for. Those were the worst times because he spelled the cottage to not let them outside.

Tierney pushed herself to her feet and followed Callum inside. Her magic begged for release, for her to choose a target and let go. But there was something forcing her to hold it back.

Portal magic, a gift she hadn't yet received.

If something happened to Callum, the twins would be stuck in the human realm forever.

Which was why they sat quietly at the table eating, their eyes never leaving their plates.

Today's plan failed, but Tierney would find a way to get them out of this. All her reasons for running still mattered. But as Tobias grabbed her hand under the table—ignoring her request to stop touching her—she realized there was another way.

She squeezed Tobias' hand, letting magic flow through their connection. Tierney would spend every moment Callum was gone teaching herself to control her power.

Until the day came when she could let it out.

She would save Tobias. She would save her parents and

everyone else. Tierney had always wanted to be just like her mother.

Now, she too had been abducted for reasons she didn't yet know.

They say history is doomed to repeat itself. Her uncle Griffin came to mind. The three kingdoms trapped prisoners in the prison realm, forever forgetting what it was they did. Tierney heard stories of Queen Regan of Fargelsi. She'd heard stories about her mother's heroics.

But they didn't have the full tale.

If you forget the very fae who caused so much turmoil, how are the kingdoms supposed to learn from it? How are they supposed to be better?

As Tierney chewed on the remnants of her stale bread, she let her magic boil and turn to anger.

Whatever it was Callum sought, she'd make sure he didn't get it.

Because if he did, something told her it would be the end of the peace the three kingdoms had fought so hard for.

She shared a weak smile with Tobias. The world saw them only as kids, but she knew they were different, more.

She could feel it in her bones.

The story continues in

Fae's Power: Queens of the Fae Book Five

Available at: michellelynnauthor.com/Power

WHAT'S NEXT?

Griffin O'Shea is Forgotten.

Maybe it's a good thing no one outside the prison realm remembers everything he did to earn his place in the dark kingdom.

Now that he's back in the world of the Light Fae, he wants to earn their trust, their loyalty, and that means going after the missing prince and princess of Iskalt, children who call him uncle. It means searching through the human realm for a vanishing village only he can see and a book full of dangerous magic and devious secrets that are better left alone.

With a human leading the search, Riona at his side, and a profound lack of magic, the chances of finding anything they seek have never been worse.

But the odds won't stop them. Nor will an illness threatening Griffin's life.

Even if he has to crawl through the portals and face the king of Myrkur on his knees, he cannot stop.

Because there are things worse than death:

Watching those he loves die before him.

Seeing the realms of the fae crumble into dust.

Returning to the prison realm means being forgotten once again. Returning without the book could mean certain death.

But when all roads point to war, Griffin has no other choice.

The king must be defeated. His vast army must be stopped.

And this time, Griffin wants to be the hero instead of the villain.

Fae's Power: Queens of the Fae Book Five
michellelynnauthor.com/Power

About Michelle

Michelle MacQueen is a USA Today bestselling author of love. Yes, love. Whether it be YA romance, NA romance, or fantasy romance (Under M. Lynn), she loves to make readers swoon.

The great loves of her life to this point are two tiny blond creatures who call her "aunt" and proclaim her books to be "boring books" for their lack of pictures. Yet, somehow, she still manages to love them more than chocolate.

When she's not sharing her inexhaustible wisdom with her niece and nephew, Michelle is usually lounging in her ridiculously large bean bag chair creating worlds and characters that remind her to smile every day - even when a feisty five-year-old is telling her just how much she doesn't know.

See more from M. Lynn and sign up to receive updates and deals!

www.michellelynnauthor.com

Also by Michelle

Queens of the Fae

Fae's Deception | *Fae's Defiance* | *Fae's Destruction* | *Fae's Prisoner* | *Fae's Power* | *Fae's Promise* | *Fae's Rebellion* | *Fae's Refuge* | *Fae's Return* | *Fae's Envoy* | *Fae's Enemy* | *Fae's End*

The Hidden Warrior

Dragon Rising | *Dragon Rebellion*

Fantasy and Fairytales

Golden Curse | *Golden Chains* | *Golden Crown*

Glass Kingdom | *Glass Princess*

Noble Thief | *Cursed Beauty*

Legacy of Light

A War For Magic | *A War For Truth* | *A War For Love*

About Melissa

Melissa A. Craven is an Amazon best-selling author of YA Contemporary Fiction and YA Fantasy (Contemporary fans will know her as Ann Maree Craven). Her books feature strong female protagonists who aren't always perfect, but find their inner strength along the way. Melissa believes in stories that make you think and she loves foreshadowing, leaving clues and hints for the careful reader.

Melissa draws inspiration from her background in architecture and interior design to help her with the small details in world building and scene settings. She is a diehard introvert with a wicked sense of humor and a tendency for hermit-like behavior. (Seriously, she gets cranky if she has to put on anything other than yoga pants and t-shirts!)

Melissa enjoys editing almost as much as she enjoys writing, which makes her an absolute weirdo among her peers. Her favorite pastime is sitting on her porch when the weather is nice with her two dogs, Fynlee and Nahla, reading from her massive TBR pile and dreaming up new stories.

Visit Melissa at Melissaacraven.com for more information about her newest series and discover exclusive content.

Also by Melissa

Queens of the Fae

Fae's Deception | *Fae's Defiance* | *Fae's Destruction* | *Fae's Prisoner* | *Fae's Power* | *Fae's Promise* | *Fae's Rebellion* | *Fae's Refuge* | *Fae's Return* | *Fae's Envoy* | *Fae's Enemy* | *Fae's End*

Immortals of Indriell

Emerge (Book 1) | *Edge* (Book 0) | *Catalyst* (Short Story)

Judgment (Book 2) | *Scholar* (Series Companion) |

Volunteer (Short Story) | *Captive* (Book 3)

Assignment (Novella) | *Heir* (Book 4) | *Betrayal* (Book 5)

Runaway (Book 6) | *Proving* (Book 7)

Ascension of the Nine Realms

The Reluctant Queen | *The Rejected Queen* | *The Rebel Queen* | *The Ruthless Queen*

www.ingramcontent.com/pod-product-compliance
Lightning Source LLC
Chambersburg PA
CBHW030527310726
48979CB00010B/1829/J

* 9 7 8 1 9 7 0 0 5 2 1 9 0 *